The Playb...
by L...

*'Trust me. I know what I'm talking about.
I saw the way he looks at you,'*

Nicholas said.

Gail paused at his tone. He wasn't joking. She opened her eyes and turned around to look at him. 'How does he look at me?'

'Like he wants to get you in his bed,' Nicholas said, his voice low, his eyes full of secrets.

Gail's stomach turned a somersault at the idea of Nicholas wanting her in his bed. She sucked in a shocked breath. Where had that thought come from? She shook her head. 'I haven't seen that from him at all.'

'Maybe because you're not looking for it,' he said, lifting a wayward strand of hair from her cheek.

'Or maybe it just doesn't seem likely to me. I'm not—'

'Don't say you're not pretty. Beauty is in the eye of the beholder,' Nicholas said.

Gail rolled her eyes. 'Okay. I'm not sexy.'

His gaze took a slow trip over her face, hovered on her lips so long they burned, then slid down to the tops of her breasts and lower. Gail felt her nipples grow taut and sank lower into the water.

His gaze returned to hers. 'That's a matter of opinion.'

Sleeping Beauty's Billionaire
by Caroline Cross

ᕲ ᗡᗡᕳ

'I wasn't trying to insult your integrity.
I'm sorry.'

Their gazes locked and the sudden silence in the room was deafening. As if from very far away Colleen heard the fire snap, followed by the faint scrape of a tree branch against the window.

'Damn it, don't look like that,' Gavin said fiercely.

She wasn't certain what it was he saw in her expression, but she was very certain she wanted to keep to herself the emotional turmoil he caused her. She lifted her chin. 'I'm not. And don't curse.'

'Don't you tell me what to do.'

Having grown up with four brothers, she was fully versed in the folly of saying anything to the male of the species that resembled a challenge. Yet she couldn't stop the imprudent streak that seemed to seize control of her tongue. 'Or what?'

His dark eyes hooded over. 'Or this.'

Clasping her upper arms, he lowered his head and in the next instant his mouth settled possessively over hers.

Available in January 2004 from Silhouette Desire

The Playboy & Plain Jane
by Leanne Banks
(Dynasties: The Barones)
and
Sleeping Beauty's Billionaire
by Caroline Cross
(Dynasties: The Barones)

A Cowboy & a Gentleman
by Ann Major
and
Beckett's Cinderella
by Dixie Browning
(Beckett's Fortune)

Delaney's Desert Sheikh
by Brenda Jackson
and
Expecting Brand's Baby
by Emilie Rose

The Playboy & Plain Jane
LEANNE BANKS

Sleeping Beauty's Billionaire
CAROLINE CROSS

*First published in Great Britain 2004
Silhouette Books, Eton House, 18-24 Paradise Road,
Richmond, Surrey TW9 1SR*

The publisher acknowledges the copyright holders of the
individual works as follows:

The Playboy & Plain Jane © Harlequin Books S.A. 2003
Sleeping Beauty's Billionaire © Harlequin Books S.A. 2003

*Special thanks and acknowledgement are given to Leanne Banks
and Caroline Cross for their contributions to the
Dynasties: The Barones series.*

ISBN 0 373 04971 4

51-0104

*Printed and bound in Spain
by Litografia Rosés S.A., Barcelona*

▼ SILHOUETTE®
DESIRE™

are proud to introduce

DYNASTIES:
THE BARONES

Meet the wealthy Barones—caught in a web of danger, deceit and…desire!

Twelve exciting stories in six 2in1 volumes:

THE PLAYBOY & PLAIN JANE
by
Leanne Banks

LEANNE BANKS,

a bestselling author of romance, lives in her native Virginia with her husband, son and daughter. Recognised for both her sensual and humorous writing with two Career Achievement Awards from *Romantic Times*, Leanne likes creating a story with a few grins, a generous kick of sensuality and characters that hang around after the book is finished. Leanne believes romance readers are the best readers in the world because they understand that love is the greatest miracle of all. You can contact Leanne online at leannebbb@aol.com or write to her at PO Box 1442, Midlothian, VA 23113, USA. An SAE with return postage for a reply would be greatly appreciated.

Special thanks to Marilyn Puett
for being the silver lining in a dark cloud.

This book is dedicated to all the wanna-be girl jocks.
I'm right there with you!

Prologue

She'd been a blue-eyed beauty with a body that could send a man's brains straight to his crotch. She'd also had a faithless heart of glass that could cut a man to ribbons.

If Nicholas Barone had been a superstitious man, he would have admitted that the Valentine's Day curse on his family continued. Almost two years ago, on February 14, he'd bought the ring and been prepared to propose to Danielle Smithson.

He remembered using his key to enter her apartment, wanting to surprise her, only to overhear her boasting to a friend on the phone that she was going to "bag the big one tonight." Justifiably confident of her allure, Danielle had feigned an attentiveness he'd later learned was purely calculated to achieve her goal. In this case, Danielle had been willing to pretend she adored Nicholas in order to get her hands on his family's money.

Bitterness still filled him at the memory of the ugly scene that had followed. When she'd been unable to deny her deception, she'd done her feminine best to placate him. Nicholas might be American through and through, but his Italian blood ran hot, and he'd sworn he would have nothing to do with her.

Even at this moment, standing in the darkness of his daughter's nursery on this January day, he felt anger roll through him with renewed strength. He looked down at the sleeping one-year-old daughter he hadn't known existed until ten days ago. Just after Nicholas had broken up with Danielle, she'd found another man with a hefty bank account and had apparently tried to pawn Molly off as his daughter.

He took a deep breath and exhaled a fraction of his bitterness. Drawing solace from the sight of Molly's innocence and vulnerability, he heard footsteps from behind him. His mother and father, he suspected. His father would deny it, but when it came to his eight children, both of his parents were professional worriers. When Nicholas recalled the shenanigans he and his siblings had tried to pull over the years, it was a wonder his parents hadn't been driven over the edge.

Feeling his mother's hand on his arm, Nicholas turned. His father, a man who'd always managed to inspire respect despite the fact that he stood under six feet tall, shook his head as he glanced at the crib. Fierce anger emanated from him. "I'll never forgive that woman for keeping your child from you. To think you wouldn't have learned you even had a daughter if Danielle hadn't died. I can never forgive her for that.''

His father's bitterness echoed Nicholas's. ''We don't need to spend energy forgiving Danielle. She's dead. I have my hands full helping Molly make the adjustment to living with me and accepting me as her father.''

His mother squeezed his arm again. ''Molly will accept you in no time. I can still help take care of her.''

Carlo Barone put his arm around his wife's shoulders. ''I don't want you overdoing. You may still turn men on their ears when you walk into a room, but you shouldn't be chasing after a one-year-old all day and night.''

Moira Barone might not have been born Italian, but she knew how to stand her ground. She lifted her red-haired head with a trace of defiance. ''If you can continue to be CEO of the top gelati company in America, why can't I chase my one-year-old grand-daughter?''

''I continue to be CEO because Nicholas is COO and I can trust him. My children have finally left home. I have earned the right to my wife's undivided attention at the end of the day. No?'' he demanded.

Nicholas hid a grin at his father's possessiveness. At sixty-three, his mother was still the light of his father's life. ''I appreciate you helping take care of her the past ten days and I still want you to be involved with Molly,'' Nicholas assured his mother. Although his mother had been perfectly willing to care for Molly, Nicholas knew his daughter was demanding. The poor child cried frequently since she'd arrived at his home.

"Because Molly has lost her mother, I know I need to create a stable environment for her. My housekeeper does an excellent job, but taking care of children isn't her forte. With my demanding position, I need a nanny. I've already contacted a couple of reputable agencies.''

His mother's eyebrows knitted in concern as she glanced into the crib. "If you're sure," she said uncertainly.

"I am," Nicholas told her.

"Nicholas is right. He will take care of the *bambina* and we will be good grandparents,'' his father said.

"I can still visit her as often as I want?'' his mother asked.

Nicholas's heart softened. His mother had already grown attached to her first grandchild despite Molly's crying jags. "Every day, if you like.''

Moira sighed, turning to Nicholas. "She is such a beautiful child. She looks just like you when you were a baby. Curly black hair, blue eyes and a stubborn chin.'' She slid a sideways glance at her husband. "You got the dark hair and stubborn chin from your father. But like your father, you're a good man.'' She met Nicholas's gaze. "You'll be a good father. Molly's a very lucky girl.''

Nicholas's heart squeezed. His mother's vote of confidence was a balm on his troubled soul. He was still reeling from the news that at thirty-five he was a father, and heaven knew, he wasn't an expert on one-year-old girls. "Thanks, Mom."

She smiled and kissed his cheek. "It's only the truth," she said, and glanced at her husband. "I'll get my coat."

Carlo squeezed his wife's hand. "I'll be with you in just a minute."

She nodded. "Just remember to keep your voice down. Sleeping baby."

As soon as his mother left, his father cleared his throat. "If you need anything, you must call me immediately."

Nicholas nodded. "I'll handle this."

"I know you will," Carlo said. "You've met every challenge put before you. I'd hoped you would find a love like the one your mother and I share…"

Bitterness suffused Nicholas again. "I found Danielle, instead."

"You're young," Carlo protested. "Your life isn't over."

"My focus now is on providing for my daughter. With a nanny, I'll have no need for a wife."

"A nanny can't take care of all of a man's needs."

"A man doesn't have to marry to take care of those needs," Nicholas said dryly.

Carlo wagged his finger. "One day you will understand the needs of the heart. But for now you're right. You must concentrate on taking care of your daughter.'' He hesitated a moment and his eyes narrowed thoughtfully. ''You were going to propose to Danielle on Valentine's Day, weren't you?''

Nicholas knew his father was remembering the Valentine's Day curse that had left its mark on more than one generation of Barones. His father had never professed belief or disbelief, just an underlying wariness. ''Yes, I was. We fought and she left town.''

A thoughtful silence followed. Carlo glanced at Molly. ''If the curse is true, this time it has brought you a gift.''

One

Gail Fenton looked at the doozy of a run in her panty hose and tried to tug the hem of her dress lower to conceal it. She wasn't having a good hair day, either, but with her noncompliant red curls, she couldn't remember ever having a good hair day. Perfect grooming probably wasn't a requirement for the job of nanny to a one-year-old, but looking like a slob during the interview wouldn't help her chances, either. Then again, if Gail felt out of place in the elegant formal living room of Nicholas Barone's luxurious town house, how must his poor little girl feel?

Nicholas Barone's assistant, Mrs. Peabody, who explained she'd come from the office to assist her boss with these interviews, looked over her half glasses. "Your résumé says you hold a degree in computer science. Why do you want to be a nanny?"

Translation: Are you nuts to give up the prestige of a computer position to change diapers? Gail was accustomed to the question and had her answer ready. "I find working with children much more rewarding. Children smile, hug and laugh. Computers don't."

"Then why didn't you major in early-childhood education or something similar?" Mrs. Peabody asked.

"My brother's influence," Gail confessed. Her brother, Adam, had wielded his influence in several areas, and with both parents gone, Gail had been susceptible to his guidance until recently. "My brother encouraged me to major in computer science because it's a marketable field and I've always been pretty good with computers. But during the summer before I graduated, I took a position as a nanny and loved it. After I graduated, I worked with Manatee Computer Services. The company recently downsized, and I saw this as my opportunity to do something I want to do—work with a child."

"Your references are excellent," Mrs. Peabody mused. "You realize this is a live-in position?" she asked.

"That's no problem for me," Gail said. "My roommate is getting married."

Mrs. Peabody nodded thoughtfully. "I think Mr. Barone should meet you. Please wait while I get him."

Gail felt a jiggle of nerves in her stomach. "I'll be here," she said with a smile.

As soon as the woman left, Gail rose and paced around the beautiful room. At her age, twenty-five, she was surprised at her case of nerves. Although she'd wanted a career change, she hadn't realized how much she wanted this job. She wanted more of a feeling of connection in her life. She stopped pacing to study a collection of family photographs on the wall.

The Barones. There was a passel of them, and their names and faces frequently graced the *Boston Globe* society and business pages. She wondered what it would be like to have that many brothers and sisters, and felt a pinch of longing. With both her parents gone, it was just Gail and her brother now, and although Adam was generous with his advice, he was busy with his own career. Gail had plenty of friends, but since college she'd missed feeling as if she really belonged.

The sound of a woman's cultured voice and a child's loud wail broke her reverie. Gail peeked out the doorway and spotted a statuesque, red-haired, older woman in what was obviously a designer dress. Not one smoothly coiffed hair was out of place, Gail noticed in awe as she absently smoothed her hand over her own mass of curls.

The woman held a howling, dark-haired little girl in her arms. She glanced up with a pained expression and met Gail's gaze. "Our Molly is still adjusting."

Curious, Gail craned her neck to get a better look at her potential charge. "A lot of us feel a little cranky when we first wake up. Amazing what a diaper change, juice and a cookie can do.''

The woman smiled and walked closer. ''A diaper change for adults?''

''Well, you must admit some adults act like their underwear is a little too tight, and they don't have the excuse of a wet diaper.''

The woman gave a throaty chuckle. ''So true. I'm Moira Barone and this is Molly. Sorry I can't offer my hand.''

''I'm Gail Fenton. Pleased to meet you and Molly.'' Gail gasped at the beauty of the screaming child. ''My goodness, she's gorgeous. Even with her face red as a tomato.''

Moira chuckled again, then shook her head. ''I think she's just getting herself more worked up.''

Gail blew into the baby's face. Molly paused in her screaming and opened her eyes, her long black eyelashes damp with tears. She stared hard at Gail, and her lower lip protruded as if she was gearing up for another cry.

''Peekaboo,'' Gail said, and moved out of sight.

Silence, followed by a hiccup.

Gail popped back. ''Peekaboo,'' she said with a smile and moved away.

Silence again. Molly turned her head to search for her.

Gail moved back into view again. ''Peekaboo.''

A slow smile curved Molly's mouth.

Moira shook her head in amazement. ''I have eight

grown children, and I had completely forgotten peek-aboo.''

''Too many garden-club meetings with society ma-trons,'' a man said as he strolled into the room with Mrs. Peabody by his side.

Gail glanced at the man and her jaw dropped. Well over six feet tall, jet-black hair, chiseled facial fea-tures and the lean, muscular kind of body that no doubt had women littering his path. He probably had to beat females off with a stick. The glint of ruth-lessness in his eyes affected her stomach. Other women would try to tame him, but she possessed nei-ther the attractiveness, sex appeal or polish necessary to match wits with or seduce a man like Nicholas Barone. Besides, she knew he'd never look twice at her. Darn shame, but that was the truth. Oh well, she supposed she could admire him from afar.

She instinctively turned to Moira. The older woman was safer. ''The power of peekaboo is greatly under-estimated, but I'm sure you would have remembered it soon enough.''

''Perhaps necessity might have jogged my mem-ory,'' Moira said, looking down at her grandchild. ''Or desperation.''

''And what would a computer specialist know about peekaboo?'' the man asked, his eyes cynical.

Gail paused less than a beat. She suspected there was a reason for the cynicism, but she disliked the attitude. Something told her he wasn't a man who worried about being liked. She met his gaze head-on, confident in her ability to care for the man's child, and just as confident about her lack of feminine appeal. "I could write a dissertation on the subject of peekaboo. The wonderful thing about peekaboo is that it requires no special equipment and can be employed at any time, just about any place. But there are some requirements for the game."

He arched a dark eyebrow. "And they are?"

"A sense of humor and a willingness to—" She broke off, her stomach a riot of butterflies at the intent way he stared at her. Gail felt heat rush through her bloodstream.

"Willingness to what?" he prompted.

She cleared her throat and prayed in vain that her cheeks weren't turning fire-engine red with embarrassment. "A willingness for the adult involved to completely ditch his or her dignity," she said, pretty sure she'd just lost hers.

His lips twitched slightly. "Is that so?" He glanced at her résumé. "Why isn't 'peekaboo specialist' on here?"

Gail laughed in a combination of relief and amusement. "I knew I'd forgotten something."

"Nicholas Barone," he said, extending his hand and meeting her gaze.

She accepted his handshake. "Gail Fenton, but I imagine you already know that."

"You imagine correctly. You've met Molly," he said, glancing down at his daughter. *"Bellisima,"* he said to the child, then dropped a kiss on her forehead.

Molly stared up at him and her lower lip protruded in a pre-wail position.

Gail couldn't blame the child. If Nicholas seemed larger than life to her, she could hardly imagine what a baby might think of him.

"Please join me in the living room," he said to Gail. "I have a few questions."

"Of course," Gail said. "It was nice meeting you, Mrs. Barone, Mrs. Peabody and Molly," she said as the tyke began to fuss. Gail followed Nicholas into the living room.

"She hasn't smiled for me yet," he muttered, motioning Gail to sit across from him on the couch. He took the large wing chair.

"She's in awe," Gail said.

He shot her a look of doubt. "Awe?"

"Well, yes. To normal people, you're quite tall, but to her, you're huge."

"Normal people," he said, rubbing his chin.

"Average," Gail corrected, thinking he was one of those men who couldn't miss a day of shaving. "Something tells me you're not familiar with the idea of being average," she said, and bit her lip. "Sorry. That was way too personal for an interview."

He nodded. "Yes, it was, but you're right. Barones aren't allowed to be average."

She saw a world of experience in his blue eyes and knew without his saying that he had always pushed himself, that much had been required of him and that he had done whatever it took.

He glanced at the application again. "I still don't understand why you would choose to be a nanny when you could work at any number of top companies.''

She bit back a groan. "I like to play peekaboo," she said. "Computers don't."

He remained silent as if waiting for the real explanation.

"When I work with computers, I don't feel as if I'm making an important contribution. But when I take care of a child, I feel as if I'm shaping the future. I love the feeling of connectedness I get from caring for a child."

"Mrs. Peabody tells me both your parents are deceased," he said.

"Yes."

"I'm sorry," he said, surprising her with the gentle note in his voice. "You have one brother?"

"Who has tried to micromanage my life."

He shot her a questioning glance, amazing her with his ability to extract information with just an expression.

"After I attended community college in Iowa, he persuaded me to finish my education here in Boston."

"How does he feel about you taking this position?"

"How he feels about it isn't important. How you, Molly and I feel about it is important."

He nodded. "Are you engaged or in a serious relationship?"

Gail paused. "That's personal, isn't it?"

"Yes, but pertinent. I've just gained custody of a daughter I didn't even know existed until a couple of weeks ago. I don't want to hire someone who can't make a long-term commitment.''

''How long-term?''

''Seventeen years,'' he deadpanned, then cracked a wry grin. ''Just kidding. After a thirty-day trial, I'd like you to sign a one-year contract.''

''A year is no problem,'' she said, an odd assortment of emotions rolling through her. Mrs. Peabody had briefed her about the way Nicholas had learned of Molly's existence, but the story still floored her. ''Your life must have been turned upside down.''

''I've had to reevaluate my lifestyle,'' he said, the fire in his eyes belying his neutral tone. ''Providing a stable environment for Molly is my top priority. Which is why I asked that personal question. *Are* you in a serious relationship that can't withstand your absence for a limited time?''

Gail thought of her wide assortment of male friends and bit back a chuckle. Serious? To them, she was one of the guys. ''I'm not engaged or serious about anyone at the moment. I have several male friends, because I play volleyball on one of the more successful teams in a Boston recreational league. I also play a little basketball.''

''Volleyball,'' he repeated, as if trying to put together a composite of her as a nanny.

''I was always better at sports than the arts, but I do a mean 'eensy weensy spider,''' she said, and grinned. ''I bet you've never asked about 'eensy weensy spider' during an interview before.''

His lips twitched. ''Can't say that I have.'' He

looked at her silently for such a long time that she had to resist the urge to squirm. "If you become Molly's nanny, I'll require complete honesty."

She saw a glimmer of the hard line he probably held at the office. He was a man who would demand and get what he wanted. "I couldn't give you anything less."

He nodded. "Good. This position will require the two of us to communicate regularly. I think it's best if we dispense with formalities. You can call me Nicholas."

Gail wanted this job, but she had an instinct about Nicholas Barone. She suspected he could charm a bear out of its den, but he also probably expected his employees to submit to his will without asking too many questions. As Molly cried in the background, Gail began to think this job might be more challenging than she'd originally thought. Although she would respect Nicholas's wishes, she needed to know he would at least listen to her ideas. "You strike me as someone accustomed to having most things your way. If I feel strongly about something, I will want you to consider it even if you don't initially like it."

He gave her a long, assessing glance. "I'm at ease with letting the buck stop with me. I don't believe in shirking my responsibilities. As much as I'd like to be, I'm not an expert on my daughter yet. I will be soon enough, but until then I'll value your input."

In that one moment her respect for him grew. His commitment to his daughter got under her skin.

"Any other concerns?" he asked.

Just that he was so good-looking she hoped she wouldn't be caught drooling whenever he came around. She shook her head.

"Good. We've already checked your references. When can you start?"

"When do you need me?" she asked, feeling a combination of excitement and some unnamed apprehension.

The sound of Molly's cries filled the air. He didn't blink once. "Yesterday."

Two nights later Nicholas sank onto the bed in one of the guest rooms. The master bedroom was being painted, so he was temporarily displaced. He hadn't slept well since he'd brought Molly home. The shock of instant fatherhood and all its accompanying concerns had kept him awake into early morning. After checking on his soundly sleeping daughter tonight, though, he felt he could finally relax. Part of it was the gut feeling that Molly felt safe and secure in Gail Fenton's hands.

If he couldn't make Molly feel secure, if his presence sent his daughter into tears, then he was damn determined to find someone who could make her feel safe. Gail had a natural warmth that he knew would comfort Molly. It surprised the hell out of him, but even he felt that same warmth in Gail's presence. He couldn't quite put his finger on it, but she projected the attitude that perfection wasn't required or expected. Nicholas had spent his life around people who expected perfection, or something damn close to it.

Through the walls, he heard the shower cut off and a feminine voice singing. The sound captured his attention. A committed bachelor whose lovers rarely stayed overnight, he couldn't remember the last time he'd heard a woman singing in his house.

Curious, he moved closer to the wall. A children's song, he concluded, catching a few of the words. "Little teapot…steamed up…tip me over, pour—"

The singing stopped abruptly and he heard a loud thump, followed by a muffled shriek. Wincing, Nicholas heard a low moan, then nothing.

He frowned, wondering if she was hurt. He pressed his ear against the wall. Still no sound. He squeezed the bridge of his nose. What should he do? What if she was lying on the floor with a concussion?

Swearing under his breath, he strode from his room to her door and knocked lightly so he wouldn't wake Molly. "Gail," he said. "Gail, are you okay?"

No sound. Nicholas turned the knob and entered the room, scanning the floor for a body. He moved toward the ensuite bath and caught a glance of Gail Fenton with a towel precariously slung over her as she rubbed her shin. "Ouch, ouch. Ouch," she whispered.

Nicholas would be missing a Y chromosome if he didn't notice her long shapely legs and the fact that the towel was one breath away from revealing one of her breasts. In other circumstances with a different woman, he would get that towel off her in a New York minute, but now he needed to make sure she wasn't seriously injured. "Are you okay?"

Her gaze shot to his and her mouth rounded in a mixture of horror and surprise. She glanced down at her body and hastily rearranged the towel. "M-Mr. Barone."

"Nicholas is fine," he said.

She clutched the towel to her. "I'm okay. I just slipped when I got out of the shower."

"It sounded painful and potentially life-threatening," Nicholas said.

She cringed. "I fall hard. It's one of my flaws. Overconfidence. I trust my balance a little too much."

"Maybe you were distracted by singing the teapot song."

Her face bloomed with color and she scooted into a sitting position. "I'll be honest," she said in a confiding tone. "I'm no Mary Poppins, so I've been practicing all the children's songs I know."

He shrugged. "Sounded good to me until you..."

"Went splat on the floor," she finished with a pained expression.

"Are you sure you didn't break anything?"

"Totally. It was very kind of you to check on me, but unnecessary. I'll just have a few very colorful bruises."

"You're sure you're okay," he said, something about her expression causing him doubt.

"Very sure. You can leave. Please."

"Let me help you up first," he said, moving toward her.

"Oh, no," she said, her eyes widening as she shook her head.

He put his hands on her arms and watched in fascination as her cheeks bloomed with vivid color again. She didn't look nearly so plain when she blushed. In fact she reminded him of a creamy white rose tipped with coral. He wondered if she blushed all over and glanced at her pink shoulders and pink chest. He looked down her pink legs to her pink toes.

"Mr. Barone—"

"Nicholas," he corrected.

"Nicholas, I won't die from this fall, but I may die of embarrassment if you don't leave."

He pulled one of his hands back, amused by her frank admission. "I don't think I've ever met anyone who blushes from head to toe."

Her mouth straightened into a firm line. "A gentleman wouldn't bring that fact to my attention."

He chuckled, thinking he was enjoying this exchange far more than he should. "I'm not a gentleman one hundred percent of the time," he said, and pulled her to her feet. "Gentlemen can be boring."

She rushed to adjust the towel around her and Nicholas caught a glimpse of the curve of her round derriere. The sight was so distracting he almost didn't catch her frown. "I disagree," she said. "A true gentleman understands the value of good manners and consideration."

"A smart man uses those to his advantage, but makes his own rules."

Gail sighed and walked around him, the towel offering more tantalizing glimpses of her rear end with each step she took. "You're not going to change my opinion. And with me clinging to this towel, I'm reasonably sure I won't be changing yours. So, thank you for your concern. I'd like to get to bed now. Good night.''

His gaze latching on to her derriere, Nicholas barely resisted the urge to say, *You give new meaning to the word* peekaboo.

Gail survived the night, even though she felt sick every time she thought about Nicholas Barone hearing her sing in the shower, then feeling compelled to pick her up off the floor and nearly catching her buck naked. Molly soon distracted her. Unfortunately one of Gail's most effective calming tricks involved her own hair, which Molly liked to grasp and hang on to. It meant the baby was attached to her for most of her waking hours. Gail told herself it was a bonding period and it would pass.

At six o'clock on the dot, Nicholas walked through the front door. ''It's Daddy!'' Gail said, trying to convey a feeling of happy excitement to Molly. Gail feared the baby and her hottie father were off to a rocky start. ''It's Daddy,'' Gail said again, heading toward the foyer with Molly in her arms.

Nicholas spotted his daughter and approached cautiously. Gail felt Molly's hand wind around a strand of her hair. A sure sign of tension. Molly popped her thumb in her mouth and stared at her father as if she couldn't decide if he were a monster.

''Hello, sweetheart,'' he said in a low voice. ''How

was your day today? Did you have a good time with Gail?''

Molly wound her hand another turn around Gail's hair and stared at her father.

''Say Da-da,'' Gail prompted the child. Then she turned to Nicholas. ''I think she's focused on verbal development now. She's making lots of sounds.''

''What is she doing to your hair?'' Nicholas asked, his brow furrowing.

''I think it's a security thing,'' Gail said wryly. ''Some kids use a blanket. Molly uses my hair.''

Nicholas moved closer. ''It looks like she's going to rip it out,'' he said, reaching to loosen Molly's grip.

Momentarily distracted by a whiff of his after-shave, Gail stared at the sensual curve of his mouth. She wondered how he kissed. Heat rolled through her. Instinct told her he was an incredible lover.

Not that she would ever find out. Not that she really wanted to find out, she told herself, feeling Molly stiffen. ''It's okay. You don't need to—'' She broke off when she felt Nicholas's fingers graze the skin of her neck as he tried to pry Molly's fingers loose.

Molly's eyes widened in alarm. She let out an ear-rattling wail of protest.

Gail winced and shook her head. ''Just let her have my hair. I don't like it that much,'' she said with a chuckle. ''She can use it.''

Nicholas pulled back his hand with a frown. ''She always seems to cry when I come around.''

Gail bit her lip. He was right. ''Maybe it's just the time of day.''

"Morning and night?" he asked skeptically.

"She probably just needs some time with you alone. Maybe you could start reading to her at night."

If Gail didn't know better, she would say she saw a sliver of terror flash through his eyes. That couldn't be right, she thought. After all, Molly was his daughter. A big, powerful man like Nicholas Barone couldn't possibly be terrified of his baby daughter. Could he?

"Maybe," he said in a considering tone, his expression guarded. "Maybe another night. I have a commitment to attend a charity function tonight. My turn to be the official Barone-family representative."

Still wailing, Molly clutched Gail's hair tightly. "It's okay," Gail cooed, rubbing the baby's back. "You're just fine." She glanced again at Nicholas, her curiosity aroused. "Do you mind being the official Barone representative?" she said.

He shrugged and his mouth tilted in a sexy grin. "Depends on the function and the woman."

She nodded. "Ah," she said, feeling a jumpy sensation at the sensual glint in his eyes. How would it feel to spend an evening receiving the undivided attention of a man like Nicholas Barone? Gail would no doubt spend the entire date stammering and blushing, unlike the confident, gorgeous women he was accustomed to. She wondered who it was tonight. "You must have a tough time choosing the 'flavor of the day.' I don't remember meeting a woman who doesn't love ice cream, so you must represent the perfect combination."

"What would that be?" he asked. "Wealth and..."

She shook her head. "Actually I wasn't thinking of wealth. I was thinking of ice cream and a favorite topping. Something hot," she said impulsively, because if ever the word was an apt description for a man, it was now. "Hot fudge sauce."

As Nicholas stared at her for a long moment, she felt a roar of embarrassment race through her. What had possessed her to say such a thing? Thinking it was one thing. Saying it was something totally different. She cringed, certain her cheeks matched the color of her hair. Was she destined to constantly embarrass herself in front of this man? "Could we just forget I said that?"

"Forget you just compared me to ice cream and hot fudge sauce?" he asked, his dark eyebrows arching.

"Uh, yeah," she said hopefully.

He shook his head and chuckled. "No. I'm sure I'll remember that for a long time."

And Gail made the futile wish that she could fall through a crack in the perfectly sealed tile floor of the foyer so her five-foot-eight-inch frame would disappear.

Two

After the last two busy days, Gail should have been comatose. Instead, she stared wide-eyed at the eight-foot ceiling of her elegant bedroom. Molly, the precious screaming meemie, had finally fallen asleep an hour ago. Caring for an uneasy, clingy one-year-old was both rewarding and exhausting. On those rare occasions when Molly smiled, it was as if the sun came out from behind a cloud.

Gail felt as if she was making progress with her little charge, but she worried about Molly and Nicholas. She had tried without success to encourage Nicholas to spend time with his daughter. He made overtures, but when Molly began to cry, and she always did, he backed away. Gail worried about how to bring the two of them together. If Molly continued to cry and Nicholas continued to pull away, she feared they would never develop the warm, loving relationship they both could have.

The warm, loving relationship Gail would have had with her father if he had lived. The memory of her father's death stirred a pang of longing to which Gail thought she'd become immune.

Abandoning her effort to sleep, she rose from the bed and pulled on her robe. She yawned, scooted her feet into her pink bunny slippers and headed for the kitchen for a cup of something hot without caffeine. As she passed Molly's room, she noticed the door was slightly ajar.

Curious, she quietly pushed the door open and spotted Nicholas standing next to Molly's crib. Dressed in a black wool suit that had taken him from early-morning meetings to another charity function this evening, he had loosened his tie and was totally focused on the sight of his sleeping daughter.

The grave tenderness on his face made Gail's heart twist. "Gotcha," she whispered.

For a moment she wondered if he'd heard her. But then he turned to meet her gaze and his mouth lifted in a slow half smile. "So you did."

Gail felt the punch of attraction all over again, but refused to let the man's sex appeal cloud her mind. "She's not crying," she said, moving closer to the crib.

"She doesn't know I'm here," Nicholas said dryly. "Otherwise, she'd be screaming her lungs out."

"Babies cry to expend energy. It's not personal," she said, and hoped it was true.

"Uh-huh." His deep voice was full of doubt as he returned his gaze to Molly.

"Well, it's true. It's not as if babies can play tennis or volleyball to work off their frustration."

"And there's no correlation to her crying every time I come around. It has absolutely nothing to do with my presence."

Gail wanted to say it didn't, but she feared her nose would grow like Pinocchio's. "Well, it wouldn't," she insisted, "if you would spend more time with her when she's awake."

"Her little life's been turned inside out lately. I don't want to upset her more, so I come every night and watch her. Maybe she'll get used to me through osmosis or something."

The combination of his wry tenderness and strength struck at Gail's heart. "Maybe you could sing to her."

He shot her a dark look.

"Just seems like there should be a way to make some progress," she said, wrinkling her brow as she searched for a solution. "Maybe you could leave something of yours in her crib. Something you wear next to your skin. Something with your scent."

"My socks?" he said.

She chuckled. "No. The objective is to help her bond with you, not chase her away. Maybe your T-shirt," she ventured.

He stood perfectly still for a long moment, then

gave a short nod. "Okay," he said, and shrugged out of his jacket and began to unbutton his shirt. He thrust his jacket at her. "Here. Hold this."

Gail instinctively clutched his jacket and felt her jaw fall open in shock. "Uh, you, uh, don't have to—" She broke off as he handed her his shirt and in one motion yanked off his T-shirt. Her gaze fastened on the breathtaking, thigh-melting view of his muscular bare chest. A dusting of dark hair skimmed down the center of his chest and abdomen and disappeared beneath the waistband of his black slacks. He carefully set his T-shirt beside Molly in the crib, his muscles rippling with the movement.

He turned back to face her. "Any other suggestions?"

None that wouldn't send her into cardiac arrest, Gail thought. She cleared her throat. "You'll get an opportunity to be alone with her when she's awake tomorrow night."

Alarm crossing his face, he did a double take. "Tomorrow night!" Molly stirred, and he lowered his voice, moving closer to Gail. "You're not quitting already, are you?"

"Of course not," she whispered. "I have tomorrow night off. I have a volleyball game."

He frowned, running his hand through his hair. "I don't know if this is a good idea. Maybe I should call a sitter."

"It requires guts and tenacity. I thought you Barones cornered the market when it came to guts and tenacity."

He looked at her for a long moment. "What do I do with her?"

Gail's heart swelled with a combination of admiration and compassion. Nicholas Barone was an incredibly powerful man, but he was willing to go to the mat for the daughter he hadn't even known existed just weeks ago. "Read to her. Pay attention to her. Women are the same at any age. They love attention. They love to be chased. They love to laugh," she said, and noticed he was standing so close to her she could see the five-o'clock shadow on his jaw. She felt suddenly light-headed.

"Women are the same at any age," he echoed, his curious gaze winding around her like a silken thread. "So what does Gail want? To be chased and to laugh?"

She had to be imagining the intensity in his gaze, because he sure as heck could not be looking at her the way a man looks at a woman he finds desirable. Dropping her gaze to clear her head, she stared at her feet and his. He wore Italian leather shoes. She wore pink bunny slippers. She backed away. "Gail wants a cup of herbal tea. I'll let you get back to your secret quality time with your daughter. Don't worry about tomorrow night. I'll leave her favorite books out for you, and if that doesn't work, you can always make up a story."

He gave her a blank look. "Make up a story about what?"

She shrugged. "I don't know. I'm sure you're creative," she said, and the naughty thought sliced through her mind that he was probably very creative in bed. Before her mouth decided to share that thought, she took another step backward. "Good night, Nicholas."

He nodded. "Gail," he said as she turned.

She stopped. "Yes?"

"Great slippers."

Her cheeks heated at the sexy amusement in his voice. His voice was so sexy he could probably read the *Wall Street Journal* and a woman would beg him to bed her. Gail bit back a moan. She definitely needed to make sure she didn't run into Nicholas late at night again. A woman needed all her faculties and fortitude to fight off that man's impact.

The following night Gail played volleyball with her co-ed team. She'd been so immersed in her new nanny position that she had a tough time concentrating at first. Her longtime buddy and teammate, Jonathan, had teased her out of her fog. After the game and a quick shower at the gym, she joined her comrades for a celebratory round of beer at a local bar. Her mind kept wandering to Molly and Nicholas. Visions of Molly, red-faced and crying, and Nicholas, discouraged and exasperated, plagued her, so she left early.

When she entered through the heavy wooden front door, she listened for sounds of screaming. Instead, she heard Nicholas's low baritone coming from the kitchen. Quietly walking down the hallway, she noticed his words were punctuated by pleasant gurgling noises from Molly. Pleasant? Gail silently mouthed the word *wow* and stood outside the kitchen.

"You like Baronessa strawberry gelato," Nicholas said. "You have excellent taste. Would you like to hear how Baronessa Gelati was started?"

Molly gave an unintelligible babble, but once again, it was pleasant sounding.

"I knew you'd be interested. Your great-grandfather Marco came to America from Italy and he fell in love with a girl named Angelica who made ice-cream desserts. The two of them eloped on Valentine's Day and they later opened a *gelateria,* which is an Italian ice-cream store. Can you say *gelateria?*"

Another unintelligible babble followed, and Gail smiled, charmed by Nicholas's ridiculous question.

"That's okay," he said. "I'm sure my father will make sure you speak some Italian. But back to the story. Marco named the *gelateria* Baronessa because their last name—our last name—means baron in English. As his wife, she was the baronessa. The *gelateria* became very popular with locals and tourists. It was a huge success. Years passed, and my father, Carlo, who earned his MBA from Harvard, took the business national, and Baronessa Gelati can now be found in the gourmet section of grocery stores all over the world." He paused. "Baronessa strawberry gelato can also be found all over you, little one. It looks like you're going to need another bath, and something tells me that won't be nearly as popular as strawberry gelato."

Gail poked her head through the doorway. "Looks like you two have been having a party."

Nicholas heard Molly shriek with joy and felt a rush of relief at the sight of Gail. Molly had been fretful for a good part of the evening. Serving her gelato had been an act of inspiration and desperation.

Gail smiled, and he felt an odd trickle of warmth in his gut. "I'm impressed," she said. "It would have taken me a while to come up with ice cream."

"But you probably would have managed to keep it neater," he said, nodding his head at the pink mess that was Molly.

"No," Gail said, grabbing a couple of paper towels and moving toward Molly's high chair. "I just would have tried to get her cleaned up before you saw her so you would *think* I'd managed to feed her without her getting it all over herself."

"So the just-fed clean one-year-old is a myth?" he asked.

Gail nodded. "If you think this is bad, you should see SpaghettiOs."

"You mean canned spaghetti?" he asked in horror.

Gail winced and chuckled. "Oops. Have I just deeply offended your Italian sensibilities? Sorry, but round noodles are great toddler food." She wiped off Molly's face and the baby began to protest. Gail put the paper towel in front of Molly's face and whipped it away. "Peekaboo," she said, and Molly smiled, reaching for the towel.

Nicholas envied Gail's ease with his daughter. Although he had hired Gail for the sole purpose of caring for Molly, he still wished he didn't feel so damned incompetent with his own daughter. As Gail lifted Molly from her high chair, he noticed ice cream on the front of the child's pajamas. "Be careful," he said. "She'll get ice cream on you."

Gail looked down and shrugged. "No problem. I'm not prissy."

That she wasn't. Nicholas was not accustomed to un-prissy women. He followed Gail up the steps, his gaze caught by the sway of her cute rear end in jeans. Remembering the sight of her bare bottom, he imagined her athletic frame naked. He suspected she would appear more toned than muscle-bound. Those thighs would wrap around a man—

He bit back an oath. This was his daughter's nanny, for Pete's sake. And she wasn't even his type. She was different from the perfectly coiffed women he dated. Her hair was wild. She couldn't completely tame it even when she pulled it back. A forbidden, instinctive image of Gail naked, with her red hair flying free, her face full of ecstasy, stole into his mind.

He frowned and bit back another oath. Maybe it had been too long since he'd taken a woman to bed. Although he'd continued to attend public events with beautiful women, he'd been too distracted about becoming a father to focus on his sexual needs.

Nicholas ruthlessly pushed his disturbing thoughts aside as he joined Gail in the nursery bathroom. Gail turned the water on full force in the tub.

"How was the game?"

"Thank you for asking. We won, of course," she said, a hint of competitiveness glinting in her eyes.

"Of course," he said. "Does that mean you never lose?"

"You have to be careful with the words 'never' and 'always,'" she said, starting to undress Molly. "But we've been undefeated for three years. It's a co-ed team, and the guys don't hesitate to blast the women when we're not aggressive enough."

"And there's no one guy who is significant to you?"

"They're all special," she said, bending down to test the water, then place Molly in the tub. "But to them I'm just one of the guys."

"They can't be that blind," Nicholas said.

She looked at him and smiled. "That was very nice, thank you. Speaking of significant others, what about you?"

"Molly is the only significant female in my present and future," he said, feeling a faint twist of bitterness when he thought of Molly's mother.

"But what about your romantic future? Surely there's someone who could be special to you."

"Nothing long term," Nicholas said. "I'm committed to keeping my relationships with women short term. I'm up-front about it, so there are no hard feelings."

Gail gave a snort of disbelief. "Yeah, right," she said as she washed Molly's belly.

"You don't believe me," he said, oddly affronted

by her response. "I'm completely clear about my intentions with a woman. No one is left wondering."

"Maybe not wondering, but hoping," she said, and rinsed Molly.

"Hoping for what?"

"Hoping you'll fall madly in love with her," she said as if it was the most obvious thing in the world.

Hard-earned cynicism cut through him. "I'll never fall madly in love with a woman again. There's no such thing as a happy ending."

Gail's eyebrows knitted together as if she didn't approve of his opinion but was holding her tongue. Nicholas suspected she found it difficult to hold her tongue when she had a strong opinion. She lifted Molly from the tub and wrapped her in a towel. In one smooth motion, she plopped his daughter in his arms. "I don't know," Gail mused aloud, glancing pointedly at Molly. "Looks to me like you got the winning hand this time."

Nicholas looked into the innocent wide eyes of his squirmy, damp daughter and felt his heart expand with protectiveness and love. He smiled at Molly. "Yeah, I guess I did."

Later that week Gail met Nicholas in the kitchen as he pulled a bottle of water from the refrigerator. His afternoon had been jam-packed with meetings to solve production problems. He was so tense his neck muscles felt like rubber bands pulled taut.

At her smile he felt the tension in him ease.

"Welcome home. I hate to jump you as soon as you walk in the door."

His neck tightened again. "A problem?"

"Not really," she said, lifting a picture frame she'd held by her side. "I just have a special request. I need a photograph of you."

"Why?" he asked, taking a deep gulp of the water.

"To put in Molly's room. You're gone all day, and I think it would be good if she has a constant visual reminder of you even when you're not here."

He shrugged. "Okay."

"Something informal would be best."

He nodded. "I'll see what I can dig up."

"And I need you to record a message to her."

Nicholas looked at her in confusion. "Record a message?"

"Sure," she said, moving closer to him and handing him the frame. "I got this today. It's so cool. We put your photo in the frame and record a message, then every time you push this button, you get to hear the message. Molly will love it."

The excitement in her voice amused and warmed him. "How do you know she won't start crying every time she hears my voice?"

Gail tossed him a sideways glance. "Because she's already warming up to you. And it's so easy. You can go ahead and record your message now."

"Now?" he said, drawing a complete blank. "What should I say?"

"Anything. You can sing part of a song. You can read from one of her favorite books. Or you can just tell her how special she is and how much you love her.''

The doorbell rang. Gail glanced at the clock. ''Oh, that'll be Jonathan. He's a friend,'' she said, answering his question before he voiced it. ''He called and said he wanted to watch a basketball game with me. You said I could use the downstairs den in the evenings if I want to have friends over. Is that still okay?''

Not really, Nicholas thought. After his hectic day, he'd enjoyed the few moments of conversation with Gail. But it wasn't fair to completely curtail her social life just because being with her had been as refreshing as the bottle of water. ''Sure,'' he said. ''I'm headed upstairs soon, anyway.''

''So you can record your message and find a photo,'' she hinted with a wide smile, then headed for the front door. ''I want to put it on Molly's dresser, so she can see it when she wakes up in the morning.''

''We'll see,'' he muttered as she opened the door.

A tall man in his late twenties swooped Gail up off her feet. ''How long were you going to leave me out there in the cold? I was starting to wonder if I was at the wrong house.''

''Put me down, Jonathan. You're just terrified you'll miss the beginning of the game,'' she said.

''There you go breaking my heart again,'' he said, allowing her feet to slide to the floor. ''I didn't want to miss one minute with you.''

''You're full of it,'' she said, dismissing him. ''The only reason you're watching the game with me is because your buddies are busy.'' She glanced over her shoulder and her gaze collided with Nicholas's. ''I'm sorry. I thought you had already left. Nicholas Barone, *my boss,*'' she added in a meaningful tone for her guest's benefit, ''this is Jonathan O'Reilly. Jonathan is one of my volleyball teammates, and also one of my best friends, despite the fact that he takes the Irish flirting thing way too seriously.''

Jonathan shot her a brief glance of mock disapproval, then extended his hand. ''It's a pleasure to meet you, Nicholas Barone. I've consumed a fair amount of your fine product over the years, and I've admired your company.''

''Thank you,'' Nicholas said, liking and not liking the man at the same time. Gail might insist that Jonathan was her friend, but Nicholas had been around long enough to sense that Jonathan wanted more than friendship with her. He resented the ease with which the man touched Gail, which was stupid. As long as Gail did her job with Molly, he shouldn't care about her relationships. ''There's beer in the fridge if you like.''

''Thanks. I don't want to chase you out of your own den,'' Gail said. ''If you'd like to join us...''

Nicholas shook his head. ''No, I have some reading to do.''

''And recording,'' she reminded him with a smile.

''And recording. Good night,'' he said to both of them, and climbed the stairs with an uncomfortable gnawing sensation in his gut. He heard the sound of Jonathan's low voice, followed by Gail's laughter, and stopped halfway up the stairs. Her laughter, robust and uninhibited, unintentionally sexy, sent a rush of shocking desire though him. Something about the sound of it was addictive, and it occurred to him that making Gail laugh could be like making her climax. The notion knocked him sideways, yet at the same time he knew it was true.

She laughed again, and the same sensation rolled through him. He frowned at his response. He couldn't recall ever becoming aroused just from the sound of a woman's laughter. Tamping down the strange but forceful urge to be the man to make her laugh, he climbed the rest of the stairs, but he didn't resist the temptation to leave his bedroom door open so he could hear her laugh again.

For the next two hours he scoured manufacturing reports in preparation for a regional meeting. His eyelids grew heavy, and he closed his eyes and leaned back against his pillow. He would rest for just a moment, he told himself, and slid into a dream that was more a mixture of images than a story...

He saw the faces of several of his top business managers and his father. Tension tightened his gut. Suddenly Gail's laughter floated across his consciousness, and he was transferred from the boardroom to his bedroom.

Her hair wild and free, Gail sat in the middle of his bed offering a smile of invitation. She wore a long-sleeved flannel nightgown that he wanted her to remove. He joined her on his bed, and as he took her mouth with his, he felt her start of surprise followed by her gradual acceptance of his kiss. Her lips were sweet and responsive.

Her murmurs of encouragement made him hard. He felt as if he'd waited a long time to kiss her, a long time to take her. Kissing her only made him want more. He put his hands over her breasts and she pressed against his palms with gratifying speed.

But she still wore her gown, and he wanted to feel her naked skin. He trailed his hands beneath the gown to her smooth legs, up to the top of her thighs, and paused in surprise. She wore no panties. The contrast of her nakedness beneath the flannel sent a roar of arousal through him. He touched her intimately and she wriggled against him.

He guided her hand to the place that ached for her touch, and she cupped him. He wanted more. Plunging his tongue into her mouth, he felt her pump him. His clothes dissolved, and there was nothing but heat and this woman. Just when the haze of his arousal began to clear, he felt her mouth pleasuring him.

The sight of her delicious mouth surrounding him nearly sent him over the edge. He was so close...

A child's cry broke the spell.

The visual abruptly vanished, and Nicholas blinked as he awoke with a crick in his neck. His papers still rested on his chest and he still wore his pants, yet he was fully aroused. What a strange dream. Had Gail really been— He heard another cry. Molly.

Automatically rising from the bed, he shook off his slumber and walked down the hall to her room. Gail stood there, holding his daughter, comforting her.

"Everybody needs a hug when they have a bad dream," she said to Molly.

Nicholas couldn't agree more. "Is she okay?" he asked in a low voice.

"I think we can't overdo the comfort measures for her yet," Gail said as she glanced at him. Then she took in a sharp breath.

Nicholas glanced down at his shirt. "I forgot to put my shirt in her crib," he said and began to remove it. He noticed that her gaze lingered on his chest before she seemed to deliberately look away. The banked admiration in her eyes stroked his nerve endings and his ego. She was attracted to him, he realized, and he sensed it was an honest attraction. As honest as a woman could be, he corrected, his cynicism rushing to protect him.

He watched Gail brush Molly's forehead with her lips, and his gut twisted as he remembered the pleasure her mouth had brought him.

In his dream, he reminded himself, and vowed to erase the erotic image from his mind.

Gail bent to return Molly to her crib, but his daughter immediately began to fuss. Gail picked her up again. "You can go on to bed. This may take a while."

"Has it happened before?"

Gail swayed from side to side to soothe Molly. "Only two other nights she couldn't seem to settle down."

He crossed his arms over his chest, frowning. "Do you think she's sick?"

Gail shook her head. "She doesn't seem to have a fever."

"What do you think it is?"

She shrugged. "I don't know. I just think she needs to be held."

"All night long?"

Gail smiled. "Maybe. So if I'm not perky tomorrow, you'll know why." She cocked her head toward the door. "Go back to bed. You have to function mentally tomorrow."

Nicholas slowly left the room and cleaned up for bed. It took him a while to fall asleep. He awakened in the dark early hours before dawn with the odd feeling that he needed to do something. Remembering Molly's difficulty going to sleep, he went down the hall to the nursery and saw Gail sitting in the rocking chair with the baby's head tucked against her shoulder. The sight stirred a strange, tender sensation inside him.

"Put her to bed," he said in a quiet voice.

Gail glanced up at him, her eyelids droopy from lack of sleep. She nodded and gingerly rose from the chair, then lowered Molly to her crib. They waited in complete silence.

A fussing sound erupted from the crib and Gail's shoulders slumped. She bent as if to pick up the baby, but Nicholas stayed her with his hand. "My turn."

Gail looked at him in surprise. "What about your sleep?"

"I got some sleep." He squeezed her shoulder. "You get yours."

"Are you sure?" she whispered.

He nodded, feeling a kind of bond with her. "We're a team. You need to sit this one out."

She held his gaze for a long moment. "If you're sure...."

"Go to bed."

Although her eyes were still blurry in a sexy, sleep-deprived way, her lips twitched with humor. "You're so good at giving orders."

"All you have to do is follow them," he said, leaning down to pick up his daughter. For the next hour he walked and rocked her. The minutes passed slowly and he vowed to make sure he shared all-nighters with Gail in the future. Just the idea of an all-nighter with Gail, however, prompted warmer, more pleasurable images. As he rocked his daughter and held her close, his mind wandered to Gail, her warmth and her ease, her laughter. Molly felt safe with her, and in a strange way Nicholas did, too.

The first rays of sunlight woke Gail. She opened her eyes and sat up in bed, listening for sounds from Molly's room. Rising from the bed, she left her room and walked the short distance to Molly's room where the door was cracked. She pushed the door open to find Nicholas asleep in the rocking chair with his daughter asleep on his bare chest.

The sight took her breath. They were both so alike, so beautiful. For all Nicholas's strength and all Molly's vulnerability, Gail sensed they both needed the same things—comfort, acceptance and a safe place. Her desire to provide both of them with those things was so strong it hurt. She wondered how her heart could be won so quickly, but she found it so easy to care for both of them.

Nicholas was such a powerful man, but Gail sensed a loneliness he kept mostly hidden. She saw a glimpse of the burden of being the firstborn in a hard-driving family. He rose to every challenge, but she suspected there were times when his duties wore on him. And now instant fatherhood had provided another challenge.

She shook her head at her thoughts. He could and would handle everything life tossed at him. He didn't need her sympathy, she told herself, but she wouldn't forget his insistence on taking a turn with Molly last night.

Moving forward, she extended her hand to touch his arm to wake him, but paused as if his skin might burn her. Disgusted with the thought, she touched him and watched his eyes. They immediately opened.

"Good morning," she whispered.

He glanced at the window, then back at her. "It doesn't look like morning."

"Room-darkening shades," she said, putting her hand on Molly's back. The baby barely moved. "I think she's finally out." She gingerly lifted her and lowered her to the crib. Molly wriggled to get into a comfortable position, then wrapped her hand around Nicholas's T-shirt and drew it against her mouth.

Feeling Nicholas standing behind her, Gail instinctively reached for him. "Look," she said, pulling him closer. "She's kissing your shirt."

Gail gazed into Nicholas's eyes and saw heart-breaking tenderness. He looked at Molly for a long moment, then turned his gaze to her. With a finger he touched her face underneath her eyes. "You need to get rid of these circles. Go back to bed."

"What about you?"

He cracked a grin and his gaze drifted over her with playful suggestiveness. "I'd love to join you, but I have to go to the office."

Gail gaped at him. "I...I didn't mean—"

He covered her lips with his index finger. "Don't worry. I'm just joking."

Gail took in the sight of his bare chest and bedroom eyes and swallowed a wail of confusion. What if she didn't want him to be joking?

Three

What he really wanted was a naked woman, a hot coupling, followed by a little peace and a glass of merlot. Weary from his full day at work and recalling a cocktail party he still had to attend at the mayor's home, Nicholas gave a heavy sigh as he stepped through his front door.

Gail and Molly greeted him. "Welcome home," Gail said, and Nicholas's wayward mind pictured her tangled in his sheets. The steamy image surprised him.

"We have two surprises for you," Gail said with a big smile.

He wiped his hand over his jaw. Something told him it wasn't going to include a hot coupling and tangled sheets. He sighed, dismissing his baser urges and turning his attention to his daughter. "Hello, Miss Molly, how are you?"

Molly shyly ducked her head. That was an improvement. At least she wasn't crying.

Gail looked down at Molly. "Okay, show him your stuff. Wave bye-bye."

Molly mimicked Gail. "Bye-bye-bye-bye-bye."

Nicholas chuckled. "Is this a hint that I should leave?"

"No. Wave back to her."

"Bye-bye," he said, waving and feeling slightly foolish.

"Bye-bye-bye-bye," Molly said, waving again.

"Good girl," Gail said. "Now here's the biggie." She whispered something in Molly's ear, and his daughter appeared to listen intently.

"Da-da-da-da," she said, and Nicholas felt his heart swell.

"Who is that?" Gail asked, pointing at Nicholas.

"Da-da-da-da-da-da," Molly said.

"What a smart little girl," he said to Molly. Encouraged by his approval, she continued to babble dada. Delighted, Nicholas shook his head. "When did this happen?"

"Today," Gail said proudly. "We pushed the message button on your photograph so many times I'm going to have to get another battery, but I don't care. This is so cool. She's so pleased with herself she can barely stop. Plus," she added, "we attended our first 'water babies' class at the health club today."

"How did my girl like it?" he asked doubtfully.

"She howled for the first fifteen minutes, but then she really enjoyed herself. I think she's part fish."

"Sounds like you two had fun today," he said, feeling a twinge of envy. "Damn, I wish I didn't have a cocktail party tonight."

A sliver of disappointment came and went in Gail's eyes. "We'll be all right."

"Yeah, but will I," he said dryly. "By the way, you can have the evening off. My father's out of town and my mother says she's experiencing grandchild withdrawal, so she's going to take care of Molly tonight."

"Okay, well, maybe Molly can show off her new tricks."

"What will you do?"

She shrugged. "I don't know. Maybe I'll give Jonathan a call."

The notion didn't sit well with him. "Or you could make this cocktail party a little more bearable by going with me," he suggested impulsively.

Her eyes rounded. "Me?"

He shrugged, walking down the hallway. "The woman who was supposed to attend with me has the flu. To tell you the truth, I'd forgotten I was committed to go until she called to cancel."

"Oh." Gail blinked as she digested his remarks. "Well, why don't you look in your little black book, or maybe yours is a *big* black book, and—"

"Because I don't feel like entertaining tonight. I'm tired," he said, tugging his tie loose.

"Then why are you going?"

"Because it's the mayor and a Barone needs to be there."

"But there are lots of Barones, aren't there?"

"Yeah, but—" He broke off and shrugged.

"Yeah, but you're the oldest and it's expected," she concluded.

He sighed. "I usually don't mind."

"I'm sure you don't," she said, her expression thoughtful. "Is it formal?"

He shook his head. "I'll wear what I have on and you can wear what you want. The bunny slippers would be a nice conversation starter."

She shot him a sideways glance. "I'm sure they would." She paused. "Okay. I'll go."

The sudden easing in his chest surprised him. He would have to think about that later. "Good. Can you be ready in about thirty minutes?" he asked, knowing her answer before she uttered it. That was one of the great things about Gail. No fuss. No muss.

Gail stared in her closet and swallowed a wail of panic. She'd just accepted a pseudo-date with Nicholas Barone. Except it wasn't even a pseudo-date, because she was a stand-in and he didn't really want to go.

Her heart hammered in her chest. So why had she accepted? He'd looked so weary and handsome, yet touched when Molly had called him da-da. She'd felt sorry for him.

That was ridiculous. He was the hottest bachelor in Boston. The man was so hot a woman needed a fire suit just to stand next to him. She looked over her unimpressive wardrobe, wondering if anything she owned was fire retardant.

She glanced at the clock and another shot of panic raced through her. She was supposed to go from nanny to appropriate escort in less than twenty-five minutes when she really needed a week for that kind of transformation.

"A week," she muttered to herself, pulling a soft brown sweater from the closet. "Who do you think you're fooling?" She grabbed a matching long brown skirt and hoped it still fit. She dug out a pair of boots. "Panty hose," she muttered and raced to her lingerie drawer. The last pair she'd worn had a run, and that was apparently the only pair she owned.

Another shot of panic raced through her. The skirt would cover the run. She glanced in the mirror at her face and hair. Some work needed there.

After several unsuccessful attempts to apply eye liner, Gail gave up and smudged some lipstick on her mouth and mascara on her pale eyelashes. She put her hair in a French-braid from which tiny tendrils were already escaping, but there was no way to prevent it. Nervous and full of regret, she walked downstairs.

Nicholas looked at her for such a long moment that she nearly turned around and went back upstairs. "Chocolate," he finally said. "You look good in chocolate."

And Gail felt almost pretty. After a short drive in Nicholas's luxury sports car, they arrived at the mayor's home. A valet parked the car and a housekeeper in a black uniform took their coats. One glance into Mayor Forwood's posh living room told Gail she had not dressed appropriately. Nearly every woman at the gathering wore the proverbial little black dress.

Gail didn't even own one. Dress at her former job had been casual, and she sure as heck didn't need a black dress on the volleyball court. Brushing aside her discomfort, she tried to project a confidence she didn't feel.

A woman wearing a black dress and pearls approached Nicholas and extended her hand. "Nicholas, we're so delighted you've come. Bill always says a party's not a party if the Barones aren't represented. And your date," she said, looking at Gail. "I thought Corinne was joining us."

"Corinne is sick and Gail was kind enough to join me at the last minute," Nicholas smoothly interjected. "Gail Fenton, this is Jo-Ann Forwood."

"It's a pleasure to meet you. Your home is lovely," Gail said.

"Thank you. Are you a colleague of Nicholas's?" Jo-Ann asked, her gaze curious.

"Oh, I just started—"

"Gail is a close family friend," Nicholas interjected again. "Did I hear you say you were thirsty?" he asked Gail.

Uh, no, she thought, wondering why he didn't want Jo-Ann to know she was his daughter's nanny.

"We must get you something to drink," Jo-Ann said. "What would you like?"

Gail drew a blank. She'd been surrounded by milk,

baby food and apple juice. She felt Nicholas's gaze on her.

"White wine," he said.

"Beer," Gail said at the same time.

Jo-Ann's eyes widened. "Beer," she echoed, then recovered her poise. "And what may we get for you, Nicholas?"

"Scotch, neat," he said.

"Very good. Excuse me while I tell the bartender," she said, and glided away.

Gail immediately turned to Nicholas. "Why didn't you want to tell her I was your daughter's nanny?"

"Because it's none of her business," he said, irritation bleeding into his tone.

"Are you sure it's not because you're embarrassed that you're here with a nanny?"

His jaw tightened and anger flashed in his eyes. "I can do what I damn well—" He took a deep breath. "Later," he muttered. "The mayor's coming."

Over the next thirty minutes Gail met six people. They all asked about Corinne, and Gail quickly grew weary of the dubious expressions on their faces as they looked at her. She was clearly a fish out of water. To be brutally honest, she didn't want to be in the water, except that for some strange reason she'd wanted to please Nicholas. The party wore on and Gail became separated from Nicholas. One beautiful woman after another vied for his attention.

Mentally waving the white flag, Gail nursed another beer and wandered into a connecting room. An elderly woman sat next to roaring fire. "Nice fire," Gail said, then politely introduced herself.

The woman smiled. "I'm Delores Forwood. Bill's my son."

"You must be very proud of him."

"Depends on the day," Delores replied. "He's a political blowhard who's going to get too big for his britches if he's not careful." Her tone was feisty.

Gail's lips twitched at Delores's bluntness. "Something tells me you try to keep him in line."

"I try, and sometimes I do, since the key to his inheritance is me. That beer looks good," she said, gazing longingly at the tall glass Gail held.

"Would you like me to get one for you?"

"Yes, but just make sure Jo-Ann doesn't see you. She'll have a conniption fit. Who are you here with?"

"Nicholas Barone," Gail said, and paused a second. "His date is sick and he needed a quick replacement. I'm his daughter's nanny."

"Nicholas Barone," the woman murmured. "He's a gorgeous man. Smart, too," she said. "Probably bored as hell. You're not his usual type."

"I got that impression," Gail said wryly.

"Maybe his taste is improving," the old woman said slyly.

Gail laughed. "Oh, I'm glad I found you. Let me get your beer," she said, and brought a tall, cold glass to the mayor's mother.

Gail enjoyed her conversation with the woman so much that thirty minutes passed before a shadow fell over her.

"I couldn't find you," Nicholas said as he stepped next to her.

Gail glanced at the clock on the mantel. "I guess I lost track of the time. Have you met Delores Forwood?"

"I have," he said, and smiled at the woman. "I should have known Gail would find the most interesting person at the party to talk with."

Delores smiled with pleasure. "You Italians are full of flattery. You're worse than the Irish."

"I won't take that as an insult since I know your husband was Irish."

"So he was. I enjoyed my visit with your daughter's nanny. If it means I get to chat with Gail, I hope all your future dates get sick."

Nicholas stared at Delores in surprise for a beat, then roared with laughter. "You're a breath of fresh air."

"Especially after spending an hour in that room. You need a backhoe to get through all that brown stuff, if you know what I mean."

Nicholas chuckled again. "It's a pleasure seeing you again, Delores, but we need to be going."

Delores patted Gail's hand. "Visit again. Anytime."

"Thank you. I will," Gail said. "Thanks for the chat."

"Thank *you* for the company. Good night, you two."

Nicholas led Gail away from the party after they

thanked the host and hostess. As soon as he put the car in gear, he glanced at her. "You disappeared."

"Not really," she said. "You were busy."

He frowned. "I'm not accustomed to having to go searching for my date."

"Oh, well, I wasn't really a date."

He slowed at a stoplight and turned to look at her. "Then what were you?"

"Your daughter's nanny operating as a last-minute substitute whom you didn't have to entertain for an engagement you didn't want to attend," she said, and told her ego not to feel pinched. It was the truth and she should be totally okay with it.

"But I'm still responsible for you having an enjoyable time," he said.

"Not really," she said. "That's gentlemanly of you, but not necessary in this situation. I think you're used to women pretty much planting themselves by your side. It's probably a territorial thing. But I don't feel that way about you."

He looked at her for a long moment. "You don't feel that way about me."

"Of course not," she insisted. "And if I did, I'd be in big trouble because there was a bunch of beautiful women elbowing their way next to you."

"I had thought that having you with me would prevent that," he said.

Gail gaped at him. He was serious. Amusement bubbled up from her throat and she laughed.

"What's so funny?"

"Nicholas, if you were looking for a woman to

intimidate all your wannabe girlfriends, you picked the wrong girl. I don't look the role. I didn't even have on the right uniform.'' She nodded. ''Light turned green.''

He returned his focus to the road and moved forward. ''Right uniform?'' he echoed.

''Little black dress. I don't own one. I'm a great nanny, a great friend. But I'm no female barracuda and I never will be.''

''I guess you're not,'' he said, but something in his expression indicated that wasn't bad. ''How did you find Delores Forwood? They usually try to hide her.''

''She was in the next room. I've learned the secret to surviving parties, you know.''

''What's that?''

''The nicest and most interesting people at a party are often in the corners, not in the middle.''

''I was in the middle,'' Nicholas said. ''Are you saying I'm boring?''

''You were there under duress,'' she said.

''I was,'' he agreed. ''The next time you go to a party, I'm following you into the corner.''

His statement hung in her brain like a veiled but delicious sensual threat. ''Okay,'' she muttered. ''But the corner's gonna get awfully crowded when all your wannabe dates follow you there.'' Nicholas just chuckled, but Gail knew as sure as her hair was red that she wouldn't be attending any more parties with him.

The following morning Gail perused the morning paper while Molly picked up her Cheerios one by one and ate them. Molly seemed to delight in finger food and relished the opportunity to exert her independence.

Gail read the front page, then the sports section, then glanced at the style section. A photograph on the front page caught her attention. A dozen local women were featured in photos for their stylish clothing. It just so happened that Nicholas was shown escorting one of them.

Gail couldn't help staring at the photograph. First she looked at Nicholas. What woman wouldn't? He was one of those men who would look just as good naked as he did in a suit. And the woman beside him in the photo was so beautiful she almost didn't look real. Gail studied the woman's impeccable clothing from head to toe, all the while entirely too aware of her own sweat suit and tennis shoes.

Nicholas's housekeeper, a middle-aged woman from Romania named Ana, came up behind Gail. "One of Mr. Barone's ladies?"

Feeling her stomach give an involuntary twist, Gail nodded. The photograph underscored the differences between her and the other women in Nicholas's life. The stark contrast shouldn't bother her. She'd always been fairly content with herself, never spending much time pining to be different. So why was she bothered now? "She's beautiful. Everything about her looks so perfect. I wonder how she does it."

"They're all beautiful," Ana said. "But Mr. Barone, he is quite handsome. The newspaper takes his picture all the time. He looks so good. But the women, he doesn't let them into his heart."

"That's what he told me," Gail said.

Ana's dark eyebrows flew upward. "He told you that?"

Gail shrugged. "Men tell me things they wouldn't normally share with a woman. They don't see me as a potential romantic partner. I'm like one of the guys," she said, and though she hadn't minded the situation before, the notion that no man viewed her in a romantic way was starting to grate on her. Silly, she told herself. Last night had just been a little tough on the ego. "I can't disagree with you about Mr. Barone, though. He's a hottie. I'm beginning to think I should get hazard pay working for him."

"Hazard pay?" Ana said.

"Sure. He's so hot he's hazardous to a woman's concentration."

Ana laughed and swiped at her. "You are joking. You have good sense of humor."

Gail wasn't joking. She had the uncomfortable feeling that any woman in Nicholas's proximity could fall for him, and based on his attitude toward romantic love, that would be a disaster. She opened her mouth to protest, but a Cheerio hit her on the cheek.

She glanced up at Molly just before another barely missed her nose. "You little bugger," she said, rising to clean up the toddler. "I've told you not to throw food. Soon enough, you'll be eating Italian food, and people don't like to dodge meatballs even from cutiepies like you."

Molly lifted her hand to toss another Cheerio, but Gail stopped her. "No, no," she said, taking the Cheerio from her tight clasp. "Breakfast is over. If you're throwing food, then you're definitely not hungry."

She quickly wiped off Molly's hands and face, then lifted her from the high chair. Molly immediately wrapped her hand around a strand of Gail's hair.

"It's so sweet the way the baby reaches for your hair," Ana said, and smiled.

"Yes." Gail looked down into Molly's trusting wide eyes. "This is one person who definitely doesn't care if I wear designer clothes or sweats." Molly adored her, but, Gail reminded herself, she would do well to remember that *Nicholas* would never fall for any woman, least of all her.

That not-good-enough feeling followed Gail around for the next two days. By game time on Thursday night, she was ready to take out her frustration on the volleyball court. She played hard, too hard, and she pulled a muscle in her shoulder in the last three minutes of the game.

Her team won, and her teammates were jazzed with her performance. They wanted to take her to their favorite bar to celebrate, but Gail's shoulder hurt too much to hang around. She drove home and quietly crept in the front door, then tiptoed down the hall. All she wanted was the peace and quiet of her room.

"How was the game?" an all-too familiar masculine voice asked from behind her in a tone that wreaked havoc with her heart.

Gail tensed. She didn't turn. She didn't want to look at him. The man had filled too many of her thoughts lately. "Great. We creamed them. Only problem is I creamed my shoulder in the process," she said, squeezing her right shoulder.

He walked to her side. "How bad is it?"

"I won't die from it."

"You'll just feel like it," he said with a gentle smile of commiseration. "Go get in the Jacuzzi in the mini-gym downstairs. It'll work wonders."

She couldn't deny that a few minutes in a hot tub sounded inviting. "Then I'll go straight to bed," she said, finally glancing at him. "Thanks."

Gail quickly climbed the stairs, stripped and pulled on a one-piece bathing suit. Self-conscious about running into Nicholas, she pulled on a sweat suit, too. She took the two flights down to the mini-gym to find the light already turned on and the hot tub bubbling in invitation.

Breathing a sigh of relief that Nicholas was nowhere in sight, she pulled off the sweat suit and stepped into the tub. She sank into the hot water and moaned as her muscles immediately began to unknot. She closed her eyes and relaxed.

"Is it your right shoulder," Nicholas said from behind her, startling her so that she jerked upright. She felt his hand on her bare skin. "You need to relax."

"It would help if you wouldn't sneak up behind me."

"I didn't sneak. You were almost asleep." He gently massaged her shoulder. "Relax."

While you're touching me? she thought. Fat chance. She closed her eyes and exhaled. As long as he stayed out of the hot tub, everything would be fine. She allowed herself to relax while his fingers soothed her knotted muscles.

She felt him shift his stance and swear under his breath. "This is too difficult from this position. I'm coming in."

Uh-oh.

Four

"**No!** That's really not necessary. You've done enough," Gail said, standing up in the tub. "More than enough."

"What is with you?" Nicholas asked, looking at her as if she had a loose screw. He stepped into the swirling water. "Why are you panicking? Do you have some kind of phobia about hot tubs or something?"

"No, but—" She broke off, flustered, feeling color rise to her cheeks. She tried to avoid looking at his naked chest, but wasn't succeeding. "Don't you think it's…well, inappropriate for us to be in the hot tub together?"

"Why?" he asked with a blank expression on his face. "We're not naked." He shrugged. "Although I admit I usually don't wear anything when I get in the hot tub.''

Gail closed her eyes and swallowed a moan. ''That's more than I needed to know.''

''Just sit down.''

Gail sighed and sank back down in the water. ''Why are you doing this?''

''I owe you after that awful cocktail party,'' he said, returning his hands to her shoulder. ''Waste of a free evening.''

''It was pretty bad,'' she conceded. ''Except I enjoyed meeting Delores.''

''Hmm,'' he said, continuing to massage her. ''So you're the POM?''

''What's a POM?''

''Player of the moment.''

''Yeah,'' she said, smiling at the acronym. ''I'll have to tell that one to Jonathan. He'll love it.''

''Was he there tonight?''

''He's always there. He's the team captain.''

''And he wants to be more than friends with you,'' Nicholas said.

Gail laughed. ''That's a good one. You're wrong, you know. Jonathan and I have been friends forever. Well, at least through college.''

''Trust me. I know what I'm talking about. I saw the way he looks at you,'' Nicholas said.

Gail paused at his tone. He wasn't joking. She opened her eyes and turned around to look at him. ''How does he look at me?''

"Like he wants to get you in his bed," Nicholas said, his voice low, his eyes full of secrets.

Gail's stomach turned a somersault at the idea of Nicholas wanting her in his bed. She sucked in a shocked breath. Where had that thought come from? She shook her head. "I haven't seen that from him at all."

"Maybe because you're not looking for it," he said, lifting a wayward strand of hair from her cheek.

"Or maybe it just doesn't seem likely to me. I'm not—"

"Don't say you're not pretty. Beauty is in the eye of the beholder," Nicholas said.

Gail rolled her eyes. "Okay. I'm not sexy."

His gaze took a slow trip over her face, hovered on her lips so long they burned, then slid down to the tops of her breasts and lower. Gail felt her nipples grow taut and sank lower into the water.

His gaze returned to hers. "That's a matter of opinion."

Her heart hammered against her rib cage. She felt as if she were going to dissolve into the bubbling water. She tried to gulp a deep, mind-clearing breath, but only managed a shallow one. The sexual intensity in his eyes scrambled her mental circuits, and of its own volition, her body leaned toward his. She instinctively lifted her mouth.

He lowered his.

She sucked in another quick breath. She was going to kiss him. He was going to—

No! Some wayward part of her rational mind

kicked in. This was craziness. She forced herself to back away. "You are very good," she said, wishing her voice didn't sound so husky.

"What does that mean?"

"I mean I'm starting to understand why women fall at your feet."

"I'd argue that they fall at my feet, but I'd love to hear why you think they do."

"You seduce without trying. It's in your eyes and in your voice. You just ooze it out of your pores. A woman would mistake that and think you meant something personal." She stiffened her backbone even though she felt like melted butter. "But not me."

"Why not you?"

She rose to her feet. "Because it would be the biggest mistake a woman could make to believe you want only her. I may be inexperienced, but that doesn't mean I'm stupid."

He rose slowly in front of her. "So what you're saying is that you're totally immune." A dark challenge glinted in his eyes.

She had the sinking sensation she'd woken a sleeping lion. "I didn't say I was immune. I just said—"

"So if I kissed you—" he moved closer "—it wouldn't affect you."

Alarm shot through her. "I didn't say that, either. I just said—"

"Let's see," he cut in, and lowered his mouth to hers.

Gail froze in shock, her eyes wide-open, her vision

blurred by his closeness. She tried to open her mouth to speak, but he used the movement as an invitation to deepen the kiss.

''Your lips are so soft,'' he muttered against her mouth, causing a delicious vibration. He rubbed his mouth from side to side against hers in a sensual motion, and she felt his warm hand gently press the small of her back. Everything about him said ''Come a little closer, I'll make you feel good.''

Just as she thought she might gather her wits, he drew even closer. His chest brushed her breasts and he dipped his tongue past her lips.

Her heart pounding, Gail was caught between a decadent urge and good sense. When he curled one of his hands behind the nape of her neck, the gentle gesture slid past her defenses. He kissed her with a combination of controlled desire and curiosity. She couldn't help wondering what would happen when he took the leash off his desire. The dark energy of passion underneath his caress sent a rush of heat through her.

This was a man who knew how to give and receive pleasure. A man with no hang-ups, no inhibitions. He exuded confidence in his sexuality.

Gail opened her mouth and, following an unbidden instinct, curled her tongue around his and sucked it deeper into her mouth.

Giving a low murmur of approval, he drew her body flush with his, and she immediately felt his arousal through his wet trunks. He began to devour her mouth with his. Something inside her demanded that she respond, stroke for stroke, caress for caress. His heat suffused her, and when he slid his hand to her bottom to guide her against him intimately, her knees grew weak. He wanted her, and the blatant signs from his body made her head spin.

He skimmed his hand up to her breast and rubbed her stiff nipple with his thumb. ''Damn, I wish you didn't have anything on. I want to put my mouth all over you.''

The hot, illicit image of his mouth on her nipple raced through her mind, causing a ricochet of need.

He took her hand and guided it down his belly to the waist of his bathing suit. He stopped abruptly and swore, tearing his mouth from hers. His eyes burned like fire as he stared down at her, his breath harsh. He didn't say it, but she could read his words on his face. What in hell am I doing?

Embarrassment and need tugging her in opposite directions, she stepped back, trying to catch her breath. She bit her lip and watched his gaze drop to her lips and linger. His gaze sent another punch of desire through her. Ripping her gaze from his, she looked down. ''This wasn't a good idea.''

''I know,'' he said.

The suggestion of desire in his voice did little to appease her ego. Some insane part of her had wanted him to disagree. ''I'm not your type.''

''I know.''

Gail scowled. He could have at least paused before he'd agreed with her. She mentally slapped herself. Was she losing her mind? She glanced at him with as stern an expression as she could manage. "I'm your daughter's nanny. I'm sure I don't have one-tenth of your sexual experience. It's not fair for you to play with me. It's like bringing an AK-47 to a fight with someone who has a water pistol."

His gaze slid over her like hot liquid. "I think you underestimate your appeal."

She felt the slow drag of seduction pull at her again and fought it. "Well, I'm not underestimating yours. Pick on someone your own size," she said, and wrinkled her brow because it didn't make sense. She waggled her finger at him. "Pick on someone who has the same experience level. Pick on someone whose breath you don't take away," she said, and turned from him, marching as if the hounds of hell were nipping at her heels.

Gail awoke after a restless night the following day. After the hot-tub incident her mind might have tried to bring her libido under control, but her body had liked the way Nicholas had touched and caressed. Her body had ached for more all night.

Her body was just going to have to get over it, she told herself ruthlessly as she sipped her morning coffee while Molly threw cereal at her. Just as Gail was putting aside the newspaper, she saw another photograph of Nicholas with a beautiful woman by his side.

She bared her teeth at the photo, then rolled her eyes at herself and turned her attention to Molly. "We're going to see Daddy today," she said as she cleaned up the baby. Nicholas had asked Gail to bring Molly to the office sometime this week.

Molly bounced up and down in her high chair as if she understood Gail. ''We're going to dress you up and take you to Daddy's office, so everyone can see you. I want to see lots of smiles,'' she said, tickling Molly's neck and causing her to giggle.

Gail dressed Molly in a cute red velvet dress with white tights and a matching red velvet hat. Molly fussed with the hat until Gail successfully distracted the toddler with one of her favorite toys. Gail quickly pulled on a brown jumper and matching boots, and scooped part of her hair away from her face with two barrettes.

With Molly safely tucked into her car seat, Gail made the short drive to the five-story glass-and-chrome building that housed Baronessa's executive headquarters. She parked in the spot Nicholas had arranged for her and carried Molly through the lobby, pointing out pictures to the baby and reading a couple of the small plaques explaining the history of the company and the awards the gelato had won over the years. She allowed Molly to push the elevator button to the top floor and once there, walked toward Nicholas's office. Molly was immediately greeted with smiles.

''She looks just like Mr. Barone,'' Gail heard one woman say as she walked past.

''When she gets older, I bet she'll attract the opposite sex with the same ease as her dad,'' another murmured.

Gail caught sight of Nicholas flanked by two stylishly dressed women. She shook off concerns about her brown jumper. She was dressed appropriately, she told herself. She was a nanny, not a runway model. Nicholas glanced up, and Gail's heart dipped. He looked at Molly and smiled.

Molly began to kick and Gail coached the baby in a whisper. "Da-da."

"Da-da-da-da-da-da," Molly called.

"I wondered when you two would get here," Nicholas said. "Don't you look gorgeous," he said, chucking Molly's chin.

His daughter coyly ducked, and it occurred to Gail that Nicholas's ability to charm was beginning to extend to Molly.

"Oh, she's just beautiful," one of the women beside Nicholas cooed. "May I hold her for a moment?"

Nicholas hesitated, glancing at Molly's fingers gripping Gail's hair. "Maybe in a little bit, Jen. There are a lot of unfamiliar faces, so we probably need to give her a chance to get comfortable. Jen, this is Gail Fenton. She's the miracle nanny."

Jen looked at Gail as if trying to imagine how she could possibly work miracles. Gail resisted the urge to feel inadequate and extended her hand, instead. "It's nice to meet you, Jen," she said.

After that, Nicholas held his hands out for Molly and to Gail's relief, his daughter went to him with no fussing. She noticed that every now and then Molly looked back to make sure Gail was still close by.

Nicholas introduced several people, including his brother, Joseph Barone, CFO of Baronessa.

Gail couldn't help noticing the stark difference in personality between Nicholas and Joseph. Nicholas's eyes were alight with humor and sharp wit, while Joseph appeared rather serious and formal. She sensed a deep sadness in him and thought she might ask Nicholas about it later.

A lovely, tall, slender woman with long, curly light-brown hair walked into the public area of the executive suite, and the crowd immediately parted for her. Her violet eyes sparkled like firecrackers, but she emanated a cool, sophisticated aura. Her expression said "Don't underestimate me."

"I heard a rumor that my niece is here. I know you've been keeping her close to home, Nicholas, so she's not getting away until I get a good look at her." She turned to Molly. "*Bellisima.* Little one, you are going to break hearts and drive my arrogant brother crazy." She looked at Nicholas and shot him a wide, wicked smile. "You are so in trouble with this one. With all the hearts you've broken, it's time for you to get a little of your own back."

"Thank you for your words of comfort and support," Nicholas said dryly. "This is my little sister, Gina. She's in charge of PR. Gina, this is Gail."

She nodded. "The wonder nanny," Gina said, and extended her hand. "I'm very pleased to meet you. Molly cried so much in the beginning that my mother was afraid you would quit. So was Nick," she murmured.

"Really?" Gail said, surprised. "It was an adjustment period."

"Yes, but most adjustment periods don't require a truckload of headache medication."

Gail smiled, liking the woman immediately. "I didn't really need a truckload," she said. "Maybe a crate. But look at her now."

Molly extended her arms to Gail.

"Mr. Barone, you have an international conference call on line one," his secretary said. "Shall I postpone it?"

Nicholas shook his head, passing Molly to Gail. "No, I should take it. Can you wait a few more minutes?" he asked Gail.

She nodded. "I brought treats in case we needed to wait."

"Good planning," he said, his gaze locking with hers as an electric understanding hummed between them.

Gail's heart bumped. It was amazing how one look from that man could affect a woman. *Any* woman, she reminded herself. In this case, she was not unique.

"They can come down to my office while they wait," Gina offered.

"Okay, I'll be there as soon as I finish the call," he said, and headed for his office.

Gina led Gail to her office on the fourth floor. "I'd love to hold her," she said as she ushered them inside and closed the door, "but Nicholas told me Molly's a little tense around new people."

"She is," Gail agreed. "I would offer for you to

give her a cookie, but she's a messy eater, and I'm afraid you might end up with wet cookie on your dress.''

Gina motioned for Gail to sit next to her desk, then sat down and wiggled her fingers. ''I'll risk the mess. I don't have any appointments today. What's dry cleaning for, anyway? Right?''

Gail pulled the treat from her bag and handed it to Gina. ''Aunt Gina wants to give you a cookie,'' she said in Molly's ear. She moved Molly to Gina's lap and gingerly disentangled the baby's fingers from her hair.

When Molly happily nibbled on the cookie, Gail exhaled a sigh of relief.

''You really have worked wonders,'' Gina said, stroking Molly's cheek. ''Both Nick and Mom told me she cried all the time when Nick first brought her home. He also told me you used to work for a computer company.''

''Molly's a lot more fun,'' Gail said. ''Although I'm starting to think I may need to adjust my image during my off-hours. Maybe cut my hair or buy some new clothes. I didn't think about it much before now, but—'' Gail stopped and shrugged, finding it difficult to explain her feelings to someone when she didn't understand them herself. Before, it had always been okay to be every guy's buddy. Before what? Before Nicholas, her conscience whispered. She frowned.

''I'm sure Molly and Nicholas are fine with your image,'' Gina said.

Her image as a nanny, Gail added, and felt a knot

of distress. She shouldn't be concerned about Nicholas's opinion of her image. Heaven knows, she'd never be in his league. Even so, she didn't like the idea of being perceived as a sexless nanny by the rest of the male population.

"If you'd really like a change, I can recommend a great hairstylist," Gina said, pulling a business card from her top drawer. "Henri's the best. Tell him I sent you."

Gail took the card. "Thanks. I'll do that."

"So how do you like working for my brother?"

"He's very smart and knows exactly what he wants. I admire how quickly he's taken on his responsibilities for Molly. Not every man would."

"True, but Nick is the oldest sibling and has always been expected to perform at a higher level than most mere mortals. He's protective of all of us." She rolled her eyes, but her expression couldn't hide a deep fondness. "I have to fight some of the baby-sister routine on a regular basis, both in the boardroom and at home."

"Looks like you're holding your own," Gail said, surprised at the connection she felt with Nicholas's sister.

A sharp rap sounded and the door whisked open. "How are my girls?" Nicholas asked.

Gail's heart tripped. What would it be like to be Nicholas's girl? She immediately felt foolish for her reaction. When would she learn? Nicholas was a player. She was not, and she didn't really want to be.

With a thank-you to his sister, Nicholas ushered

Gail and Molly to the elevator. He joined them on the ride down and pulled Gail to a quiet corner in the lobby. "Listen," he said, "I need to apologize."

Her chest tightened with a weird knot of dread. "Apologize for what?"

"For the way I acted last night." He shook his head. "I don't know what got into me. Maybe it was insanity brought on by lack of sleep."

Gail felt the knot in her chest tighten painfully. "You're saying you kissed me because you were insane and sleepy." She tried to remember when she'd felt more insulted.

"I know it's lame," he confessed. "But I can't come up with any reasonable explanation for my behavior."

Such as you were at least remotely attracted to me, she thought. She felt a slow sizzle of anger burn through her blood.

"I need to apologize to you," he went on. "You are very important to Molly and me, and I don't want to mess that up. Molly is my primary concern and I don't want to jeopardize her care."

Gail nodded slowly, feeling her temperature rise. "You're right."

He let out a sigh of relief. "I'm glad you understand."

"I understand completely. I have the same problem. I can't come up with one logical reason why I kissed you last night. I've never gone for the arrogant, playboy type. Never," she said with emphasis.

He blinked. "You haven't?"

His surprised expression soothed her battered ego. "I sure haven't. I totally agree with you. Last night was a crazy aberration. You're not my type at all," she said, and planned to mentally repeat those statements until she washed all erotic, seductive images of Nicholas Barone from her mind.

Five

His daughter's nanny had a date.

The prospect irritated the hell out of Nicholas, but he kept his grumpiness to himself. During the past few days, he'd watched Gail undergo a transformation before his very eyes. Someone had cut her hair in a sexy, layered style that celebrated her curls, instead of trying to tame them. Yesterday he could have sworn that when she came home, she was wearing makeup.

Nicholas shouldn't care. As long as she took good care of Molly, then it was none of his business what Gail did during her off-hours. He was just concerned about her. With seven younger siblings and four of them sisters, he came by his highly developed pro-tectiveness honestly. He felt the same kind of protectiveness for Gail that he felt for his sisters, he told himself as he reread a paragraph in an article on the future of the economy from the latest edition of the *Wall Street Journal.*

Molly had gone to sleep early and Nicholas was settled in for a much-needed peaceful evening in front of the fire in the den.

He heard the click of high heels on the staircase. Gail. Curiosity burning him up inside, he craned his neck for a peek at her, but he couldn't see. He casually repositioned himself in another chair just inside the den and waited until she moved closer.

When he saw her, his eyes nearly fell out of his head. The *Wall Street Journal* slipped from his fingers.

What had the woman done to herself? Her wild hair fell in sexy tendrils around her face, and she had on enough makeup for three women. Still, the eyeliner emphasized her eyes in a sultry way. She wore a purple dress that faithfully clung to every curve and stopped several inches above her knees, revealing her shapely legs. Her red lips were pursed in a moue of unhappiness as she glanced down at the high heels with an expression of complete exasperation.

"Might as well be walking on a pair of stilts," she muttered, then glanced up and abruptly met Nicholas's gaze. He felt as if he'd been punched in the stomach. A wave of self-consciousness crossed her face, then she lifted her chin as if to fight it off. "How do you like my new look?"

Nicholas blinked and stood, shoving his hands into

his pockets. The sight of her mouth accented with red lipstick brought his forbidden visual to the forefront of his mind. He cleared his throat. "It's different. You look very different."

Her face fell. "You don't like it," she said.

"I didn't say that," he said quickly. "I'm still just taking it all in. Who cut your hair?"

"Henri. Gina recommended him."

I should have known, he thought, resisting the urge to grind his teeth.

"He was just as good as she said he was. He recommended a complete makeover, hair, makeup, clothes. I haven't quite perfected the eye-makeup techniques yet."

"That probably takes practice," Nicholas said in the most neutral tone he could muster.

"But Henri also recommended this dress. I had nothing like it in my wardrobe. What do you think?"

"It fits," he said. "It fits like a glove. And the color is good on you."

"Thanks," she said with a smile. "I love my job as nanny, but it just recently occurred to me that guys perceive me as, well, asexual partly because of my job. I'm already everyone's favorite buddy, so I thought I might need to counter the nanny image.

"Henri also recommended a magazine called *Goddess*," she continued. "It sounds kinda silly, but the idea is to unleash your inner goddess, so I'm trying some of the suggestions from the magazine."

He nodded, but he had no earthly idea what she was talking about.

"But some of the suggestions," she said, shaking her head, "I just can't see myself doing."

"Like what?"

She shot him a doubtful look. "Are you sure you're interested?"

"Trust me. This is a helluva lot more interesting than the article I was just reading about the economy."

"Okay, I can get used to wearing thong underwear and learn how to walk in heels even though it may kill me, but one of the articles featured suggested pickup lines for women to use with men. I can't imagine myself saying some of them."

Nicholas felt his neck tighten with an inexplicable tension. "Give me an example."

"I can imagine going panty-less for one evening, but I just can't imagine going up to some guy I don't know very well and saying, 'Oops, I forgot my panties.' Is it just me or is that a little over the top?"

Nicholas couldn't prevent his gaze from skimming down over her hips. No panty lines. Was she naked beneath that man-eater dress? His neck tightened again. "I guess it depends on what kind of man you're trying to attract."

"What do you mean?"

"I mean some men prefer understated, natural beauty. Some men are attracted to modesty," he said.

"Really?" she said, tilting her head to one side as if considering the notion. She bit her plump lip, then shook her head. "But don't you think most men like that are in their sixties or seventies?"

Nicholas's head began to throb. "Not necessarily."

"Well, think about it. If a woman came up to you and said, 'Oops I forgot my panties,' you must admit you wouldn't forget her, would you? I've been forgotten and passed over by men my entire life. I think it's time that stopped. Do you think if I stand in front of the mirror and practice, I might eventually be able to say it?"

"Say what?"

"Oops, I forgot my panties," she said, getting her coat from the closet.

God, I hope not, he thought. He was saved from responding by the ringing doorbell. A dozen warnings and cautionary statements raced through his head as she put her hand on the doorknob. Wear your coat the entire time. Slap him if he touches you. Keep your legs crossed. He swallowed them all except one. "Be careful."

She glanced back at him and met his gaze for a long moment. "I've been careful since the day I was born. A goddess is wild and wise."

Watching her whirl out the front door, Nicholas instinctively made the sign of the cross. What had gotten into his daughter's sweet, innocent nanny? If her date tried to act out half the scenarios that had raced through Nicholas's head, then she wouldn't be home until February.

Pacing the den, he swore under his breath. He should have hired the middle-aged woman in ortho-pedic shoes. That woman wouldn't have given him acid indigestion. She probably wouldn't have allowed

Molly to nearly pull her hair out by her roots like Gail did, either, though, he reminded himself.

Pushing his fingers through his hair, he told himself he needed to remember that Gail might try to be wild, but underneath the sexpot trappings, she was sensible and careful. She would never use that crazy pickup line about panties. Never, he told himself, and wondered why he felt jumpy.

He forced himself to sit down and pick up the paper. This was going to be a peaceful evening. A relaxing evening, he told himself, and began to read the article he'd put aside.

With every other sentence, however, a question plagued him without mercy. Was she wearing panties or not?

Gail decided to pretend that Nicholas was her uncle. It was the only way she was going to survive such close proximity with the sexiest man she'd ever met. They talked every evening about Molly, his day, her day. It would be too easy to slide into a futile crush on him.

Since he was her theoretical uncle, she decided she would also share her quest to unleash her inner goddess with him. Talking about thigh-high stockings removed all the forbidden mystery and would further ensure that she would be able to keep her head on straight.

''Molly's going to walk any day,'' she told Nicholas as she grabbed a soda and joined him in the den for their nightly conversation.

He looked at her in surprised pleasure. "Really? Any day?"

"Any day," she said with a nod, sitting across from him on the leather sofa. "She loves it when I hold her hands above her head and get her moving."

He sank into a chair, loosened his tie, unbuttoned the top button to his shirt and took a long swallow from his glass of red wine. "I don't want to miss it," he said.

Her heart squeezed tight and she smiled. "That's gonna be tough. I don't think Baronessa's will let you stay away that long."

He frowned. "True. Maybe you could videotape it."

"It's possible, but I have no idea when and where she'll decide to take her first steps."

He took another swallow of wine. "Okay. Just promise you'll call me the minute she walks."

"What if you're in a meeting?"

"Interrupt," he said.

She nodded and lifted her fingers in a quick little salute. "Whatever you say."

"Good. I love the acquiescence. Nice change," he said with a sexy grin.

"It's temporary. Don't get used to it."

"Should have known," he said wryly.

"Goddesses only acquiesce when it suits them," she told him.

He looked at her and gave a slow nod. "Ah, we're back to that."

"We were never really away."

He raked his hand through his hair. "What's the latest?"

"You don't have to pretend interest," she said.

"Oh, I'm dying to know."

"You're making fun of me." She stood, her feelings oddly hurt.

"I'm not," he insisted, also standing. "I'm interested. Tell me the latest."

She hesitated, then slowly sat down. "You've probably never had a very hard time with this because you've always been very—" She broke off. She refused to call him "hot" to his face again.

"Very what?" he prompted.

"Very appealing to the opposite sex. I'm sure you've never had any trouble attracting women."

"True, but I may not have attracted the right kind of women. Case in point was Molly's mother. She was always looking for a bigger paycheck. In fact, the only reason she didn't come back to me when she found out she was pregnant was because she'd found another man with a bigger bank account and she told him that Molly was his daughter. I attracted a female barracuda."

The bitterness in his voice was so strong she could almost taste it in the air she inhaled. "Do you still love her?"

He looked stunned. "Hell, no. I stopped loving her the day I broke up with her."

"Then why do you let her continue to control your love life?"

His brow furrowed thoughtfully. "What do you mean?"

"I mean you're so determined not to have a committed relationship with a woman that you could miss the chance to experience real love."

He turned silent and brooding, taking a sip of his wine. "I'll take that under advisement. What about you? If you dress like a tart, what kind of guy do you think you'll attract?"

Gail gaped at him. "I'm not dressing like a tart."

"Okay, that was a slight exaggeration," he conceded in a grudging tone.

Gail continued, "Besides, I have different goals than you do. I've spent my entire life being regarded as one of the guys. I want to be..." She hesitated, feeling a flush of self-consciousness. "I want to experience my femininity. I'm younger than you and—"

Nicholas choked on his wine. "Younger? You make me sound ancient."

"Well, not exactly ancient, but I think of you almost as an uncle and—"

"Uncle?"

"You *are* ten years older than I am."

"That doesn't make me old enough to put out to pasture."

"I wasn't suggesting that," she said, wondering if she'd gone a little too far with the mention of the uncle thing. She shook her head. "We've strayed from my original point. The whole goddess thing got started when I took a sexy quiz."

Nicholas went very still. "With whom did you take this quiz?" he asked in clipped tones.

"With myself," she said. "The magazine had a quiz to test your sexiness, and the reason I'm trying to do some of this goddess stuff is because I flunked it. I flunked the sexy quiz. I bet you've never flunked a sexy quiz in your life."

Nicholas gave a long-suffering sigh. "That quiz didn't prove anything. The only sexy quiz worth a damn is conducted in bed with a member of the opposite sex."

He would know, Gail thought, feeling that assurance in every feminine pore of her body. He would know everything she didn't know about being sexy. "Well, as I've previously mentioned, you're an expert in this area, and I'm trying to become more expert, if that's possible."

He nodded and took a long drink of wine. "So what's the latest?"

"Just girl things, like an eight-hour lipstick designed to last through marathon lovemaking. The magazine does tests," she said, feeling a little silly.

"Did you buy some?" he asked her, his gaze intent.

Her cheeks heated, but she nodded.

"Found someone you want to test it on?"

"Not yet," she said, lifting her chin. "But I'll be ready when I do."

While Nicholas attended a managers' meeting at corporate headquarters two days later his assistant slipped into the room and gave him a note.

Your daughter is walking all over the place.

A rush of pride and joy raced through Nicholas. Molly was walking. He excused himself from the meeting and put his first vice president in charge. He grabbed the car keys from his office, told his assistant he would return later and immediately drove home.

He threw open the door and headed for the den, where Gail was holding Molly's hand as the toddler marched around the room. Gail spotted him first.

"Look, Molly! It's Daddy!" she said.

Molly's face lit up.

"Show Daddy how you can walk," Gail gently urged.

Her brows furrowed in concentration, the toddler wobbled toward him with no assistance from Gail.

Nicholas dropped to his knees to catch her. He praised her and cherished the wet kiss she plastered on his cheek. His daughter was beaming. His heart felt so full it almost hurt to breathe. When Molly had first come to live with him, a secret part of him had feared she would remain sad and afraid for a long, long time. Just a few weeks in Gail's care, however, had turned her around. Nicholas wondered if Gail had any idea of her impact.

"A few weeks ago I never would have dreamed she would be walking so soon," he said, allowing Molly to cling to his hand as she continued to practice her new skill around the room.

"It was time," Gail said.

"But all she did was cry in the beginning."

"She just needed time to regroup. You probably wouldn't understand it since you seem to operate on a different level," she said with a wry gentleness, "but most of us humans need a little time to catch our breath when we suffer a loss."

"What do you mean I operate on a different level?"

"I mean a lot has been expected of you and you have always risen to the occasion. You don't appear to stumble or fall very often."

He filed that in a corner of his brain, determined to think about it later. Lifting Molly and holding her against him, he met Gail's gaze. "You've done a great job with her. She wasn't at all easy in the beginning."

"Thanks, but there's something really special about knowing such a vulnerable little person needs you." She smiled. "It makes you willing to do just about anything for them."

"Well, thank you," he said, knowing the words weren't adequate. "From both of us."

"My pleasure."

"Maybe we could celebrate tonight by going to Baronessa's for ice cream."

Gail's face fell. "I can't, but you two should definitely go."

Nicholas frowned. "Why not?"

"It's my night off, and I have a date."

"Oh. Maybe another time," he muttered, irritated that she had a date, irritated that another man was going to have the opportunity to be with her tonight, irritated that he was irritated.

Nicholas returned to work and arrived home in time to watch Gail leave for her date. She wore a short black dress, more elegant than some of the others she'd acquired, and he noticed she'd improved her makeup technique. Her perfume lingered after she left, and he stood in the foyer inhaling it until he realized what he was doing and felt like an idiot.

Tired from her day of walking, Molly fell asleep early, so Nicholas nixed the idea of visiting his family's *gelateria*. He wasn't much in the mood, anyway. Nor was he much in the mood to watch a Boston Celtics game or read the newspaper in front of him. The hour grew late, and his imagination went through the roof. He wondered what Gail was doing.

He wondered if this guy she was out with cranked her engine and if she had decided to give her lipstick the eight-hour lovemaking test. He wondered if this guy would try to find out if she was wearing panties, or a thong or nothing beneath that black dress.

His gut tensed at the images, and his skin felt too tight for his body. He should be thinking about the woman he would be seeing tomorrow night, not Gail. He was attending a cocktail party with one of the most beautiful women in Boston. It should be easy to switch his focus away from Gail. So, why wasn't it?

Just after midnight he turned off the television and walked toward the stairs. He heard a sound outside the front door. The door whooshed open and Gail, drenched from head to toe, stumbled inside. Her makeup was smeared and her hands were trembling.

"What in hell?"

She gave a short smile. "Had a little disagreement with my date."

An ugly suspicion seeped through him. "What do you mean?"

"He insisted that I go back to his apartment with him and I disagreed. He got pushy…"

Nicholas tensed. "How pushy?"

She wrinkled her nose. "You know if you don't want somebody's tongue in your mouth, you definitely don't want it down your throat. And you definitely don't want him going fishing under your dress. He was worse than a toddler. I must've said no a dozen times. Maybe he was deaf. And I didn't try any of the goddess come-on lines."

Fury raced through him. "What's this guy's name? He sounds like he needs to learn some lessons about how to treat women."

Gail looked at Nicholas in surprise. "His name was Jeremy, but—"

"Are you sure he didn't hurt you?"

"Absolutely sure." Taking off her coat, she looked down at her shoes and winced. "High heels were not designed for a one-and-a-half-mile trek through Boston. I'm going to have the worst blisters in the history of my existence, and this guy was not worth it. Could you please turn around? I can't bear to have these stockings on one more minute."

Nicholas turned, still infuriated. "Maybe you should let me screen your dates."

"My dates *are* screened. I ask the guys on the volleyball team, and they get the scoop. This guy was new in town, though." He heard her sigh. "Oh, thank God, the stockings are gone. I think I really offended him when I told him to take a cold shower."

She seemed less shaky now. Relief trickled through him. "Did you really walk that far?"

She nodded. "No cabs available this late in the rain."

"You should have called me," he said, moving closer to her.

She sighed. "I couldn't do that. You're my boss."

"Damn it," he said, taking her arm. "Your safety is important to me and Molly. If you ever get in this kind of situation again, I insist that you call me."

She paused, her gaze meshing with his. "It's not likely to happen again, but if you really mean it—"

"I do."

"Okay. Now all I want is a hot bath."

"Jacuzzi?" he offered, pushing a damp strand away from her face, wanting to take her in his arms and frustrated that he shouldn't.

Her eyes darkened with the same forbidden desire that he felt in his gut. She shook her head, but he could read the memories of their shared passion written on her face. "The Jacuzzi is a big no-no for me," she said. If her eyes could talk, they would have said, in the sexiest way possible, "And you're the biggest no-no, of all."

Nicholas felt the growing, dangerous urge to show Gail just how pleasurable her no-nos could be.

Six

Nicholas was out with one of his beautiful women. It should be a long evening. Dinner and the opera. Gail told herself she wouldn't have wanted to attend the opera, anyway.

"You are lots more fun than any opera," she said to Molly as she fed her SpaghettiOs.

Molly opened her mouth and gave a pasta smile.

Gail winced. "We are definitely going to have to work on your table manners."

The doorbell rang, and the housekeeper called out that she would answer it. "Wonder who that is," Gail said to Molly when she heard several female voices. She'd barely blinked before four women filled the doorway. She immediately recognized Gina, and though all the women had distinctive features, she could see a Barone family resemblance.

"We're here to see the *bambina,* and we're not taking no for an answer," the most petite woman said. With dark-brown hair and brown eyes, she was exquisitely pretty.

"Stop it, Maria," Gina said. "You're scaring Gail. The least you can do is introduce yourself."

The young woman immediately stepped forward with a friendly smile and extended her hand. "I'm Maria Barone, the youngest. We couldn't stay away when Gina told us about Molly. Nick says she's walking. You must bring Molly to the *gelateria.*"

"We were going to come last night, but I had a date and Nicholas is at the opera tonight."

"Oh, he's gone," another of the women said in delight. "That means he won't be able to hustle us away too quickly. I'm Rita, number seven in birth order." The energetic woman laughed. "Don't worry. There won't be a quiz. Gina, Maria and I live in the same brownstone. I hope you don't mind us barging in. Since I wasn't working and none of us had plans for the evening, we decided we had to get a look at our niece. Nick has been very protective of her."

The quietest of the group stepped forward. "I'm Colleen," she said. "I've heard many good things about you from my mother. She says you've done wonders with Molly."

"Thank you," Gail said, overwhelmed but delighted to meet Nicholas's sisters. With this group, she wouldn't have even a minute to think about him and his date. "I'm pleased you could visit. Molly and I didn't have anything planned except finishing SpaghettiOs and a bath."

"SpaghettiOs," Maria echoed, making the sign of the cross. "My father would wig out. But he's not here, so he doesn't need to know. May I feed her?"

Gail gave the spoon to Nicholas's sister and moved to the side so that she was still in Molly's line of vision. "You don't live with your other sisters?" she asked Colleen.

Before Colleen could reply, Gina stepped forward, shaking her head. "Colleen left the convent a couple of years ago, but she decided it would be a shock to her system to live with us after living with nuns."

Colleen chuckled. "I think they were more concerned about my moral influence."

"It's hard to combine wild and wise," Gail said, envying the family closeness, "but it could be fun to try."

"Henri gave you a copy of *Goddess* magazine, didn't he?" Gina asked, apparently recognizing the lingo. "I love your new haircut."

"Thank you. Yes, he did. I don't think I've reached true goddessdom yet. I ended up walking home from a bum date last night."

Gina gasped. "Oh, no. Are you okay?"

"Fine. Your brother's very protective."

All four sisters groaned, then burst into laughter. "Tell us something we don't know," Rita said. "When we first moved into the brownstone, he and my father wanted to hire an on-site chaperon."

"Gosh, it must be nice having such a big family," Gail said, unable to hide the secret longing she'd had for years.

"It's got ups and downs," Colleen said. "What about your family?"

"Both my parents have passed away, so it's just my brother and me."

Colleen murmured sympathetically and patted her hand. "Well, we can adopt you."

"Sure," Gina said. "We can intrude in your business, show up unannounced and tell you how to run your life. We're very experienced at that."

"Sounds great to me," Gail said.

"Oh, I like this one," Rita said with a smile. "And I bet you have a great effect on Nick."

Gail's heart stopped and she shook her head. "I'm not at all his type."

"Why not?" Maria asked, cleaning Molly's face with a wet cloth.

"Well, for starters, I'm not beautiful," Gail said, rising when Molly began to fuss. "Cleanup's gotta be done fast with this one."

"Who told you you're not beautiful?" Maria asked.

"No one needed to," she said, uncomfortable with the discussion. "I'm just not his type."

"He must think you're important if he's protective of you," Gina said. "Otherwise, he wouldn't bother."

"Oh, I'm very important because Molly needs

me,'' she said as much for herself as for Nicholas's sisters. ''Who wants to help give her a bath?''

''Me,'' the women said at once, and Gail was relieved she'd successfully changed the subject. She couldn't help liking the women for their gentleness with Molly. Each of them took a turn caring for her. After they put Molly to bed, they surprised Gail by each embracing her at the door before they left.

Afterward Gail sat at the kitchen table and daydreamed about what it would be like to have such a large, caring family. She suspected they didn't know how precious their bond was. The yearning to belong knotted her chest, and her eyes watered.

Dismayed at her emotional reaction, she sniffed back her tears and pulled open her latest issue of *Goddess*. Surely that would distract her.

Nicholas entered the quiet house and leaned against the wall, giving a sigh of relief. The evening had been interminable. Corinne had looked incredibly beautiful and classy. She had hung on every word, agreed with everything he said, and he'd been bored out of his mind.

Gail paid attention to him, but she didn't hang on every word, and she sure as hell didn't agree with everything he said. He closed his eyes and squeezed the bridge of his nose. This situation was growing more insane with each passing day. He had thought an evening with Corinne would wipe Gail from his mind, and Corinne had indicated she would be more than willing for him to stay the night at her condominium.

He should have stayed. He should have allowed her to take care of his needs, but the prospect had left him lukewarm at best. Lord, he hoped nothing was wrong with him, he thought, pushing away from the wall and heading for the kitchen. He pulled a bottle of wine from the cabinet and tugged the cork from the bottle. He inhaled the aroma from the cork, then poured himself a glass of the merlot.

He took a long, slow sip and savored the full-bodied flavor. Glancing at the table, he noticed a magazine open on the table. Gail or his housekeeper must have left it there. Curious, he walked over and looked at it. The title of the article grabbed his attention immediately: "50 Wicked Ways to Seduce Your Man."

This was definitely not his housekeeper's magazine. Nicholas checked the front cover. *Goddess*. He should have known. He flipped back to the article and scanned the list of suggestions. "Lick his earlobes... Blindfold him and skim all his sensitive places with just your hair... Lick his belly button... Lick his..."

Growing warm, he could easily imagine Gail letting her wild hair fall over his bare body. He grew hard.

If Gail was reading this, he wondered with whom she planned to try out the fifty wicked seductions. The idea of her trying *any* of them with any man but him drove him nuts.

"This is not good, old man," he muttered to himself. He scanned a few more of the wicked suggestions and groaned. He shut the magazine and swore under his breath. How in hell was he supposed to sleep now?

"Your sisters visited last night and your mother called," Gail said to Nicholas the next morning as she set a cup of dry cereal on the high-chair tray in front of Molly.

"My sisters visited whom? You and Molly?" he asked.

She nodded, her eyes wide. "All four of them."

"Did they overwhelm you?" he asked, pouring himself a cup of coffee. After taking his cold shower, he'd had a hard time going to sleep, so more than ever he needed a jolt of caffeine.

"No, I liked all of them. It must be wonderful having a large, close-knit family."

"Most of the time," he said. "What did my mother want?"

"She's having a cocktail party tomorrow night and wants you to come. She also asked me to come and bring an escort."

Nicholas gulped his coffee, nearly scalding his tongue. He was starting to feel as if there was a conspiracy against him. First his sister had encouraged Gail to get a makeover from Henri. Now his mother was inviting Gail and a man of her choice to a cocktail party. "She did?"

"Yes, but I don't have to go. Someone needs to watch Molly and—"

"We could leave after Molly goes to sleep and Ana can watch her," he said.

She eyed him carefully. "Are you sure? After all, I'm not family. I'm an employee."

She seemed determined to remind him of that. "But you're a personal family employee. If my mother invited you, then you should attend. And if you can't think of an escort—"

"Oh, I can," she said quickly. "And he's been checked out by all the guys on the volleyball team. Very nice guy. A doctor. He already asked me out, so I just need to see if he's available tomorrow night."

Nicholas's coffee tasted suddenly bitter in his mouth. "Okay. If it doesn't work out, let me know." He watched her from behind his cup, and desire twisted a knot in his belly. "When I came home last night, I happened to see the article you'd been reading."

"What article?" she asked, her face blank. Realization hit, and her cheeks turned pink. She looked away. "Oh, that article."

"Have you found anyone on whom you want to try out those fifty wicked seductions?"

She bit her lip, keeping her gaze focused on Molly's cereal. "Not yet, but if I keep trying, then maybe…"

"Maybe?" he prompted.

"Not maybe," she said with a resolute expression. "If I keep looking, then I know I will."

Her determination gave him heartburn. Damn it. If

she was going to try wicked things with a man, then he wanted to be the man. Warning bells clanged in his head, but he ignored them. It had been a long time since Nicholas had wanted a woman the way he wanted Gail. "Number thirteen looks interesting," he said, dumping his coffee into the sink.

She whipped her head up to stare at him. "Excuse me?"

"I said number thirteen looks interesting," he told her, moving closer. He brushed his daughter's head with a kiss, and trailed his finger over Gail's open mouth. "Watch out. Don't catch a fly," he joked. "Did anyone ever tell you that you have the kind of mouth men fantasize about?"

She shook her head.

"Hmm. See you tonight," he said, and headed for the door with a hard-on and an ounce of satisfaction from her stunned expression.

As soon as Molly allowed, which turned out to be during her afternoon nap, Gail zipped in front of her bathroom mirror to stare at her mouth. She poked at it and stretched it, trying to see what Nicholas had seen. She had the kind of mouth that men fantasized about? Why? she wondered. Her lips were a little plumper than average, she supposed, not small and dainty. But then there wasn't much about her that was small and dainty, she thought wryly.

She kept looking at her mouth and wondered what kind of fantasies men had. The magazine's list came to mind, and she watched herself blush in the mirror.

Giving up on the appeal of her mouth, she headed back downstairs to find out exactly what number thirteen was. Not that she would ever take part in it with Nicholas, but it would just be interesting to know.

"Straddle his lap and give him a deep French kiss just before you—"

Woo-hoo! Gail felt her temperature skyrocket and slammed the magazine closed. So that was what Nicholas liked. She closed her eyes and a hot visual filled her mind. She wondered if she would be able to do that, especially with Nicholas. Gail took a deep breath, opened her eyes and reopened the magazine again, studying the article with new eyes. What would it be like to do all fifty wicked things with Nicholas?

That evening Molly was fussy due to teething, so it took some extra time and effort to get her settled. By the time the baby was sleeping, Gail was tired and her shoulders ached. Nicholas had stayed late at the office, but she knew he had arrived home because she could hear him moving around in his bedroom. The flood of images that had crossed her mind earlier that afternoon invaded her mind again.

Gail shook her head. "Uh-uh. I'm not going there again," she told herself, and turned toward her bedroom. Just as she opened her door, Nicholas stepped into the hallway. She automatically stopped.

"How was Molly today?" he asked, moving toward her.

"She was teething a little, but she was still mostly intent on perfecting her new skill. She was walking like she was planning a hike to China."

"Bet she wore you out," he said. "Why don't you join me for a glass of wine downstairs?"

Why don't I? A dozen sensible reasons immediately sprang to mind. The expression in his eyes sent those same reasons scattering. "That sounds nice. Just for a few minutes," she added more for herself than for him.

She followed him downstairs to the den, where he opened a bottle of red wine and poured each of them a glass, then turned the Boston Celtics basketball game on low volume. Gail hadn't perfected the art of appreciating red wine. She took a big swallow and wrinkled her nose.

He chuckled, sitting beside her on the sofa. "You don't like it?"

"I'm not used to it. I was raised by a teetotaler. I'm trying to acquire the taste," she said. "Any tips?"

"Sip it. If you really want to enjoy fine wine, you don't gulp it the same way you do a soft drink."

"Okay," she murmured, looking at him over the rim of her glass. She took a tiny sip, which went down more smoothly. His gaze locked with hers and she felt her chest tighten. She searched for a way to break the tension. "How was your day?"

"Long, but productive. We're in the process of unveiling another flavor of gelato for Valentine's Day. Everything needs to be coordinated with Operations. PR and Marketing often ask the impossible."

"But you deliver," she said, instinctively knowing he did. She absently rubbed her sore shoulder.

His eyes glinted with sensual promise. "I try." He pointed to her shoulder. "What's going on there?"

She shrugged. "Just a twinge I get every now and then from that night I overdid it at the volleyball game."

"Turn around. I'll rub it," he offered.

"Oh, no, that's okay. It's not that bad. It's just—"

"C'mon," he coaxed, setting his wineglass on the coffee table. "I'll make you feel better."

A delicious shiver ran down her spine. If any man could make a woman feel better, she would just bet it was Nicholas. "I'm not sure an employer should—"

"We're more team than employer/employee. Would you let one of your teammates rub your shoulder?"

"I guess," she said, thinking that her teammates didn't have bedroom eyes. The background noise of the game was comforting, not mood music, she told herself. She gave in to temptation and turned around so that her back was to him.

She felt him move so close she could feel his breath on the nape of her neck. Her heart jumped. Maybe this was a stupid idea, she thought. He lowered his hands to her neck and she pushed away her protests. His fingers kneaded her tight muscles. His hands were pure magic.

Closing her eyes, she couldn't hold back a moan.

"Good?" he asked.

"Yes," she whispered, and another moan escaped.

"That's a sexy sound," he murmured.

She hadn't intended to make a sexy sound, she

thought. "I didn't realize how tense my shoulders were until now."

He said something in Italian.

"What does that mean?" she asked.

"You have beautiful hair," he said, continuing to massage her shoulders and neck.

"Before or after the haircut?" she asked.

"Both, but you don't try to restrain it as much since you got the cut."

She laughed. "I've been trying to restrain my hair since I could hold a rubber band."

"And now it's time to let it go wild," he said, shifting so that he could prop one leg on the sofa and pull her between his thighs.

Acutely aware of the way his body surrounded hers, she only managed a nod. He slid his fingers underneath the neckline of her pullover, and she felt another rush of tantalizing pleasure. He lightly skimmed his fingertips around the front of her neck and down to her collarbones, then returned to her shoulders.

When she inhaled, she caught the seductive scent of his aftershave. An edgy kind of restlessness skipped through her. Although his hands soothed her shoulders, other parts of her felt jumpy, sensitized, hungry. She took a sip of wine, then another.

He kneaded his way down her spine, then slipped his hands up under her shirt and slowly moved his fingers over her back. He skimmed his fingers under her bra strap, but didn't undo it.

The mere suggestion of him touching her bare skin

and bra made her nipples tighten. The instant response took her off guard. If he affected her this much with a mere back rub, what would happen if he tried to seduce her?

The thought made her even more restless, and she shifted. He paused at her movement and she heard a quiet intake of breath before he continued. It took less than a moment for her to register his arousal against her derriere.

Was that possible? she wondered. Her mouth went dry and she sipped the wine in earnest. His fingers slid from the center of her back to her rib cage. She held her breath, a forbidden part of her not wanting him to stop. The game continued to play in the background, although she couldn't have told the score if her life had depended on it. He rubbed his thumbs on her back while his fingers slid upward to just below her bra. She held her breath again, wondering if he would touch her breasts.

He slid his hands down again and she bit her lip in frustration. Her body humming with unspent need, she shifted against the restless feeling.

He stopped again and murmured something under his breath.

She would have asked him what he'd said if she could have found the words, but her pulse was pounding as if she'd just run a marathon.

He skimmed his hands upward again just beneath her breasts. He slid his fingers underneath the edge of her bra and she waited breathlessly for him to continue. He stroked the underside of her breast, and she felt a growing heat between her thighs. When his fingertips finally brushed her taut nipples, she sighed with relief.

She took another sip of wine to combat the dryness of her mouth.

"Good?" he asked, his voice vibrating deliciously against her ear.

She nodded.

"You mean the wine?" he asked in a voice that taunted and teased.

"Everything," she had to admit.

He unsnapped her bra, pulled her back against him and cupped her breasts. "You know how you're sipping that wine," he said, rubbing her nipples between his thumb and forefinger so that she felt a corresponding tug in her secret places.

"Yes," she said, feeling hot all over.

"That's how I want to sip your nipples."

The image was so erotic she nearly dropped her wineglass. He saved it, wrapping his hand around hers, then he set the glass on the table next to his.

She turned to meet his gaze. "What are we doing?"

"Nothing we both don't want to do," he said, and pulled her mouth to his. He moved his mouth from side to side, then dipped his tongue into her mouth to taste her. He continued to move his hands over her breasts.

He overwhelmed her with such a plethora of sensations that she couldn't assimilate them all. His mouth on hers, his tongue seeking and seducing, his hands arousing. Acting on instinct, she responded to his kiss by curling her tongue around his. He gave a low groan of approval, sank backward on the sofa and pulled her body on top of his. When he cupped her bottom to rock her pelvis against his, her mind went fuzzy. She balled her fists, not knowing what to do with her hands.

"Touch me," he told her.

"Where?"

"Anywhere," he dared her. "Everywhere."

She hadn't thought her heart could race any faster. She wondered if she was dreaming. This was the one vision she'd been afraid to dream. She feared that even the power of dreaming about Nicholas would put her under his spell.

She squeezed his shoulders with her fingers and wished she was touching his bare skin. He rocked his pelvis against her and she shuddered at the hardness there. He pulled her slightly upward. Meeting her gaze, he lifted her shirt so that her breasts were bared.

"Number thirteen with clothes," he told her, then lifted his mouth to her breast.

The room began to spin. It was too easy to lose herself in the sensation of his mouth on her nipple, his hands guiding her bottom over his hardness. If only she was naked. If only he was, too. He would be thrusting inside her, rubbing the ache he created.

He pulled her mouth down to his and took her with his tongue the same way he would take her body. Gail was so turned on she couldn't think, could hardly breathe.

He pulled his mouth from hers, his breath harsh. "Come with me to the cocktail party tomorrow night," he said.

The possessive tone in his voice thrilled her. "I— I—"

"Say yes," he coaxed her.

She wanted to, but something prevented her. Her brain felt as if it were moving more slowly than paint dried. She tried to concentrate. "I—" She broke off. Dr. Gallimore. "I can't," she finally said. "Dr. Gallimore has already agreed to go with me."

Nicholas met her gaze. "Break the date."

"I can't," she said, regret burning through her like acid. "It wouldn't be fair. I've already asked him."

"But you would rather be with me," he said, everything about him daring her to deny it.

Much to her irritation, she couldn't deny it. Her body was still pulsing with desire for him. "Did anyone ever tell you that you can be just a little bit arrogant?"

"No."

"Well, you can," she said, pulling her shirt back into place and trying not to think about how much she wanted to be as close to him as humanly, physically possible. "How would you feel if I broke a date with you?"

In one smooth movement, he rose to a sitting position and slipped his hand through her hair. "Once we had each other, you wouldn't be able to imagine yourself with anyone else."

That was exactly what she feared. She swallowed

over a knot of anticipation. "Why are you interested in me? In the realm of sexual experience, I'm a guppy and you're a shark. You eat guppies for breakfast."

He gave her hair a gentle tug, and his lips tilted into a grin so sexy she felt as if she was stuck in a permanent free fall. "I could make you like being my breakfast."

Seven

Nicholas pulverized the ice chips between his teeth as he watched the good doctor with Gail. The man couldn't seem to keep his hands off her. Not that Nicholas could blame him. Still, Nicholas felt the not-very-nice Sicilian urge to break one of the man's fingers when he saw it and four others curled around her waist.

In a sea of black, Gail stood out in a classy cream suit that gracefully followed her curves. She looked like vanilla ice cream topped with caramel sauce, and Nicholas wanted to be the man consuming her.

Family and friends mingled pleasantly in his parents' Beacon Hill home, but Nicholas wasn't in a sociable mood.

"You don't look like you're having a good time,"

his sister Rita said as she joined him beside the bar. "Why didn't you bring Corinne?"

He shrugged.

"Uh-oh," Rita said. "Another one bites the dust?"

"Tell me, what did you think of Corinne?" he asked Rita, confident she would offer a frank opinion.

"She's beautiful. Like all the rest."

"But not very real," he said.

Her eyes widened. "I'm surprised you noticed. I figured you were blinded by her beauty."

Nicholas saw the doctor touch Gail's hair, and he bit down on another piece of ice.

"For a man who can practically turn hay into gold with his investments, you don't seem to have the same luck with women."

Nicholas glanced at his sister. "Thank you for sharing your insight," he said dryly.

"Well, you did well with Gail," she said, as if trying to console him.

"What do you mean?"

"She's obviously a terrific nanny, but she's also a nice person. She didn't bat an eye when all four of us descended on her a few nights ago. In fact, she did everything she could to make Molly at ease so we could feed her and give her a bath." Rita nodded. "See, you do a great job selecting employees, too."

"Speaking of love life, why haven't I heard about you hooking up with a doctor?"

Rita rolled her eyes. "Because I work with them, so I know the truth about doctors. Some of them are terrific, but many of them are shallow, egotistical and crass.''

Nicholas glanced over at Gail and her doctor friend and felt a shot of good cheer for the first time that evening. ''Really? Did you know Gail is here with a doctor?''

''Hmm. He'll probably get called away for an emergency.''

Rita's words proved prophetic. Less than five minutes later, Nicholas noticed the doctor checking his messages. He appeared to be explaining something to Gail. Nicholas left his drink at the bar and moved toward the two of them.

''Hello,'' Nicholas said, extending his hand to the man with a kind face and prematurely receding hairline. ''Nicholas Barone. Gail takes care of my daughter.'' And lives with me.

''Pleased to meet you. I'm Dr. Gallimore. I was just telling Gail that I hate to duck out, but I received an emergency call and I need to leave.''

''How unfortunate,'' Nicholas said. ''I'll make sure Gail gets home safely.''

''Unless I can take you home on my way to the hospital,'' Dr. Gallimore said to Gail.

The good doctor was hoping to at least get a kiss, Nicholas could tell. He resisted the urge to grind his teeth. ''Gail hasn't had a chance to meet the rest of the family, yet. Don't you worry about her. I'll personally make sure she gets home tonight.''

''I hope your patient is okay,'' Gail said, squeezing the doctor's arm.

The man nodded, his attention on Gail. "I'll call you, and next time we do this, I'll make sure there are no interruptions."

In your dreams, Nicholas thought with a complete lack of charity as he watched the doctor leave. Without missing a beat, he turned to Gail. "You've met my sisters and my brother Joe. My uncle Paul is here tonight. And there's Derrick, Daniel and Emily. But not Claudia."

Gail shook her head. "Do you have a notepad? There's no way I'm going to remember all these names without writing them down."

"Don't worry. I'll remind you," he said, tucking her arm in his.

Gail spent the next several moments getting acquainted with some of Nicholas's extended family. His quiet uncle Paul was very different from Nicholas's gregarious father. She met one of Paul's sons, Derrick, vice president of Quality Assurance for the Baronessa manufacturing plant located just a few miles west of Boston. Gail immediately liked Derrick's friendly sister Emily. The more time she spent with the Barones, the more Gail couldn't help wishing she had a large, loving family just like theirs.

"What can I get you to drink?" Nicholas asked.

"Just some ice water," she said, wanting to keep a clear head tonight. Although she wasn't sure it was possible when she was the object of Nicholas's undivided attention. When he looked at her, she felt like Cinderella at the ball. She just wondered what was going to happen at midnight.

"One water," he told the bartender, then scooped up the glass. "Let's take a break," he said, and led her into a small room off the main parlor that had a large fireplace.

"I still haven't met your other brothers."

"Reese and Alex? Neither of them is here. Reese is out sailing the world. He and my father don't see eye to eye, but that's another story. And Alex is a career navy pilot."

Her eyes widened. "Does anyone in your family do anything boring?"

He chuckled. "My mother might have preferred that."

She wrinkled her brow in concentration. "Didn't you mention another cousin? A twin?"

"Derrick's brother, Daniel. You don't need to meet him," he said in a velvet voice as he held her gaze.

She felt a jump in her stomach at the sensual expression on his face. "Why not? What does he do?"

"He's a professional adventurer and ladies' man."

"And how does that make him different from you?" she asked, unable to hide her amusement.

"Well, I do have a day job," he said, cupping her elbow as he led her toward the back of the house, away from the crowd. Stopping in a darkened alcove that overlooked a beautiful private deck, he turned toward her and looked deep into her eyes. "I don't want you distracted."

Gail felt that free-falling sensation in her stomach again. She took a gulp of water. "Distracted from what?"

"From me," he said, taking her glass from her hand and placing it on a small antique table.

Gail looked down at the beautiful wood. "If my glass leaves a water stain on your mother's table, I will seriously croak."

Shaking his head, he chuckled and pulled a coaster from the small drawer. "I don't think any other woman has mentioned water stains when I was getting ready to kiss her."

After he repositioned the glass on the coaster, he turned back to her, standing close enough that the bottom of his black wool slacks brushed her legs. She couldn't believe that wanting expression in his eyes was meant for her. She sucked in a quick breath of air and inhaled his aftershave. His proximity made her feel dizzy.

"I just can't believe you really want *me*," she whispered.

"I can show you, and I promise you won't have any doubt," he said in a low voice, sliding his hand around her waist.

A shiver of anticipation ran through her. She knew he could. Gail also knew anything with Nicholas would be temporary. He'd made that perfectly clear. Although she was afraid her feelings for him wouldn't be temporary, she tried to imagine nixing the opportunity to be involved with him and couldn't.

"But what about the fact that I work for you?" she asked, clinging to a few threads of common sense.

"We're both adults. We can handle it."

But what about when it's over? she wanted to ask, but couldn't. "Why me?"

"You make me warm," he told her in a sexy, confiding voice that tied her in knots. Then he took her mouth. His kiss spoke of a man's want and need laced with something tender that she couldn't quite name. All of it got to her.

She opened her mouth and he slid his tongue inside. Pleasure and every good feeling she'd wondered if she would ever experience rippled through her, and she didn't want it to end. Pushing aside her doubts and sensible protests, she sighed and sank into him. His chest was hard against her breasts, and one of his long legs slid between hers.

She felt his hands slide down over her hips, lower, lower. It occurred to her that a woman wouldn't need liquor with him around. The way his mouth moved on hers made her light-headed. Distantly she felt him lift her skirt and then his hands glanced the bare skin of her thighs and her derriere. He stopped and swore.

"What are you wearing?" he asked, pulling back slightly, his eyes dark with desire.

She felt a rush of self-consciousness. "Garter belt," she managed. "Thong."

He swore again and dragged his mouth over hers, plunging his tongue inside. He slid both his hands beneath her skirt and filled his hands with her. "I want you," he muttered against her mouth. "I want to pull this skirt off you and take you right this minute."

His blatant sexual invitation melted her inside and

out. Her breasts felt heavy and achy, and between her legs, she grew moist. His tongue plunged into her mouth at the same time his fingers slid beneath her thong and found her most delicate sensitive place. His finger slid inside her and she clung to him, shuddering. A shocking tidal wave of need rumbled through her. She wanted. She had never wanted this much. "What are we doing?" she whispered.

"Not enough," he muttered, and pulled her down the hallway into a small darkened room. Shutting the door behind them, he backed her into the wall and took her mouth again.

Her world was spinning on its axis. She had no concept of where she was, only that she was with Nicholas. His mouth, his hands, his heat. He shoved her skirt upward and pushed her thong down, immediately seeking and finding her wet and swollen femininity. He ate at her mouth, and the wildness of his need took her breath. The silent darkness of the room added to the intimacy. All she wanted was to get closer, to please him, to assuage the ache he was building inside her.

He drew her hand to his waist, and she fumbled with his belt and zipper. When she slid her hand inside his briefs to his erection, he moaned, and the sound vibrated inside her mouth. "Damn, I should wait, but I can't," he said, and pulled protection from his pocket. Before she could blink, he lifted her against the wall and plunged into her.

Gail gasped at the invasion, at the size of him. Her eyes watered at the burning sensation.

He swore. "You should have told me."

She took a careful breath, trying to adjust to his size. "Told you what?"

"That this was your first time."

"I wasn't thinking about it being my first time. I was too busy thinking about you."

He groaned and allowed her to sink more fully onto him. He took her mouth in a kiss that managed to combine carnal need and compassion. When he pulled his mouth slightly away, she whispered, "Don't stop now."

She could almost feel lightning crackle through him. He began to move, squeezing her bottom as he thrust in a mind-robbing rhythm that sent her higher and higher. The coil in her nether regions grew tighter until she felt herself explode. The room was black, but inside her closed eyelids, she saw the red burst of the sun as she clung to him.

Seconds passed and she felt him thrust and stiffen, his climax rippling through her. After he caught his breath, he pulled back and allowed her to slowly slide down him until her feet touched the floor. Her knees buckled and Gail reached for him.

Making a sound of reassurance, he pulled her against him and held her for several moments. "Okay?" he asked.

For Gail, everything was still spinning. "I think so."

He flicked on a light and she instinctively covered her eyes. She heard him groan and peeked through her fingers. He was staring at her nakedness.

She crossed her thighs in a useless act of modesty.

Shaking his head, he moved closer and took her mouth again. ''I want you again,'' he told her, sending a shiver of need through her. ''But I want to take my time.'' He gently adjusted her skirt and found her thong on the floor. ''You look like you've just been sexually mauled and liked it. My family will take one look at you and they'll know what we've been doing. This is between you and me, and I want to keep it that way.'' He rubbed his finger over her bottom lip. ''There's a bathroom at the opposite end of the hall. Tell me where your purse is. If you put on more lipstick and pull yourself back together, maybe we can time things so we say goodbye and make a quick exit.''

''This lipstick was supposed to last through eight hours of lovemaking,'' she said, her mind a jumble. She wondered how he could think straight after what they'd just done.

''I hope you got a money-back guarantee,'' he said with a grin.

She looked away from him in hopes of regaining her equilibrium. She took in the small, elegant writing desk on the other side of the room, the shelves filled with books, and the fresh flowers on a small, antique table. ''Where are we?''

''My mother's office,'' Nicholas said, straightening his tie.

Embarrassment and alarm hit her like a cold glass of water. ''We just…'' She groped for an adequate description. *Made love* wasn't right. Everything else that came to mind didn't fit. "We just *did it* in your mother's office? How can you be so calm?" A terrible thought crossed her mind. "Or maybe this isn't the first time you've…"

He shook his head. "This is the first time I've ever 'done it' in my mother's office. It's the first time I've 'done it' in my parents' house. I'm damn well not calm, because I want you again. At the moment that desk is looking like a good place to start, but I think you deserve better than a desk for your second time. If you want to practice fifty wicked ways to seduce a man, then, *cara,* I'm your man."

Twenty minutes later she stood in the middle of her bedroom with Nicholas, and she was still trying to gather her senses. She saw the undisguised desire in his eyes, and her chest felt so tight she wondered when she would breathe normally again.

He skimmed his hand down her arm, then twined his fingers with hers. "Are you okay?"

"I'm not sure. I haven't had time to think."

He slid his hand around the nape of her neck. "I'm going to give you some more time not to think," he said, lowering his head and brushing his lips from side to side over hers.

Gail immediately felt a melting sensation. She fought it. "I, uh, I think I need to know the rules."

His brow furrowed, but he continued the mesmerizing movement of his lips. "What rules?"

Gail swallowed. "Well, like, is this a one-night—"

"No," he immediately said, then plunged his tongue into her mouth.

The possessiveness she tasted in his kiss made her light-headed. "Okay," she said in a breathy voice.

"Then how long—" She broke off, uncomfortable with the question.

"We've got at least a list of fifty to get through," he told her.

Her heart stuttered, and she bit her lip. "How are you going to get through a list of fifty with me when so many other women are panting to be with you?"

He leaned back slightly, and the intent, aroused expression in his eyes pulled her under again. "I've never had anyone just for me before. I want to keep this just between you and me. Exclusively."

She had seen his strength, and she'd glimpsed his vulnerability, and although he wasn't making any forever promises, she wanted to be with him more than anything. "I want to be just for you," she said.

He took her mouth in a kiss that sent shockwaves of pleasure through her. Shaking his head, he seemed to try to pull himself under control. He lifted a finger to touch her swollen lips. "If you keep looking at me that way, it's going to be hard for me to treat you like a virgin tonight."

Another woman would have played it safe, would have walked away. After all, how could she possibly avoid heartache in this situation? Gail had no choice. Nicholas was everything she'd ever wanted in a man, but she'd always been too afraid to do anything more than dream about it. He was everything. Everything except forever. Even during their heated coupling at his parents' house, she had never felt more desired, never felt more like a woman.

Swallowing her inhibitions and fears, she mentally stepped up to the plate. She slid her tongue over his finger. "Don't treat me like a virgin," she whispered.

It took only a second to register the passion her words unleashed in him. Gail felt the thrill of lighting an explosive device as Nicholas unbuttoned her jacket and tossed it aside, then quickly dispensed with her skirt. "As you requested," he said, and ditched her bra at the same time he kissed her.

Their words, spoken and unspoken, surrounded them like a protective barrier against the outside world. He was safe with her. She would be safe with him. At least for now.

Allowing herself to sink into his kiss, into his seduction, she kissed him back, twining her tongue with his. She felt him touch her nipple with his thumb and forefinger, while he ran his other hand from the back of her head down to her bottom.

She started to step out of one of her heels and he shook his head. "Leave them on," he told her, and the sexy order raised her temperature several degrees.

"You look great in a suit," she said, "but I want to feel your—"

She didn't even complete her sentence before he pulled loose his tie and shoved aside his shirt, kissing her all the while. The room felt as if it had turned upside down, and the air around her seemed to crackle with electricity. He moved against her and she felt his nakedness, his hard chest, flat abdomen and urgent arousal.

He propped her against the bed and leaned down to draw her nipple deeply into his mouth. "I want to touch you everywhere at once," he muttered, sliding his hand between her legs. When he slid a finger inside her and rubbed his thumb over her most sensitive spot, she felt herself bloom under the caress. She in-

stinctively spread her legs farther apart for his min-
istrations, and he groaned in approval.

"So hot, so sweet, so tight," he said. He lifted his
gaze to meet hers. "You told me not to treat you like
a virgin."

Her mouth went dry at the expression on his face.
He looked as if he were going to consume her. She
nodded.

He knelt down in front of her and pressed an openmouthed kiss on her belly, then moved his tongue
lower and lower still. He consumed her intimately;
his tongue and mouth sent her over the edge time and
time again. She gasped at the sharp pleasure.

When she didn't think she could stand another
peak, he stood up and thrust inside her, his gaze making her feel as if she was some kind of prized captive.
Shocked, but unafraid of her wantonness, Gail relished every move he made inside her. The sensations
built again, but she wanted to feel his release, to see
the pleasure on his face.

So hot she was burning inside and out, she clung
to him and felt the instant his climax rolled through
him into her. He stiffened and his eyes drooped to a
sexy half mast, his gaze latching on to her. He swore,
but it sounded almost like a prayer, and his pleasure
sent her over the edge again.

He sank with her onto the bed, his body still joined
with hers. A riot of sensations and emotions raced
through her. She was so overwhelmed she felt the
urge to cry. Alarm slammed into her. Heaven help
her, she couldn't cry. He would be horrified.

Shell-shocked, she focused on the hard strength of
his chest against her breasts, the pounding of his heart

against her rib cage and his fingers sifting through her hair.

"Are you okay?"

Her heart twisted at the gentleness in his voice. For all his fire and passion, Gail knew Nicholas couldn't take without giving. It wasn't in him. And she lo— She broke off that line of thought as quickly as possible. She took a careful breath.

He lifted up slightly to look at her. "You didn't answer me."

She inhaled again. "Give me a…"

"Minute?" he finished for her.

"Week," she said around a soft chuckle.

He grinned, then turned thoughtful. "You told me not to treat you like a virgin."

She heard the concern in his voice and couldn't help falling for him even more. "And you followed instructions very well," she said. "You consumed me and made me like it."

"Careful," he said. "Talking like that could get me started all over again."

She swallowed and met the challenge in his eyes. "You consumed me and made me like it," she repeated.

Eight

When Gail awoke the next morning, she immediately grasped the meaning of "love hangover." Although she was an athlete and she'd strained muscles from overexertion before, her body ached in ways she'd never imagined.

She looked at the large vacant spot beside her where Nicholas had been and rubbed her hand over the pillow where he'd rested his head. A rush of conflicting emotions assailed her. She began to think about all she'd told herself not to consider last night.

She and Nicholas had stepped over the line, and now they were lovers. Secret lovers. Sitting up in bed, she felt more twinges, some in her heart. In a way, she understood his desire to keep their relationship secret. Everything else in his life was so public. Plus, there was the fact that she worked for him. Part of her, however, couldn't help wondering if he was, in some way, ashamed of her, or at least ashamed of his desire for her.

Gail felt a sharp jab of pain and closed her eyes against her thoughts. "You can't go there," she whispered. "You can't think that way."

From the moment she'd met Nicholas Barone, she had known he was way out of her league, but she was determined not to be a wuss about it. This was no Cinderella and Prince Charming relationship that would culminate in marriage, she told herself sternly as she rose from her bed.

This was the affair of a lifetime, and if that knowledge pinched her in hidden places, she was going to have to get over it. She might even fall in love with Nicholas....

Might. She glanced in the mirror over the cherry dresser and made a face. Her conscience mocked her. If she wasn't already in love with Nicholas, would she have given herself to him so freely last night?

Gail's heart contracted, and panic sliced through her. She had fallen in love with him. Maybe it was a virgin thing, she thought desperately. Maybe all women thought they were in love with the first man.

But Gail knew better. Deep down she knew, and the knowledge rocked her. She was in love with Nicholas Barone. She had witnessed his strength and vulnerability up close and personal. She had experienced his humor and his passion. Sure, he was charming and knee-weakening gorgeous, but it was the private man who'd gotten to her. He was strong, but she felt oddly protective of him.

So she loved him, she admitted to herself unabashedly. Now she just needed to keep it a secret.

During the day Gail fought back her little doubts, but when Nicholas arrived home, he made all her concerns disappear. Every night. They shared evenings at home with Molly and one time even ventured to Baronessa Gelateria on Hanover Street in the north end.

The building maintained the look and charm of an old-time soda shop, complete with diner stools and booths. Gail loved it on sight.

Maria greeted the three of them with a wide smile. "It's about time you visited. We even have hot chocolate or cappuccino if you're feeling a little cold."

Gail couldn't help thinking about the hot kiss she and Nicholas had shared just before they'd left his town house moments ago. "I'm not cold," she said, refusing to meet Nicholas's taunting gaze. "Molly and I would love strawberry gelato."

"Make that three," Nicholas said as he followed Maria to a booth in the back of the moderately busy store.

"You got it," Maria said, pulling out a high chair for Molly. "I'll send Kyle to serve you."

Nicholas tucked Molly into her chair, then sat across from Gail in the booth. "I'm surprised you didn't ask for hot fudge sauce," he said, rubbing his leg against hers.

She glanced up at him and felt her heart leap at the expression on his face. "You shouldn't flirt with me in public if you want to keep our relationship a secret."

"But it's so hard to resist. Your face turns this lovely shade of—"

"Fire-engine red," she said, glowering at him while she gave Molly a spoon to play with.

"And since I've seen you naked, I know the blush starts in your face and travels down your neck to your shoulders." He lowered his voice, and his gaze took the same trip as his words. "Then your breasts turn pink and so do your nipples."

Gail willed her cheeks not to heat. "My nipples do not change color," she whispered.

"No, but they get hard when I look at them or put my mouth on them."

Gail decided two could play this game of sensual torture. "Just as you get hard when I look at you, touch you or put my mouth on you."

He held her gaze for a long moment. He slid his legs between hers. "You mean like I'm getting right now?"

"Are you?" she asked, amazed at how easily he aroused her. Suddenly warm, she pulled off her sweater as Kyle, their waiter, delivered the gelati.

Distracted by Nicholas's gaze, she managed to respond appropriately to Kyle and cover Molly with a large bib.

"So what are you going to do about it?" Nicholas asked, feeding Molly a spoonful of gelato.

"What am I going to do about what?" she asked.

He nailed her with an expression hot enough to burn down the building. "About how you affect me."

She lifted her spoon to her mouth and looked at the gelato. "You may not remember number thirty-seven on the list."

"Probably not. My circuits were smoked by number twenty-nine."

"Number thirty-seven involved ice cream," she said, and licked the creamy dessert from her spoon.

"Ice cream and what else?"

"Something I would get arrested for if I did it in public," she said with another long lick and a smile. He tugged at his collar and she could practically see the steam rising from his head. The knowledge that she could get him so worked up was deeply gratifying.

Serving another spoonful to Molly, he shot Gail a look that told her payback would be hell. "Speaking of the list of fifty, I disagree with one of them. I don't like your lipstick."

She blinked. "Why not?"

"Because I would rather you wear a lipstick that leaves a mark everywhere you kiss me," he said. "Everywhere."

Her belly tightened at the primitive prospect of marking Nicholas, of making him hers. "We maybe could add that to the list," she said. "Would I get to choose where I get to kiss?"

"Yeah, but I would try to influence you."

She just bet he would. Gail resisted the overwhelming urge to apply the dish of cool gelato to her heated cheeks. The sensual images she and Nicholas had stirred had temporarily fried her brain.

"No hot goddess comeback?" he taunted.

"I always said I was out of my league with you," she returned, thinking he had no idea how serious she was.

"You underestimate yourself."

"We'll see," she muttered, wondering how much longer she'd be able to hold his attention.

His brow furrowed. Apparently he'd caught the serious note in her voice. "What do you mean?"

She shrugged and angled her head in the direction of Maria, who was coming toward them.

"Everything okay?" she asked.

"It's fine. You're running the show with the same finesse as Grandmother Angelica did."

Maria's lovely brown eyes softened. "That's high praise coming from you," she said.

"You've earned it."

"Thanks. Are you sure everything is okay? Your conversation looked a little intense."

"I was telling Gail that the gelato is actually made in the basement," Nicholas said without missing a beat.

Maria nodded. "He's right. We do it all right here on the premises. We're committed to maintaining the atmosphere and quality of the original shop." She threw an assessing glance over her shoulder. "I would show you the basement, but we're getting more crowded by the minute. Next time," she promised Gail, and whirled away.

"Excellent diversion," Gail said to Nicholas.

"Maria is passionate about the gelateria. She worked here with Grandmother Angelica until Grandmother died last year."

Gail looked up at the large black-and-white photo of Nicholas's grandparents opening the shop. Love and hope were written on their young faces. "They loved each other very much, didn't they."

Nicholas nodded. "Marco loved her enough to steal her away from another guy. Then they eloped."

"How romantic."

"They had their share of struggles," he said thoughtfully. "But they had one of those once-in-a-lifetime loves that not all of us find."

Gail's heart twisted at the closed expression on his face. She wished he could feel that kind of love for her. She wished he would look at her and see how much she loved him. Her stomach turned. If he knew how strong her feelings for him were, he would probably drop her faster than gelato melted on the Fourth of July. Oh, her silly wishes. She needed to stop making them.

Later that night, after they'd made love in her bed, Gail flipped over onto her stomach to look at him. She rested her hand on his strong chest. "Tell me another Barone story."

Nicholas groaned. "Not another one." A family story had somehow become part of every evening they shared. She made love to him with the force of a tornado, then demanded a story.

She poked out her lip in a playful pout. "But you tell great stories. I love hearing about your family."

"Why?" he asked, opening his eyes to study her.

She glanced away. "Because I don't have much family and you do."

Something about the heartrending expression she tried to hide from him grabbed at his gut. "You haven't told me much about your childhood."

"There's not that much to tell. After my father died, my brainy brother, Adam, got a scholarship to boarding school here in Boston. Then he got a full scholarship to Boston College."

"But what did you do?"

"I went to school, played sports and did a lot of baby-sitting before my mom got sick." She slid a furtive glance at him. "I warned you that I didn't lead a fascinating life." She sighed. "There was this Greek family that lived down the street for a couple of years. I think they had six or seven kids, and they kind of adopted me while they lived close by. It was so noisy at their house and so quiet at mine."

"You liked the noise," he concluded, toying with one of her curls.

She nodded.

"You would have enjoyed dinner at the Barones, then. Just about any meal at the Barones," he said, correcting himself. "Breakfast could get noisy, too. I remember how much I savored the peace and quiet when I got my own place."

"Funny how you always want what you don't have," she murmured.

The faraway expression in her eyes tugged at something deep inside him. For all the forbidden heat of their sexual interludes, Nicholas hadn't fooled himself into believing he wanted Gail just for the sex. He would probably die before he admitted it, but he felt safe with Gail. She wouldn't turn on him. She wouldn't lie to him. She would hurt herself before she would hurt him.

Her full acceptance of him touched him in a way he'd never experienced before. Although he was convinced love wasn't in the cards for him, he had protective feelings for Gail. He wanted to take away the lost expression on her face. He loved making her laugh.

"Enough about you," he said in a teasing tone. He knew she hated talking about herself. He tugged her on top of him. "You are insatiable for my stories, and I'm determined to keep you satisfied."

Her lips curved into a smile. "That's nice to know. Tell me more about Marco and Angelica."

"Marco was living with another family and working in their restaurant when he fell in love with Angelica. Angelica was supposed to marry a man named Vincent, and the family taking care of Marco assumed he would one day marry their daughter Lucia. When Marco and Angelica eloped, the family was very angry, and Lucia was so furious she put a curse on my grandmother and grandfather."

Gail gasped. "No!"

He smiled at her indignation. "Yes. When we talk about it, and we usually don't, we call it the Valentine's Day curse."

She frowned. "Why Valentine's Day?"

"Because throughout the years, some tragic things have happened on Valentine's Day. Angelica miscarried her first baby on Valentine's Day, then several years later, on the same day, one of her and Marco's infant twins was abducted."

She shook her head. "How terrible. When you said Marco and Angelica went through some rough times, you weren't exaggerating." She paused, lifting her finger to touch his chin. "Do you believe in the Valentine's Day curse?"

"Logically, no," he said.

"I hear a but in your voice."

He remembered his breakup with Molly's mother on Valentine's Day. With Gail naked on top of him, the warmest, most sensual covering, that breakup seemed very far away. "Logically, no," he repeated.

"Hmm," she said, clearly not satisfied. "Maybe I'll get more out of you another time."

"You can try," he invited, fascinated by her. One moment she was the supreme nurturer. The next she was the ultimate temptress. And from the look in her eyes, she was his.

She lowered her mouth to his chest, kissing her way down to his belly. Sweeping her hair across his thighs, she pressed her cheek against him intimately, then turned her head and took him into her mouth.

The sight of her mouth pleasuring him was so

erotic he almost couldn't bear it, but he couldn't make himself look away. She stirred his body, his mind and, heaven help him, if he wasn't careful, she would get into his heart.

The following afternoon, Nicholas sneaked a kiss from Gail in the kitchen while she fed Molly. "I missed you," he said.

Her heart dipped. "I was here all day long."

"That was the problem. You weren't with me."

She smiled, so pleased by his words she could barely stand still. "I was with your daughter."

He gave an expression of mock disgust. "If you weren't going to be with me, then I guess it's okay that you were with her."

Gail chuckled and shook her head. "You're spoiled."

"I keep trying to get you to spoil me."

"Don't you think you've succeeded?"

"Occasionally," he admitted, tugging her toward him. "I'm a Barone. I like to succeed all the time."

She rolled her eyes, her heart still hammering in her chest. "If I showed up at your office, I would only distract you."

"I know. I had this great idea to add to the list. You on my desk—"

"Da-da-da-da-da-da," Molly said, banging a spoon on her high chair.

"I think somebody else wants some attention," Gail said.

Nicholas moved toward his daughter and kissed her forehead. "*Bella bambina,* how was your day?"

Molly gave a wide grin and reached out to touch his face. Gail noticed that Nicholas didn't back away for fear of getting messy, and she loved him a little more for it. She watched the two of them for a few minutes, then Nicholas cleaned Molly's face and hands.

"I'll give Molly her bath tonight," he said as he picked her up. "By the way, I got a call from a member of the Boston Historical Society today. I'd forgotten that I'd offered my home for the January board meeting. It's in a few days, so I just wanted to give you fair warning. Another member will plan the meeting. That was the only way I would agree to it."

Gail nodded as she wiped off the high-chair tray. "How long does it last?"

He shrugged. "Only two or three hours, but Corinne will probably be in and out a couple of days before."

Gail stopped midmovement. "Corinne?" she echoed, her heart sinking.

He glanced at her. "Yeah."

A dozen possibilities flew through Gail's mind; the first and second stung sharply. He wanted to see Corinne again. He was growing bored with her. She frowned. Then why had he said he missed her?

Nicholas moved closer to her, staring at her while the baby touched his face. "You stopped smiling."

Why was she so obvious? She sighed. "It's nothing."

"You're lying to me," he said, his voice dark with disappointment.

Even now she hated the idea of disappointing him. "I just—" She broke off, trying to find a way to protect her pride. "I was just surprised to hear you mention Corinne."

Realization crossed his face. "There's nothing going on between Corinne and me now. This was planned months ago. She's a member of the Historical Society, too, and she roped me into agreeing to use my house if she did the planning." He brushed her mouth with his. "It's nothing. I'll prove it to you later tonight."

By the middle of the night Nicholas had indeed proved his desire for Gail as he had on many previous nights. He had told her another story and managed to pry out of her that she hadn't attended her high-school prom because her mother had been sick.

Perhaps she should be reassured. She could see that he felt more for her than physical need. But now in the darkness when she was all alone, the doubts crept in like a cold draft under the door. He came to her bed nearly every night, and he acted as if he couldn't get enough of her, but she couldn't erase the fact that he also always left well before dawn.

He never stayed until morning.

Nine

The doorbell rang and since Gail knew Ana was busy, she scooped up Molly and walked into the foyer. Molly rubbed her soggy-cracker face against Gail's sweater just as Gail opened the door to the most beautiful woman she'd ever seen. Her straight blond hair skimmed the shoulders of a cashmere camel coat. Her blue eyes were enhanced with just the right touch of cosmetics. No blemishes marred her ivory complexion, and her lips glimmered with a silky pink sheen. All Gail could do was stare, because this woman could have written the book on how to look like a goddess.

"I'm Corinne Gladstone. I'm here to do some last-minute plans for the Historical Society meeting. You must be the nanny," she said, extending her hand, then eyeing Gail's stained sweater and apparently thinking better of it, withdrawing. "And you must be Nicholas's adorable daughter, Molly," she said, smiling at the baby.

Molly ducked her head.

"I'm so glad to finally see Molly. I haven't been able to see Nicholas as much lately because he's so devoted to his daughter. I imagine this Historical Society meeting will get things back on track. Would you mind getting the housekeeper for me?" She paused. "I'm sorry. I didn't catch your name."

"Gail Fenton," Gail said, fighting the sensation that Nicholas's home had been invaded. Or perhaps fighting the fear that Nicholas would lose his fascination with her now that Corinne was back in sight. "I'll get Ana.

"Oh, would you like to hold the baby?" Gail offered, holding Molly out to the woman's perfectly manicured hands.

Corinne looked aghast at the cracker- and juice-covered child. "I'm not sure…" she began.

Molly stiffened and let out a wail of protest.

Corinne's eyebrows shot up and she immediately stepped back. "Oh, my. She is a little handful, isn't she. Nicholas was wise to hire a nanny. Well, I won't keep you, Jane," she said in a dismissing tone. "If you'll just get Ana for me, please."

"Gail," she said, correcting Corinne. "Not Jane. Gail."

"Oh, Gail," Corinne said with a sheepish smile. "I wasn't thinking. Sorry. I should tuck your name up here," she said, tapping her forehead. "Future reference. I'm very fond of Nicholas. You and I may end up seeing a lot of each other."

Plastering a smile on her face, Gail gritted her teeth so hard she wondered if she was going to break one. She nodded and sought out Ana, then took Molly upstairs. Corinne obviously thought Gail was no threat to her plan to snag Nicholas, or she wouldn't have dropped such huge hints.

Glancing into the mirror, Gail caught sight of her makeup-free face, cracker-smeared sweater and the baby on her hip. She was definitely not in goddess mode, she thought. Even if she tried her hardest, she could never achieve Corinne's beauty.

Did that also mean that Nicholas would never look at her as anything other than temporary? The silent answer echoed inside her, making her heart hurt. How had she fallen so hard for Nicholas so quickly? she wondered. And soon she would have to pretend it didn't bother her if he stopped wanting her. She would have to pretend it didn't matter if Corinne was successful in luring him back to her. A tight knot of distress formed in her stomach. Molly leaned toward her and pressed a messy kiss on her face.

Gail's heart softened. "Nice to know you don't care if I'm not goddess material, sweetie."

Gail kept her doubts to herself over the next two days, despite Corinne's frequent unexpected visits. She did her best to hide her fears from Nicholas, too.

When the night of the meeting finally arrived, she stayed upstairs. She entertained Molly in the nursery until it was bedtime. When Molly finally drifted off to sleep, Gail watched television in her room, but couldn't later have recalled a single show. After she heard the meeting break up and the members depart, she sighed with relief. Minutes passed, but Nicholas didn't come upstairs.

A disturbing image filled her mind. Nicholas downstairs with Corinne, getting reacquainted. Gail couldn't stand it. Pulling on her tennis shoes and sweats, the nursery monitor in tow, she found Ana and asked her to keep an ear out for Molly. Ana agreed, and Gail slid out the back door.

Nicholas had a roaring headache.

He'd never realized before how ingratiating Corinne could be. Although the woman was stunning to look at, her laughter affected him like the sound of fingernails on a chalkboard. He wondered how he'd ever missed how superficial she seemed. Or perhaps he hadn't cared. Why did he now? The answer immediately hit him. Gail. It was Gail's fault. Nicholas had spent years dating debutantes and models, but Gail was the first *real* woman he'd held in his arms.

Eager to see her, he went upstairs to her room and knocked on the door. No answer, so he opened it. She wasn't there.

Frowning, he checked on Molly and found the baby sleeping peacefully. Then he went downstairs to Ana's room.

''She asked me to watch the baby while she went out for a while. It was after your meeting and I'm watching TV, so it's no problem," his housekeeper said. "She gave me the baby monitor."

Feeling an inexplicable shaft of uneasiness, Nicholas nodded. "Did she say where she was going?"

Ana shook her head. "But she gave me her cellphone number. She was wearing gym clothes and tennis shoes."

"Okay. Thanks, Ana. I'd appreciate if you'd listen for Molly a little longer while I take care of something."

"Of course, sir."

One mystery solved, he thought, stripping off his tie as he went to his room. Gym clothes meant Gail had gone to the gym. He wondered if she'd called one of her friends to meet her there. Such as Jonathan. The notion twisted his stomach.

Gail had been quiet the past couple of days. He hadn't failed to notice. But when he'd tried to pry the reason out of her, she'd successfully diverted his attention with an erotic suggestion.

Quickly he changed his clothes and jogged to the gym, just a few short blocks away. He checked the raquetball courts and scrutinized the players at a volleyball game as it ended. Peeking in all the rooms, he finally came upon a lone figure shooting baskets on a half court.

Her curly red ponytail bounced as she ran and jumped, shooting, rebounding. Her sweatshirt lay abandoned on the side of the court, and she wore a cropped shirt and sweatpants that rode low on her hips. The no-nonsense outfit shouldn't have been sexy, but he remembered touching that smooth abdomen, kissing her there. She moved like a woman possessed, so focused she looked as if she was practicing for a pro game.

The ball bounced off the rim and Nicholas impulsively ran forward to catch it.

Gail turned, her eyes widening in surprise.

"Are you trying to give one of the Celtics a run for their money?" he asked, dropping the ball and dribbling.

She gave a smile that didn't quite reach her eyes. "Safe to say I'm not in their league."

"You say that a lot," he commented, continuing to dribble the ball. "You're not in their league. Not in my league."

She shrugged, moving toward him. "It's true," she said, and snatched the ball from him. "At least in some ways."

Nicholas watched her sink a hook shot. "Not the important ways," he said, feeling an odd rush of sensual excitement and competition. Her strength turned him on. He moved toward her and blocked her next shot, grabbing the ball and making his own basket.

She quickly retrieved it and cast him a reassessing gaze. "I didn't know you played basketball."

"You thought I was better in the boardroom than on the court?"

She shrugged and smiled. "Well, you're not playing for the Celtics, either," she said, then scooted around him and sank another shot.

He grabbed the ball and met her gaze. "Your face glows like that when we make love."

Her eyes widened and she stopped, finally unable to look away from him.

"Why did you leave without telling me?" he asked.

She glanced away. "You were busy with Corinne."

"The least you could have done was save me from her."

"I've seen Corinne. I didn't think you'd be suffering," she said dryly.

"She doesn't laugh like you."

That got her attention. Gail returned her gaze to him. "What difference does that make?"

"Big difference. Do you know that making you laugh is almost as much fun as making you climax?"

She blinked, speechless for a moment, then swallowed hard. "I'll never be like her, even if I try."

He frowned. "I don't want you to be."

"I don't think you understand. I'll never be as pretty. I'll never be as polished or sophisticated."

"I don't think *you* understand. Corinne could never be you, even if she tried."

Gail gave a short chuckle of amusement. "I don't think Corinne wants anything I have."

"What about me?" he asked.

Gail looked as if he'd knocked the breath out of her. "I don't really have you."

"You have me wanting to be with you tonight," he said, moving closer to her.

He watched a flood of emotions come and go in her eyes before she closed them tight. He put his arms around her and drew her against him. "Why did you leave?"

She lowered her gaze. "So you wouldn't hear me making loud meow sounds," she whispered.

He chuckled. "I can't believe she inspires that kind of response from you. She's harmless."

"She told me she planned to get the relationship between you and her back on track and that I would probably be seeing more of her," Gail said with a dark scowl.

Surprised at Corinne's plans, Nicholas shook his head. "She's dreaming, believe me. I have no—" He stopped. He could feel himself growing impatient. He'd come to think of his time with Gail as his island away from the madness. He resented any intrusion. "Why are we talking about Corinne when we should be together back at the house?"

"You don't like the basketball court?" she asked, seductive mischief glinting in her eyes.

"The place doesn't matter that much to me. I just thought we'd be more comfortable in my bed."

She did a double take. "Your bed. You always come to my bedroom."

"Do you have a problem with coming to my bed?" he asked, giving in to a primitive need for possession, but refusing to examine it.

Her eyes darkened with emotion. "Let me get my sweatshirt."

* * *

Hours later, after Nicholas had thoroughly made love to her, Gail lay in his bed and soaked in every sensation, from the large, firm mattress and the Egyptian-cotton sheets to the overriding feeling of his body close to hers and the steady rise and fall of his chest as he slept.

Her mind made noisy thoughts in the quiet darkness, and she allowed herself to think behind doors she'd kept closed. What if she was to lie here next to him every night? What if he was her partner? What if he was her husband?

Her heart jumped at the thought and she stared at his face in repose, half fearing her forbidden thought would wake him. What if it was her right to greet him every day and kiss him? To make love to him every night and smooth his brow when he was bothered about Barone business? What if she was truly his woman? And he was truly her man?

The images that played in her mind were so sweet she felt an urge to cry. Was this what she had wanted her entire life, but been afraid to wish for?

She closed her eyes at her thoughts. She needed to get herself under control. Nicholas wouldn't like the direction of her thoughts at all.

She took a careful, shallow breath and knew what she had to do. Nicholas always left her in the middle of the night. Even though every fiber of her being rebelled against it, Gail knew she would have to do the same.

Opening her eyes, she leaned toward him and brushed the barest of a kiss over his brow. Then she bit her lip and with agonizing care, slid out of Nicholas's bed and left for her own room.

The following evening after Molly was down for the night, Gail and Nicholas shared a dinner by firelight in his bedroom. Gail wore an apricot-colored chemise and coordinating silk robe and had fixed her hair and makeup as if she was going on a date. She was learning that one of the secrets to feeling like a goddess was dressing the part. She wasn't sure what was responsible for the warmth suffusing her—the fire or the fact that Nicholas hadn't taken his eyes off her since she'd joined him in his room.

"You're staring," she said, taking the next-to-last bite of honey-glazed salmon. The pink delicacy nearly melted in her mouth. "This is delicious. Ana is amazing." Still feeling his gaze on her, she felt her pulse race. "You're still staring."

"I'm trying to decide which look I like best," he said, encircling her ankle with his hand like a sensual chain. "The jock at the gym…"

Gail wrinkled her nose.

"You looked sexy."

"Yeah, right," she said in utter disbelief.

"Or the nanny…"

She rolled her eyes. "Now that's gonna knock 'em dead."

He squeezed her ankle. "You look warm."

"As opposed to hot?" she asked.

He grinned, sliding closer to her. "You want to look hot?"

Gail felt her cheeks heat. "I realize it's a stretch."

He shook his head. "Not a stretch at all. When you first put on a short skirt and too much makeup, you nearly gave me a heart attack."

"Too much makeup," she said in consternation.

He took her fork from her hand and served her the last bite of salmon. "Well, you have to admit it was more than you usually wore."

Gail swallowed the bite. "Anything was more than I usually wore."

"It made you look different."

"That was the idea. How did it make me look?"

He paused, looking as if he was editing his word choice. "Like a woman who could drive a man crazy. Like a bad girl."

An illicit thrill raced through her. "Really?"

He chuckled. "I can't believe you're that pleased."

She sat tall. "Hey, for someone who has been one of the guys forever, this is monumental."

"They don't know what they're missing. If I have anything to do with it, they won't find out," he said, his gaze possessive as he lifted the glass of wine to her lips.

Gail swallowed a gulp of wine. That possessiveness made her heart trip. It gave her hope, hope she tried to stamp out like stray sparks from a fire. "So do I look like a bad girl tonight?"

He cocked his head to one side, studying her. "Yes and no."

"Does that mean I've gotten better with makeup application?"

He chuckled again and shook his head. "You look like a woman who could drive a man crazy," he said, then his gaze turned serious. "But you also look like a woman a man could trust." He tugged her onto his lap. "I should take you out to dinner, but I'm selfish as hell about you. I don't want to share. When I come home, it's like we have our own little island, and I don't want it polluted by the outside world."

"Polluted how?" she asked, touched that he would confide in her.

"Questions from the media, questions from my family, stupid speculation. I want to keep this between you and me as long as we can," he said, lifting his hand to her cheek.

And then what? she wondered, but swallowed the question. The look in his eyes was so powerful it overshadowed everything else. She could almost believe he might somehow, some way, grow to— No! She had to stop the thought.

Loosening the belt of her robe, Nicholas pushed it from her shoulders and lowered his mouth to hers. "Being with you is habit-forming."

Gail pressed her mouth to his, boldly sliding her tongue inside, hoping she was a habit he would never break. She unfastened his shirt and slid her hands over his chest.

He skimmed a lazy finger down her throat and breast just inside her chemise to her tight nipple. She let out a little sigh.

"Damn," he muttered. "You've already got me hard. Do you have any idea how sexy it is knowing all I have to do is touch you and you're mine? I bet you're already wet," he said, and slid his hand between her thighs to find the tell-tale dampness.

He rubbed his thumb over her hot spot and French-kissed her. Groaning, he pulled back slightly. "I'm going to take this slow if it kills me."

"What if taking it slow kills me, too?" she asked.

He shook his head and raked his fingers through his hair. "You're not making this easy."

"I didn't know that was my job," she murmured, sliding her hand down to his crotch.

Swearing under his breath again, he stilled her hand, his gaze full of promise. "We're taking this slow. You'll like it," he said, and lifted her to his bed.

And much to her delight and impatience, he did indeed take his time. He kissed her nipples until they were stiff peaks against his tongue, then he drew them deep into his mouth. He pressed openmouthed kisses down her rib cage to her belly. Lower still, he searched her secrets with his magic tongue.

Gail was so aroused her body glistened with sweat. She arched against him, seeking more and more of him. He took her with his mouth with shocking carnal intimacy and left her trembling but determined to drive him just as far as he'd driven her.

When he slid up her body, she held his head between her hands and kissed him deeply. She sank her fingers into the crisp waves of his hair and luxuriated in the sensation of his hard chest against her breasts.

Overwhelmed with her feelings for him, she tried to convey herself with her mouth and body.

His body moved restlessly against hers, and she flowed down the front of him and took him into her mouth. He began to mutter in Italian, and the sound was like the most sensual music. She tasted the honey of his arousal, and he tightened his hands on her shoulders, signaling her to stop.

She looked up at him. "What are you saying? Tell me."

"Angel, witch," he muttered, his gaze dark with unspent passion. "You're both." He pulled her up his naked body and positioned her just over his hardness. His velvet gaze holding her more effectively than a locked cell, he thrust inside her. "Ride me," he told her in a low voice that ran through her blood like an explosive.

He guided her over him, his body straining, hers taking him in. The sensation of feminine power rocked through her. She wanted nothing more than to be as close to him as possible. The rhythm of his sensual invasion made her pulse pound in all her secret places. With each thrust, he rubbed where she was most sensitive.

Panting, she felt her vision grow hazy and she clung to his shoulders. Her climax whipped through her, taking her like a hurricane. She cried out his name. She felt him take one last thrust inside her, his powerful body arching into hers. She came in fits and starts, trembling with pleasure until she was so weak she sank onto his chest.

Rocked to her soul, she tried to catch her breath, tried to catch a remnant of sanity, but there was only Nicholas, and she wanted only to be his.

"I love you," she whispered, the words bursting from her heart of their own volition. "I love you." The secret wouldn't be stifled anymore.

Her heart was still racing so fast she wasn't sure if she'd said the words aloud. Had she? Nicholas lay perfectly still. He still held her in his arms, but she sensed something different in his body.

Her stomach knotted. Had she told him she loved him?

Gail looked into his eyes and immediately had her answer. He held her, but his gaze had never been more remote. It didn't seem possible. They'd been so incredibly close just moments before.

She lifted her hand to his jaw, and though he didn't move, he looked away from her. Gail knew she'd made a terrible mistake.

Ten

Gail held her breath when she heard Nicholas climb the stairs the next night. He'd stayed late at work, and when his footsteps slowed outside her door, she hoped with all her heart that he would knock. She waited, but there was no knock. She heard him check on Molly, but he never came into her room.

His silence cut like a knife. Nicholas Barone wanted warm smiles, acceptance and hot nights, but not her love. She closed her eyes against the pain.

I don't believe it, she thought as she got out of bed. It wasn't just the sex. Heaven knew, Nicholas could get that from any woman. He might not realize it, but the reason he'd wanted her was that she loved him. It might make him uncomfortable, and he might deny it until there was another tea party in the Boston

Harbor, but what Nicholas Barone wanted and needed was the love of a good woman. And Gail was that woman.

She paced the plush carpet of her bedroom floor. She had half a mind to barge into his room, turn on the lights and shout that she loved him and wasn't ashamed of it. No more furtively biting her lip to keep from saying it in the darkness and hoping he wouldn't read it in her eyes. The cat was out of the bag, and part of her was relieved.

Part of her was terrified.

He hadn't verbally told her to leave his room last night, but he'd wanted space. After the closeness they'd shared, that had hurt. She understood he needed some time to think, to digest what their bodies had said to each other. He needed to recalibrate his distrustful attitude toward women, and that wasn't going to be accomplished in moments. She understood that.

If she gave him time to think this over, he would come around, she told herself. It was the only possible thing he could do. It was obvious that she loved him and he wanted her love, and if he didn't love her this second, he would grow to love her. The bond between them was too powerful, too compelling. He would come back to her.

At least, she hoped he would.

"Nick, didn't you hear me?" his sister Gina asked, a furrow between her brows. "Is something wrong? I've felt like I've had to repeat everything I've said."

He shook his head and raked his hand through his hair. He stood, unable to sit for another moment.

"Everything's fine. I just didn't get enough sleep tonight."

Gina raised an eyebrow. "Out with Corinne again?"

"No," he said immediately, dismayed at his sharp tone.

Her eyes widened. "Oh. Somebody new?"

"It doesn't have to be anybody. A man can have lots of things on his mind."

She frowned. "Is there something at work I should know about?"

He sighed. His sister was incredibly intuitive and persistent. She'd needed both qualities to succeed in the family company, where he knew he and his father had sometimes underestimated her. "The company's great. You should know that more than anyone."

"Then if it's not Molly, it's got to be a woman," she said, half sitting on his desk.

"Maybe this is none of your business."

"Maybe I could help," she returned without batting an eye. "You've dated so many women since Danielle I couldn't begin to name them, but you haven't seemed happy until the last few weeks. If you've found something worth keeping, don't let it go."

Nicholas stared silently at his sister, and she seemed to get the message. She lifted her hands. "Okay, sorry to intrude. Here are the dates for the upcoming national promotions. If you need anything further, you know my extension," she said, leaving a file on his desk and exiting his office.

He shoved his hands into his pockets and looked down on Huntington Avenue. If his little sister could tell what was going on, then he had gone a damn sight farther than he'd intended.

He was ready to jump out of his skin. He'd let Gail get too close and now he was paying for it. He'd told himself he would never again get so involved with a woman that she affected his concentration.

Nicholas had always prided himself on his ability to compartmentalize his life, especially where women were concerned. Too, he was known for his ability to maintain control and keep his personal life private. The knowledge that his sister could tell that something was going on bothered the hell out of him.

Gail wasn't the first woman to profess her love to him in the heat of passion. She was just the first woman he believed actually did love him. The others had wanted something. Gail did, too, but she wasn't angling for marriage. She didn't consider herself attractive enough for him to consider marriage to her. No, she wanted something more dangerous than marriage or money. She wanted to be his friend and lover. She would hand him her heart on a platter, but she wanted his in return.

And the mere thought of that scared the hell out of him.

For the next two nights Nicholas stayed late at work, and after checking on Molly, he passed by Gail's room. Knowing she was so close struck him with such a strong feeling of longing that his chest hurt with it. Troubled, he went to his room and tried to sleep, but visions of Gail interfered. In his half dreams, her laughter drifted over him like a caress, her kisses stirred him, and he awoke hard with wanting.

Following the same procedure the next night, he carefully closed Molly's door. Inhaling, he caught a whiff of a familiar alluring scent. He turned and saw Gail standing in front of him. His heart caught.

"How are you?" she asked quietly, her eyes full of emotions that beckoned and pushed him away at the same time. It would have been so easy, so natural, to walk into her arms, but he didn't.

"Okay," he said. "Just busy."

"I've missed you," she whispered, moving toward him. "You look tired. Can I get you a glass of wine?" she asked, lifting her hand to his jaw.

Her presence soothed a multitude of rough places inside him. She shouldn't have that kind of power over him, he told himself. "No. I just need to hit the sack."

He tried to look away from her gaze, part-siren, part-friend, but he couldn't. When she stood on tiptoe and brushed his lips with hers, he couldn't back away.

"Have you talked yourself into believing you don't want to be with me anymore?"

He wanted to taste her so much it hurt. He ached to slide his hands around her and carry her to his room. He ached to lose himself in her. "Don't make more of what's between you and me than it is," he said as much to himself as to her.

He heard her sharp intake of breath and saw by the look in her eyes that he had hurt her. Necessary pain, he told himself, even though he felt as if someone had slipped a knife in his side. She had gotten too close.

By the end of the week Nicholas was running on empty. It was Friday and although he knew Gail would be at the house, he couldn't find the energy to stay in the office any longer.

As he put the key in the front door, he noticed a light flickering in the den. The television must be on. His stomach dipped. Gail was up, probably waiting for him. In no mood to confront or resist, he pushed open the door, fully expecting her to call out his name.

Instead, he heard a male voice coming from the den. Curious, he glanced around the corner and saw Gail's friend Jonathan with his hand on her hair. He heard Jonathan murmur something, then lower his head and pull Gail into his arms.

Something inside him turned to ice. He stood there, watching Gail in Jonathan's arms for a full five seconds. Flickers of the betrayal he'd felt with Danielle assaulted him.

Gail pulled back, and her face was visible to Nicholas. Her gaze met his for a heartbeat. She opened her mouth as if to speak, but Nicholas didn't stick around to hear. He turned away and strode up the stairs. Cold fury raced through him as he shut his bedroom door behind him. Realizing he was still wearing his overcoat, he ripped it off and jerked his tie loose.

He unfastened his shirt with such force two buttons bounced on the floor. He shouldn't give a damn whom she held or who held her. He shouldn't care. That was the point of this entire week, to make him not care so much.

He heard a knock on the door and ignored it. His

pulse was pounding in his ears. He pulled off his shirt and went to a mini-bar to pour a glass of scotch. He couldn't trust a woman. When would he learn?

A knock sounded again, but he again ignored it. The same way he should have ignored the itch Gail had generated inside him. He knocked back the scotch and relished the burn down his throat.

His door flung open. "We need to talk," Gail said, her eyes lit with purpose.

"No, we don't," he said. "Leave."

She shook her head and closed the door behind her. "Ever since I told you I love you, you've acted like a jerk."

"I thought you had decided we were more serious than we really are. You cleared that up tonight."

"You saw Jonathan comforting me. Yes, I was crying."

"You don't owe me any explanations," he said, pouring himself another drink. "Our relationship was no strings." He shrugged. "You can go do anything you want with Jonathan."

She froze. "It would be okay with you if he and I became lovers?" she asked, her face turning pale.

"You can do whatever you want. It's no concern of mine."

Her eyes turned shiny with unshed tears. "I can't believe you're saying that to me. I don't want Jonathan. I want you."

The image of Gail in Jonathan's arms replayed in his mind over and over again. He was stunned and horrified at the depth of his pain. "It doesn't matter. If you want to stay with me, we can have a good time. We always have before."

She gasped at his callous remarks. She could bear a lot, but he intuitively knew she couldn't stand for him to belittle what they'd shared. He saw the moment she began to close herself off to him. A shield came over her eyes. She looked away from him and wrapped her arms around herself. "I'm going to have to think about what to do," she finally said in a quiet voice.

"What do you mean?" he asked, unsettled by her lack of emotion.

"I mean I have to figure out if it would be best for me to leave."

It surprised the hell out of him, but the prospect of her leaving hit him broadside. "You can't leave," he told her. "We have a contract."

She met his gaze. "With a thirty-day trial period." Her lips lifted in a brittle smile. "A lot has happened, but thirty days aren't up."

"You wouldn't use that against me," he said.

"Use what?" she retorted. "How could I use anything against you? I'm starting to think you're a closet misogynist. Or maybe you're a masochist. You refuse to believe that a woman could love you and be willing to do anything for you. You refuse to trust when you've been given every reason." Her eyes grew shiny again, and she closed them, lifting her hand as if to collect herself. "I need to figure out the best thing to do. You may not need me, but Molly does. At least for now," she said, and whirled out of the room, leaving him to face some hard questions about himself.

Nicholas drank enough scotch to drown out the questions and bitter rumblings of regret. It was enough to leave him with a vicious hangover the next morning. After a long shower he made his way to the kitchen, his head pounding. Rubbing his hand over the hollow feeling in his chest, he nodded at Ana. "Good morning."

She smiled. "Almost noon, Mr. Barone. You never sleep this late. I hope you're not catching the flu."

He shook his head. "No, but I could use some coffee."

"Coming right up," she said, and placed a cup in front of him as he sat down at the table.

"Thank you. Where's Molly?" he asked, thinking it was extremely quiet.

"She's with your mother. Gail said she needed to take the day off and arranged for Molly to visit with your mother."

Nicholas paused mid-sip. "Did Gail say where she was going?"

"No."

"Or when she would be back?" he asked, getting an ugly feeling in his gut.

Ana shook her head. "No. She just said she was taking a drive." Ana glanced out the kitchen window. "It's a nice day for a drive. No snow."

He gave a noncommittal murmur and walked toward the den, nursing his coffee. He wondered if Gail was with Jonathan. In the clear light of day, he knew she wasn't. He'd been hard on Gail. It had been damn tough for him to see her in Jonathan's arms, but he knew her eyes didn't lie. She hadn't lied when she'd confronted him in his bedroom.

She hadn't lied when she'd said he couldn't trust her even when he had every reason to trust. Amazing what a scotch-induced night of sleep could do to his reasoning capability. He remembered the shuttered look in her eyes. She had closed him out. He deserved it. What the hell could he do about it all now?

He drank two more cups of coffee and swallowed a gallon of regret. Edgy with the need to talk with Gail, he thought about calling his mother to find out where she might have gone. The phone rang just as he went to pick it up.

"This is Boston Community Hospital. May I speak to Nicholas Barone."

Alarm raced through him. "This is Nicholas."

"We have your name in case of emergency for Gail Fenton. We found it in her belongings at the emergency room."

Nicholas felt his heart stop. His coffee cup fell from his hand to the floor, shattering. "Gail? What happened?"

"She was in an automobile accident. She's unconscious and a doctor is evaluating her condition. We tried to contact her brother, but we haven't been able to reach him."

"I'll be right there," Nicholas said, and dropped the receiver into the cradle.

As Nicholas paced the emergency waiting room, he wished Gail had been taken to Boston General. He had connections there, namely his sister Rita. Here, he was relegated to waiting and to the stock answers from the nurses.

The bitter taste of regret and fear filled his mouth. What if Gail was seriously injured? Worse yet, what if she didn't make it?

Nicholas broke into a cold sweat, and the hard realization he'd unsuccessfully dodged the past weeks hit him head-on. He didn't want to lose Gail. Not to an automobile accident, not to another man, not to anything. She had become the most important person in the world to him, and he didn't want to lose her. He didn't even want to begin to think about a future without her.

Frustrated as hell that he couldn't be with her, he approached the nurses' station again. He wanted to make sure Gail was getting the best possible treatment. "I think Miss Fenton would respond better to treatment if someone familiar to her is with her."

The nurse glanced up. "She's conscious now. Exam room three. I'll ask if you can see her. Sir!"

Nicholas walked past the indignant nurse. Let the woman call Security. He'd waited long enough. He rounded the corner, strode down the hall and walked into exam room three. A nurse and doctor stood over Gail as she lay on the table. They immediately looked up at him.

"I'm the contact in case of emergency for Gail Fenton."

Gail sat up and gaped at him. "Nicholas?"

"Keep your head down, Miss Fenton," the doctor said. "We want you to remain as quiet as possible for the next couple of hours. You've been banged up and you need to give yourself a chance to heal."

Gail's heart pounded. She was still dizzy from the concussion and her head felt as if it was going to split open. She wondered if she was seeing things. Was that really Nicholas?

"Miss Fenton is recovering from a concussion, and

we're making sure there is no internal bleeding from her accident,'' said the doctor. "It's important that she remain quiet. I may admit her for the night.''

Gail closed her eyes. She couldn't think about Nicholas right now. Her head was hurting too much. Her heart was hurting too much. She might have been hit on the head, but her memory was perfectly sound. She recalled every hurtful word he'd uttered to her last night.

"That's good. Close your eyes and rest,'' the nurse said, patting her arm "We'll let you know when we get the results from X-ray.''

She heard the door whoosh open, then close. A moment passed before she felt another touch on her arm, but Gail knew it wasn't the nurse this time.

"What happened?'' Nicholas asked in the gentlest voice she'd ever heard him use.

She inhaled his scent and pushed aside a twist of bittersweet longing. The purpose of her drive had been to get herself together and to put her feelings for Nicholas behind her. So far she hadn't done a very good job. "A guy with a Jeep ran a red light. He wasn't hurt. They tell me I'm lucky, but my car was totaled.''

"We can replace the car.''

"The guy who hit me was insured, so it shouldn't be a problem.''

"I was worried about you,'' he said in a low, intimate voice.

"I'll be okay,'' she said, refusing to read anything into his words.

A long pause followed. "Things need to be different between us.''

Her stomach tightened. "Yeah, you've made that perfectly clear."

"No. I haven't made myself clear at all."

"Oh, I would say you have," she said, unable to keep her eyes closed any longer. "You told me I had taken our relationship far more seriously than I should have. You told me I could go to bed with Jonathan. You didn't care. You told me—"

He swore, his face flinching in remorse. "I was an idiot, and I'm sorry."

Looking at him hurt her heart. She looked away from him. "No, you were right. I took things more seriously than I should have. I'm going to try to put what happened between us in the past," she said, although she still hadn't figured out how to accomplish that. "I don't have as much experience being blasé about…" She couldn't finish. Her head throbbed with renewed vigor.

"No," he said, touching his finger to her cheek. "I don't want you to change. I was the one with the screwed-up attitude. Look at me."

She closed her eyes. "I can't. My head is killing me."

"Okay, then just listen. I was wrong. I've been wrong. I didn't understand what was happening to me. I didn't expect you to become so important to me. I didn't expect anyone to become so important to me. I fought it. I have never felt so safe and yet so incredibly aroused by a woman."

A bubble of hope formed in her chest. Gail was afraid to open her eyes. What if she was suffering from a delusion?

"I love you," he said, and she felt his lips brush the back of her hand. "I need you."

She swallowed over the lump in her throat. This couldn't be true. This couldn't be happening. She'd dreamed it, but it wasn't really possible. "For Molly," she said more for herself than for him.

"Yes, I need you for Molly. But if I didn't have Molly, I would still need you for me."

Now she *knew* she was dreaming. She looked up at Nicholas and saw a deep love glowing in his eyes. Her heart was hammering in her chest. "I think you'd better get the doctor. I think I'm imagining things because I just heard you say that you love me and need me."

"That's because I do."

She felt her eyes well with tears. "Could you do me a favor? If this is real and you really mean it, could you tell me tomorrow when my head isn't hurting and I don't feel dizzy?"

His eyes were full of fierce, yet tender emotion. "I can tell you I love you every day for the rest of my life if you'll let me."

Yup, she was dreaming.

The doctor and nurse observed her for a couple of hours more, then released her with instructions for Nicholas. Back at his town house Nicholas insisted she stay in his bed with him, but he didn't make love to her. The following morning when she awoke, she felt battered, but slightly better. Her cheek still resting on the pillow, she opened her eyes and took a quick inventory of her body and head.

She immediately noticed, however, that Nicholas wasn't there, and her chest tightened in distress. Had she imagined the things he'd said to her yesterday? Had he said them impulsively and thought better of it?

Slowly sitting up in bed, she felt her stomach twist and turn. The door opened and Nicholas appeared wearing a pair of jeans and an unbuttoned shirt and carrying a breakfast tray. "Good. You're awake," he said with a smile that made her heart turn over. "Hungry?"

"I hadn't gotten there yet," she said. "I was making sure my brain and body were working correctly."

"And?"

"I'm moving a little slow, but I'll get there. Good grief," she said as he pulled the silver cover off a plate filled with scrambled eggs, bacon, potatoes and toast.

"You eat while I shower," he said, dropping a kiss on her forehead on his way to the connecting bath.

Gail temporarily pushed aside her uncertainties and devoured a good portion of the meal. After returning the dishes to the kitchen, she went to her own bathroom to splash some water on her face and brush her teeth. She nearly plowed into Nicholas when she rounded the corner into her bedroom.

He caught her by the shoulders and looked into her eyes for a long moment. "Does your head hurt?"

"Not too much," she said, her pulse picking up at his intense expression.

"Are you dizzy?"

"No," she said. No more than I usually am when you're touching me.

He lifted his hand to her cheek. "I love you, Gail."

Her heart somersaulted. "Are you sure?" she asked, having difficulty believing it.

"Never more sure."

"But why? I'm not a model or anything impressive. I'm just me."

"Ah, Gail," he said, shaking his head and pulling her against him. "I can see I'm going to have to prove to you that you're the most impressive woman in the world. I'd given up on having a relationship with a woman that would last longer than one basketball season. I don't know how you do it, but you make it okay for me to be human and not perfect every minute. At the same time, when I'm with you, I want to be better. I can trust you." He pulled back slightly and looked at her. "I never thought I'd be able to trust a woman like I trust you. I just know that you're always going to look out for me. I stopped feeling lonely when you came into my life."

His words rocked through her, leaving her speechless.

He gave a sigh of exasperation. "I'm not saying this well."

"Oh, you're doing great," she assured him, her eyes glistening with tears. "I'm just having a hard time believing it. I want to, but I feel like I need to be pinched or need some witnesses to tell me I'm not dreaming."

"Okay," he said, and gently pinched her. "Does that help?"

"Some," she said, looking at him through the tears. She knew her eyes were filled with the love for him that had grown inside her despite her attempts to squash it.

"Okay. About the witnesses. How about a hundred of them in one week?"

She gaped at him. "A hundred. Wh-what…"

"At our wedding," he said, his gaze utterly serious.

Overwhelmed, Gail moved her head in a circle. "Wedding," she squeaked, feeling light-headed. "You just said two W-words. Wedding and one week. And I'm not supposed to get dizzy."

"Do you love me?" he asked, and there was no room for compromise in his eyes. There was no need.

"Of course I do," she said, his arms holding her while her knees grew unsteady.

"Then make me the happiest man in the world and marry me."

Her heart could only offer one possible answer.

Eleven

Exactly one week later, with her brother, Adam, by her side, Gail walked down the aisle of the beautiful chapel of St. Christopher's Cathedral. The smaller chapel provided the perfect atmosphere of intimacy for the hastily arranged wedding.

Between Nicholas's mother and sisters, Gail had hardly lifted a finger. Bustling around, eager to take care of every detail, the women showed obvious delight that had moved her to tears. Gail had spent more than a few moments drying her eyes the past week. Nicholas's entire family had embraced her immediately and made it clear that she not only belonged to Nicholas, but she also belonged to the Barones. One night she told him that his family was the cherry on top of the sundae as far as she was concerned. He'd told her that was okay with him as long as he was the main dish, and then he'd proceeded to make love to her.

She'd found her dress at a local designer's shop, and the owner had been more than happy to make the necessary alterations for a Barone bride. Her old college roommate, Rose Trent, had been so thrilled she'd cleared her schedule to be one of Gail's bridesmaids, alongside Gina and Colleen. Rita and Maria had volunteered to keep the baby happy during the ceremony.

Gail looked at Nicholas and felt her heart leap. Her brother joined her hand with Nicholas's. ''Take care of her and she'll take care of you,'' he said.

''I will,'' Nicholas said, his gaze encompassing Gail and Adam. Then his eyes were only for her. The priest led them through their vows, and Gail felt Nicholas's promises resonate all the way to her bones.

The ceremony was sweet and brief, and before Gail knew it, she was wearing a wedding ring on her finger and the priest was pronouncing them husband and wife.

Nicholas lifted her veil.

''It went so fast,'' she whispered. ''I wanted to be able to remember every second.''

''You won't have to remember,'' he told her. ''I'll remind you every day that I love you, Gail. Every day,'' he said, and sealed the promise with a kiss.

Her tears of joy overflowed. She had finally found home in this man's heart.

After hugs from Nicholas's family and so many photographs Gail was certain she was left with a permanent smile, the group adjourned to an exclusive downtown club for the reception.

Nicholas coaxed her onto the dance floor for their waltz. The romantic tune and the love she saw in his gaze was stamped on her memory forever. More hugs followed as he introduced her to members of his extended family.

After the first crush passed, he pulled her away from the crowd. "Hey, even in football you're allowed a few timeouts," he said to the protesting guests. He guided her behind an ice sculpture for a glass of champagne. "To you and me," he said, lifting his glass to hers in a toast.

She smiled, clinking her glass with his. "To you and me."

"I'm ready to leave. I've shared you enough," he said.

Surprise raced through her. "We've only been here thirty minutes."

"Tell the truth. Would you rather stay here or take off with me?"

Her heart swelled and she leaned into him to feel his strength and warmth. "That's easy. The party's lovely, but you're the main attraction for me. I'd rather take off with you."

Nicholas lowered his mouth to hers and stole a kiss. He pulled back with a reluctant sigh. "One more hour, max," he said. "Then you're all mine." He slid his arm around her and they both looked out on the crowded dance floor. "Looks like everyone is having a good time."

"Your mother sure knows how to throw a wedding,'' Gail said, still amazed at Moira Barone's ability to put such an event together so quickly.

Nicholas gave a wry grin. ''She says she's been planning this since I turned twenty-one. The power of positive thinking, I guess.''

Gail laughed, spotting Carlo and Moira dancing. She saw Colleen with a tall, dark-haired man. ''Hey, who is that with Colleen? Is he a Barone?''

Nicholas narrowed his eyes. He shook his head. ''Not a Barone. Hell if it isn't Gavin O'Sullivan,'' he said with a mix of surprise and pleasure in his voice. ''I don't know if you've met him yet. He's probably been waiting until the crowd thins out a little to greet us. He was a good friend of mine in school. He's come a long way. When I first knew him, he was a foster child. Now he's the billionaire owner of a luxury hotel chain.''

''Wow. I've never seen Colleen look like that before. She's almost lighting up like a Christmas tree.''

''Hmm. Interesting. I think the two of them had something going in high school, but my mother didn't approve because—'' Nicholas broke off. ''Incoming,'' he said with a wry chuckle. ''Looks like we've been discovered.''

Gina, dressed in silk with Molly happily ensconced on her hip, peeked behind the ice sculpture. ''Inquiring minds want to know. When are you cutting the cake? If you don't cut it soon, I fear your daughter is going to help. She can't take her eyes off it.''

''Da-da-da-da,'' Molly said, then reached for Gail.

Gail took the baby in her arms and kissed her soft cheek. ''Do you think it's time for cake?'' she asked

Molly. "Do you know how messy you're going to get?"

"I'm armed with wet towelettes," Gina said.

With much coaching from the guests, Gail and Nicholas cut a slice of the beautiful three-tier cake and fed each other a bite. Nicholas took a sly, secret lick around her finger, sending her an illicit thrill. Without batting an eye, he waved Gina and Molly closer, and he and Gail fed the baby a couple of bites.

"She can have a few more bites, but not too much if you want her to go to sleep tonight," Gail told Gina, who would be caring for Molly while the bride and groom honeymooned in Italy.

"Three more bites," Gina said with a sly wink. "Everyone except you two will want their sleep tonight."

Gail felt her cheeks heat.

"You're blushing," Nicholas said against her ear.

"It's not very nice of you to point that out."

"Knowing that you blush over your entire body is a tremendous turn-on. Knowing I'm the only man to see your body blush turns me on even more," he said, curling his hand around her waist.

She instinctively put her arms around him, and a few of the guests gave wolf whistles of encouragement. Gail withstood the good-natured teasing and affection, then escaped down the hall for a quick trip to the powder room. She ran into her brother along the way. "Having a good time?"

He embraced her. "It's a great party. I just want to make sure you're okay."

Her heart twisted at the concern in Adam's eyes. "I couldn't be happier. I'm still amazed."

"You always wanted a big family," he said with a grin.

"I did," she confessed. "The Barones are wonderful. But the real draw for me is Nicholas. He takes up such a big space in my heart. I didn't know such a thing was possible."

Adam hugged her again. "I'm glad you're happy. If you ever need anything…"

"I know I can call you," she said. "I think some of your friends' names were put on the guest list. Were any of them able to come?"

"Yeah, I was able to talk Steven Conti into coming when I told him your old college roommate Rose Trent was going to be here. He's wanted to hook up with her for a long time. He mentioned something about how some of his family aren't big fans of the Barones, but clammed up when I asked him about it."

"I can't imagine why anyone wouldn't love the Barones," she said, confused.

"Spoken like a loyal bride," Adam gently teased.

She swatted playfully at him. "He was one of your roommates in college, wasn't he?"

Adam nodded. "He's one of the dotcom millionaires who stayed on top after a lot of them crashed and burned. If I can find him, I'll make sure I bring him around to say hi."

"Make it soon," she said with a smile. "Nicholas wants to leave soon."

"I'll see what I can do. In the meantime, I'll eat some cake and see if any of the Barone cousins are interested in going out with the bride's brother," he said with a wink and headed back to the reception.

Gail continued down the hall in search of the powder room. She took another turn, then another, at last finding it. Colleen Barone was already there, pressing a cool towel to her face.

"Are you okay?" Gail asked, concerned at the sight of Colleen's flushed cheeks.

"I'm fine," Colleen said, appearing self-conscious. "I just…" She swallowed. "I just saw someone I didn't expect to see."

"Gavin O'Sullivan?" Gail asked.

Surprise crossed Colleen's gamine features. "How did you know?"

"I saw you with him. Nicholas told me that you and he had once—"

Colleen pressed her hand to her throat. "That was a long time ago. I just didn't expect to see him here and to feel so…" She took a deep breath and shook her head. "Enough about that. You're the beautiful bride, and Nicholas looks so happy. I've never seen him this happy. I think we have you to thank for that."

Gail's eyes immediately filled with tears. "You're so sweet to say that. Your family has been so kind to me." She embraced Colleen.

"You've made it easy," she said sincerely, returning Gail's hug.

"Oh, no. I hope I don't cry again," Gail said. "I feel like a hyper sprinkler system."

Colleen chuckled. "I'll leave you to catch your breath and get back to the party. Will you be long?"

"Just a couple of minutes," she said, and watched Colleen leave. After she freshened up, she walked down a long hall, but didn't hear signs of the reception. She was all turned around. Her brain must have been jumbled by all the excitement. Hearing voices in a room, she decided to ask for directions. She pushed open the door and saw Maria in the arms of a tall man.

"I haven't been able to look at anyone but you," he said, his voice filled with wonder.

Gail blinked. Maria? The man looked familiar. Surprised, she stood still for a moment, trying to place him. Who was he? Then recognition hit. Steven Conti. But her brother had just told her he was interested in Rose.

Gail felt a surge of protectiveness for Maria. She bit her lip, not knowing what to do. The two of them were so focused on each other that they hadn't noticed her. Steven appeared totally transfixed by Maria, and she by him.

Her heart contracted at the sight of them. She knew the feelings behind the electricity they shared. She and Nicholas shared the same electricity and love. Steven lowered his head and kissed Maria passionately. Gail looked away with the odd sense that she was watching some kind of world-shaking intimacy take place between the couple. Feeling like an intruder, she quietly backed away.

Distracted by what she'd seen, she took several wrong turns before she managed to find the reception. Nicholas greeted her as soon as she entered the door. "I looked in all the corners for you. I even chatted with Delores Forwood. She told me I'm the smartest man in the world to marry you," he said, reminding her of the time they'd attended the mayor's party.

She smiled. He made everything feel better for her.

"Very nice lady. I'm embarrassed to admit I got lost coming back from the powder room."

He gave a low chuckle and pulled her into an embrace. "That's enough of a sign for me. It's time for me to take you away from all this."

Hours later Gail lay naked in her husband's arms in the lavish honeymoon suite. She sighed with pleasure, relieved that the hustle and bustle was over. "You never really told me why you didn't want to wait past Valentine's Day for our wedding."

"I don't believe in the Conti curse, but—"

"Conti?" Gail interrupted, surprise racing through her. She looked up at him. "Conti curse?"

"I told you about the Valentine's Day curse."

"Yeah, but you never mentioned the Contis."

"The Contis were my grandfather's godparents and they expected him to marry their daughter, Lucia, but he eloped with Angelica."

"Oh, now I remember. Sounds sticky," she said, shifting to her side so she could look at Nicholas's face. She would never tire of looking at him and listening to his voice.

"If that weren't sticky enough, the Contis' son, Vincent, had hoped to marry Angelica."

She winced. "So the Contis weren't very happy with the Barones."

"That's putting it mildly. I told you how Lucia Conti put a curse on the Barones."

Gail digested the information and couldn't help remembering the passionate kiss that Steven Conti and Maria Barone had exchanged. She wondered if she should tell Nicholas, but she didn't want to cause unnecessary concern.

He pulled her on top of his long, sexy body. "Enough about the Contis. I've got you now."

The sexy growl in his voice heated her blood like sun on a summer day. She smiled and slipped her fingers through his hair. His arousal rubbed against her intimately. "We still haven't finished the list."

He took her mouth with a quick, but lethally seductive French kiss. "Did you have a particular one in mind?"

"Yes, I did," she said, struggling with the distraction of how close he was to being inside her. "It involved Baronessa gelato, my mouth and your—"

He thrust inside her, taking her breath.

"Tomorrow," he said, moving in thigh-melting rhythm. "We will get through that list," he promised, and the look on his face made Gail believe him.

"What about when we finish the list?" she asked, sighing when he took her breast into his mouth at the same time as he thrust deeper into her.

"We'll make another one," he said. *"Mia moglie. Il mio cuore."*

He sounded and felt so good she almost didn't need to know what he was saying. Almost. "Translation?" she asked, her mind and body steeped in her connection with him.

He placed her hand on his chest over his heart. "My wife. My heart."

Overwhelmed by a flood of emotion, she bit her lip to hold back tears of joy. "I've been practicing. *L'amero per sempre,*" she whispered. "I hope my pronunciation isn't so bad that I sound like I'm talking about brussel sprouts, because I'm not.''

His eyes lit with passion and understanding, and she felt the velvet cord of their love twine them even closer together. ''I will love you forever, too,'' he said, and Gail counted her blessings, because she knew that she and Nicholas had found the love of a lifetime.

*   *   *   *   *   *

SLEEPING BEAUTY'S BILLIONAIRE
by
Caroline Cross

CAROLINE CROSS

always loved to read, but it wasn't until she discovered romance that she felt compelled to write, fascinated by the chance to explore the positive power of love in people's lives. She grew up in Yakima, Washington, the 'Apple Capital of the World,' attended the University of Puget Sound and now lives outside Seattle, where she works (or tries to) at home despite the chaos created by two telephone-addicted teenage daughters and a husband with a fondness for home improvement projects. Pleased to have recently been No. 1 on a national bestseller list, she was thrilled to win the 1999 Romance Writers of America's RITA Award for Best Short Contemporary Novel and to have been called 'one of the best' writers of romance today by *Romantic Times*. Caroline believes in writing from the heart—and having a good brainstorming partner. She loves hearing from readers and can be reached at PO Box 47375, Seattle, Washington 98146, USA. Please include an SAE with return postage for a reply.

One

"Hey, Colly, what's the matter? Why're you stopping?"

Colleen Barone only dimly registered her second cousin Matthew's inquiries. The nine-year-old's voice seemed far away as, her feet rooted in place, she stared transfixed at the tall, black-haired man who had just entered the reception hall.

Gavin O'Sullivan. Even among the throng of notable guests helping to celebrate her brother Nick's wedding—and so far she'd seen four U.S. senators, the current governor of Massachusetts and two of his predecessors, a bushel of Fortune 500 CEOs and a smattering of Hollywood movie stars—he stood out. And while Colleen wished it was merely because of his chiseled good looks or the impeccable tailoring of his expensive black suit, she knew better. There was simply something about the aloof way he held himself, the serious line of his sensual mouth, the reserve in his coffee-colored eyes, that set him apart.

But then, that was Gavin. Always so intense, so unpredictable, so alone.

Of course, there'd been a handful of brief exceptions to the latter. Once upon a time, for the three years they'd played soccer together at Madison Prep, he and Nick had been best friends. And then later, during her second year of college and his last, he and Colleen had shared for a little while what could only be called magic.

An ache, brief but savage, squeezed her heart. It had been twelve years since their last meeting, and the relationship had ended badly. Yet suddenly she longed to cross the space separating them, slip her hand into Gavin's and say something to make him smile.

If only it was that easy…

"Colleen!" Matthew's earnest voice coupled with his sharp tug on her hand jerked her back to reality.

Tearing her gaze from the man across the room, she looked down at her young companion. "What?"

He rolled his eyes. "I'm hungry, remember?"

As if someone had hit a switch, the totality of the reception hall snapped into focus for her. She heard the band playing, registered the noisy, shifting presence of the hundreds of guests, saw the impatience on her young relative's face. "Oh, Mattie, I'm sorry. Of course you are." Pushing away an edge of dismay— just how long had she been staring at Gavin, anyway?—she summoned a smile. "Lead the way."

"All *right*." His equanimity restored, the youngster tightened his grip on her hand and set off like a tugboat at full throttle. He chugged steadily past clumps of chatting guests and skillfully avoided knots of family members, not stopping until they finally arrived at the buffet, a vast spread laid out over a river of tabletops covered with crisp white linen.

The boy's gaze darted from the steaming casseroles to the heaps of Italian meat sliced paper thin, from stacks of golden calzones to platters of strawberries dipped in pale chocolate. He exhaled with gusty appreciation. "Wow."

Wow was right. In her usual over-the-top fashion, Colleen's mother, Moira, had made certain there was enough food on hand to feed all of Boston. Yet Colleen, who'd typically forgotten to eat that day and had been ravenous only a few minutes earlier, realized she no longer had an appetite.

The reason was obvious, and she felt a prick of annoyance at herself. Not that she intended to let on. Although Matthew probably wouldn't care, she refused to allow Gavin's unexpected presence to affect her behavior. After all, the time they'd been together had happened many years ago; neither of them was the person they'd been.

She knew she wasn't. After a difficult, pain-

ful struggle she'd learned to accept herself.
She'd carved out a life rich with friends and a
job where she felt she made a difference. And
though there were times she was lonely and
she still had her share of doubts and fears,
frustrations and longings—life after all, was a
constant and ever-changing challenge—in the
ways that mattered most she was at peace for
the first time ever.

So quit acting like a drama queen and eat,
her practical side chided. Squaring her shoulders, she handed Matthew a gold-banded china
plate, then took one for herself. "It looks
good, doesn't it?" she said as she began serving them.

"Oh, yeah."

Thirty-five minutes and one return to the
buffet line later, Matthew leaned back and exhaled in satisfaction. "That was really, really
scrumpdillyitious," he announced.

Her lips quirked. "Yes, it was." Which was
perfectly true as applied to the pathetically
small amount she'd managed to get down. She
set down her fork, grateful she could finally
quit rearranging what was left on her plate.

Matt started to wipe the back of his hand

across his mouth, then apparently thought better of it as she raised an eyebrow at him. Sighing, he took a cursory swipe of his face with his napkin, tossed the linen square on the table and idly began to swing one leg.

He was silent for what was for him an uncharacteristically long moment. "Colleen?"

"Hmm?"

"Do you feel okay?"

She glanced over at him in surprise. "Sure."

"You're not mad at me or something?"

"Of course not. Why would you think that?"

He stared with sudden fascination at a spot of Alfredo sauce he'd dripped on the tablecloth and gave a slight, one-shouldered shrug. "I dunno. It's just…you're sort of quiet. For you. And you didn't eat very much, either. And earlier, when we were coming to get our food and then you stopped, you got a real funny look on your face. Kind of like Jordan Crenshaw did when I dared him to eat a dead frog."

"Gosh." Ignoring a concern that her earlier turmoil had been so apparent, she deliberately made her voice light. "And here I thought I was looking pretty good today."

Matt's head jerked up. "Oh, yeah! You do! For a girl. That is…" Flustered, he broke off. Heat stained his cheeks, but at least he was looking at her now, even if his expression was far too earnest. "It's just…I mean…it's just that usually you don't act like other grown-ups."

She'd certainly heard that before. Only normally it was from people her own age. "Ah." What the heck. She might as well take the plunge. "In what way?"

"Well…" He cocked his head, considering. "You really listen to me when we talk. And you never make me feel like you'd rather be somewhere else, with somebody else."

She blinked, gratified.

"And you don't act like you're smarter than me just because you're old."

That certainly put things in perspective; she swallowed a sudden bubble of laughter and did her best to look solemn. "Gee, maybe you'd better find me a cane. I wouldn't want to topple over when I stand up and fall in the punch bowl and embarrass us both."

For half a second the boy looked horrified. And then he realized she was kidding, and his eyes took on an impish gleam. "Naw. You're not *that* old." He did his best to match her deadpan delivery. "But if you were gonna fall down, we're a lot closer to the wedding cake. Now, that'd be really cool."

"Matthew!" Her protest was ruined by her sputter of laughter. "No wonder your mom says you're a menace."

He looked inordinately pleased. "Really? She said that?"

"I'm afraid so."

Before she could add that her cousin Janice had then said how crazy she was about the little rascal, his gaze settled on something behind her and he straightened like a bird dog who'd spotted a covey of quail. "Hey, it's Jeremy and Sean!" Like Matt, the two boys were distant cousins from Colleen's mother's side of the family and had recently become objects of Matt's veneration by virtue of having birthdays and officially becoming teenagers. "Can I go say hi?"

"Of course."

She didn't have to tell him twice. He shot

to his feet and disappeared almost before she gave her consent.

Fondly Colleen watched him go, relieved when the older boys welcomed him warmly. Looking away as a waiter approached, she declined an offer of champagne, taking a sip of her water, instead, as the young man quickly cleared away her and Matthew's plates.

The reception really had turned out to be a lovely affair, she reflected. A few tables away her brother Joseph was involved in an intense conversation with Uncle Paul, while her younger sisters, Rita, Gina and Maria, stood clustered together near the buffet, hands gesturing and faces alight as they chatted with one another.

Out on the dance floor, Nick glided into view, his arms securely cradling his bride, Gail. Hands clasped, heads together, the two were engrossed in each other. Colleen felt a wash of pleasure at their obvious happiness. Before meeting Gail, Nick hadn't had the easiest time when it came to love and romance.

A tendency that seemed to run in the family, she mused as she found herself searching the crowd for Gavin's black hair and broad shoulders. Assuring herself the sudden hollow feeling in the pit of her stomach was relief rather than disappointment when he was nowhere to be seen, she brushed a crumb off the table and told herself firmly she'd played hooky long enough.

At the very least, she should go check on ''the aunts''—the contingent of widowed, black-clad, elderly ladies all gathered together at one big table like a flock of crows. Or, if she really wanted to feel virtuous, she could always seek out her mother....

Quit that, Colleen. Swallowing a sigh—was she ever going to outgrow the irreverent streak that too often got her in trouble?—she pushed back her chair, stood, squared her shoulders and turned.

And found herself gazing straight into the unsmiling face of Gavin O'Sullivan.

It wasn't fair. Twelve years, and she looked exactly the same, Gavin thought grimly. Dainty. Delicate. A doe-eyed waif with flawless skin and the hint of a dimple in one soft cheek.

The only thing different was her hair. Gone

was the ebony sheaf that had once fallen in a silken tumble to her waist. In its place was a cropped, tousled cap that somehow made her neck seem more fragile, her straight little nose finer, her densely lashed blue eyes even bigger.

Not that he gave a rip. His sole reason for seeking her out was to get this encounter over with. He'd come to celebrate Nick's wedding, and he was damned if he was going to spend his time worrying about inadvertently bumping into her. Better by far to take the direct route, where he called the shots. Just to make sure that she or anyone else who might recall they'd once had a thing for each other would be absolutely clear he was long over her.

He summoned the polite, impersonal smile that was his stock-in-trade in social settings. "Hello, Colleen. It's been a long time."

For a second longer than was strictly polite her gaze remained riveted on his face. Then she seemed to catch herself and, as if recalling her manners, smiled and said, "Gavin. How nice to see you."

He'd forgotten what an appealing voice she had. Soft, a little husky, with a warmth that wrapped gently around whomever she was addressing like a well-worn flannel blanket. Too bad it was merely part of her act.

"Does Nick know you're here?" For an instant she sounded almost nervous, but then her voice evened out and he knew he must've imagined it. "Have you talked to him yet?"

What did she think? That he was still some ill-mannered inner-city kid who didn't know how to behave at a fancy wedding? "Sure. I saw him when I went through the reception line."

"Oh. He must be so pleased that you came."

He shrugged. "I wouldn't know about that. I do know I've enjoyed seeing him again."

"Of course." Although her pleasant expression didn't alter, a shadow darkened her eyes, and he knew she'd heard the slight but deliberate emphasis he'd put on *him*.

He felt a flick of satisfaction.

In the next instant he asked himself what in hell he was doing. It had been years since their breakup, damn it. And while being dumped by Colleen had been hard at the time, it was nothing compared to some of the other things he'd endured in his life. Losing a girlfriend just wasn't in the same category as being raised, if it could be called that, by an alcoholic single mother in one of Boston's toughest neighborhoods. Or getting himself not just through high school but also through college. Or even having to learn about art and culture later in life because such "civilized" things had taken a back seat to survival when he'd been younger.

What was more, the intervening years had been good to him. He'd transformed himself from a dirt-poor charity case to a rich, respected, successful hotelier whose extensive holdings provided jobs for hundreds of people.

And he certainly hadn't lived like a monk while he'd done it. In the time since he and Colleen had parted ways, he'd dated his share of women. Most of them, at least lately, tended to be either up-and-coming actresses, members of what was left of European aristocracy or international supermodels.

So maybe he should try not to act like some petulant kid; maybe he could even see his way clear to give little Ms. Barone a break. After all, there was a chance, slight though it was, that he might not be where he was if she hadn't chosen to stomp on his heart all those years ago.

"Dance with me," he said abruptly as the band struck up a new song.

Her eyes widened and for a second something that looked almost like panic gleamed in their sapphire depths. "I beg your pardon?"

What the hell. So he wasn't a saint; but what could it hurt if by acting like an adult he also gave her a taste of what she'd thrown away? He deliberately softened his voice. "Dance with me, Colleen. Please?"

She hesitated another instant, then her face smoothed out as she apparently decided he was now upwardly mobile enough to warrant her attention. "All right." Flashing him a quick smile he might have deemed shyly beguiling had she been anyone else, she headed for the dance floor.

He fell in behind her. Refusing to debate the wisdom of what he was doing, he forced himself to concentrate on the slow but catchy beat of the love song the band was crooning—and not the supple line of her back. By the time they reached the outer circle of dancers, he was ready. Taking Colleen's slender hand in his much bigger one, he slid his other palm to rest on the small of her back, pressed her close and led her into the dance.

Given the awkwardness of their reunion, the acrimony of their former parting and the disparity of their heights, their coming together should have been more than a little graceless.

Instead, from their first step they were perfectly matched, melting together in a rhythm that was as instinctive as breathing—or sex.

"Oh, my," Colleen murmured.

"What?" Even to his own ears, he sounded a little terse, but then, the last thing he'd expected was the pleasure that was currently sizzling along his nerves.

"I'd just...forgotten." She raised her chin and met his gaze, an unexpected and oddly self-effacing expression on her fine-boned face. "It's been a long time since I danced. I'd forgotten how nice it is."

Nice? That was the last word he'd use to describe the awareness tingling through him like ungrounded electricity. "Yeah. Right."

She cocked her head. "When did you finally learn?"

"What?"

"To dance. As I recall, you didn't... before."

Now there was a diplomatic choice of words. For a second he was tempted to make her squirm, to politely inquire, "Do you mean before you discarded me like yesterday's newspaper, with no more explanation than we didn't suit and you didn't want to see me anymore?"

But then he reminded himself of his decision not to be petty. Which was no doubt good since a second later the band launched into a complicated instrumental riff that sounded as if it might keep them together longer than he'd been counting on.

What wasn't good was the discovery that he wanted in the worst way to look away from Colleen's gaze so that he could bury his face in the delicate curve where her neck met her shoulder and drink her in, inhale her scent, taste her skin, savor the flavor of her on his tongue. Just like that, any sort of distraction, including conversation, seemed like a damn good idea. "I took lessons. Arthur Murray."

"You're kidding." She couldn't hide her amazement.

Annoyed and not sure why, except that it pissed him off royally to be lusting after a woman he didn't like, he retorted, "I'm dead serious. Elliot insisted."

"Elliot?"

Terrific. If ever there was a subject he didn't care to discuss with her, this was it. "Elliot Sutherland," he said repressively. Determined to distract her long enough to retake control of the conversation, not to mention his treacherous body, he executed a complicated series of steps.

She followed effortlessly, not missing a beat. "I apologize if I ought to recognize his name, but I don't," she said easily. "Is he a friend?"

"Yes."

She continued to look at him, the picture of interest—and endless patience. Clearly, she wasn't going to drop the subject.

"Elliot was my boss." *And the closest thing to a father I ever had.* Not that she needed to know that. Or would care if she did. "He owned the Independence Hotel downtown and he gave me my first real job in the business." Not to mention the mantle of his chosen successor. Thanks to Elliot's having noticed Gavin's savvy business mind and solid work ethic, today Gavin stood before Colleen a wealthy hotelier with five-star lodgings all over the country. He'd done his best to make Elliot proud, adding hotels to the chain over the years. But he never lost sight of his humble beginnings.

"Elliot's and my backgrounds were similar, so he took an interest in me. In addition to teaching me everything I know about business, he also insisted I learn some other things."

"Like how to dance?" she said softly.

"Yeah. Like how to dance. And dress. And use the right fork and choose the right wine at dinner." Try as he might, he just couldn't keep the trace of sarcasm out of his voice. "Hell, he even made sure I'd know how to behave at a big society wedding."

She flinched, just as he'd intended. Yet rather than experiencing satisfaction, he felt more than a little ashamed of himself. Colleen might be a spoiled, social-conscious snob, but he was no bully. Nor was he likely to make her regret giving him up if he kept behaving like a callow jerk still smarting from a long-ago rejection.

Which he wasn't. He'd gotten past that a long time ago.

Yeah? Then prove it. See if you can't locate a little of the Irish charm Clarice and Caroline and Angelina and the rest of your dates are always prattling on about.

He drew Colleen slightly closer. Ignoring the treacherous leap of his pulse, he swung her around and reversed direction as they reached the edge of the dance floor. "So what about you?" he inquired, doing his best to sound mildly curious and nothing more. "Did you get your teaching degree?" Given her chic little haircut and stylish suit, it was easy to imagine her teaching French or Nineteenth-Century Romantic Poets to a giggly group of teenage girls at some posh private school.

Some of the tension left her body. "Yes, I did."

"So what are you doing these days?"

"I run a counseling program for gifted but at-risk kids at Jefferson High."

He missed a step. "You *what?*" Surely he hadn't heard her right.

Her voice held a totally unexpected hint of wryness. "Don't look so horrified."

"I'm not. Just…surprised." That was putting it mildly. Jefferson was his alma mater, a tough school in an even tougher neighborhood. Given Colleen's privileged, sheltered, parochial-school background, he would've thought she was joking if not for the calm, steady way she was gazing up at him. "When did you start?" Even if she was being serious, surely this had to be something recent, some sort of fleeting, poor-little-rich-girl scheme to help the needy and downtrodden.

"This is my third year."

For a moment he was so stunned he couldn't think what to say. "And your family—your parents—are all right with it?" he finally managed. He simply couldn't imagine the fashionable Moira Barone allowing such a thing.

Colleen gave a slight shrug. "They're not wild about it. But then, they were so overwrought when I decided to leave the order that they consider my subsequent errors in judgment these last three years minor in comparison."

Her voice was so matter-of-fact it took a moment for her words to sink in. "You left… What order? What the hell are you talking about?"

All solemn blue eyes, she looked up at him. "I'm sorry. I just assumed you knew."

"Knew what?"

"After we broke up…and after college, I joined the Sisters of Charity. For seven years I was a nun."

Two

"Hey, lady." The cabbie turned to give Colleen a quick, questioning glance over his shoulder, then twisted back around to peer through the windshield at the street ahead. "You sure you gave me the right address?"

Jarred from her thoughts, she contemplated the back of the man's balding head and told herself to focus. "Yes, of course. Why do you ask?"

He snorted with disbelief. "You're kiddin', right?" He lifted a hand off the wheel and gestured at the surrounding area. "Take a look around. In case you haven't noticed, this ain't exactly Beacon Hill."

She dutifully turned her head although she already knew what she'd find outside. With each block they passed, the sidewalks grew narrower, the store signs less refined, the building facades dingier. More and more steel and iron grills secured by chains and padlocks protected businesses; more upper-story windows were barred.

Wryly she conceded the cabbie had a point; the area didn't bear the slightest resemblance to either Beacon Hill or the upscale neighborhood where Nick and Gail's wedding reception had just been held.

Yet as she noted the eclectic mix of people on the street, some standing and chatting, some coming and going from various bars, cafés and delis, some clearly intent on getting somewhere else, she felt a distinct fondness for the area. It might not be squeaky clean nor even particularly attractive, but it was very much alive, with no pretensions. It was also home.

"You're right. It's not Beacon Hill. But we

are in the right place. My street is the third one after the next light. When you reach it, go right, and my building is a few blocks down, just past a small park.''

The man parted his lips as if to make yet another disapproving observation, then seemed to think better of it. He shrugged. "Whatever you say."

Colleen swallowed a smile, suspecting his sudden lack of opinion had more to do with the sizable tip he'd been promised by her father than a sudden appreciation of the neighborhood. Carlo Barone had not only insisted on calling her a cab, but had told the driver he'd get an extra twenty if he saw her to her door. Then, ignoring her protests, he'd pressed a wad of bills into her palm as he'd handed her into the back seat, given her a tender kiss on the cheek and told her to take care of herself and "not be such a stranger."

Dear Papa. They'd always had a special bond, no doubt in part because she'd been the only girl among the four boys in the family until she'd been five and Gina had arrived. Even so, it had been a distinct shock when she'd eventually come to realize that her de-

cision to join the Sisters of Charity had sprung
not from a true vocation on her part, but from
a desire to fulfill her father's long-held dream
for her and, to a lesser extent, to please her
mother.

And? prompted the gentle voice of her conscience.

She shifted on the vinyl-covered seat. Ever
since she'd admitted to herself—and God—
that she wasn't meant to be a nun, she'd
vowed she'd always be honest with Him and
herself, no matter how difficult or humbling.

*So quit avoiding the other reason you knew
you weren't meant to stay in the order. Admit
that despite the passage of time, you never
completely quit having feelings for Gavin.
That for all these years, a part of you has continued to long for him—the sound of his voice,
the scent of his skin, the warmth of his
touch…his presence in your life.*

The shudder of pleasure she hadn't allowed
herself at the time swept through her now as
she recalled how it had felt to be held in his
arms on the dance floor tonight. She squeezed
her eyes shut, thanking the Almighty for lend-
ing her the strength to appear composed, to

keep the conversation light, to not make a fool of herself and blurt out to Gavin that she'd never stopped missing him.

She also thanked God for helping her keep her chin up when, moments after telling Gavin she'd spent most of the past decade as a nun, he'd fled. Or close enough. Conveniently for him, the music had ended a few seconds after her revelation. Murmuring an uninflected, "I see," he'd glanced at his watch and grimaced. "I'm sorry to be abrupt, but there's a phone call I need to make." He'd looked up, flashing her a duplicate of the polite, impersonal smile with which he'd first greeted her. "It's been nice seeing you, Colleen. Thanks for the dance." Then he'd turned and walked away, leaving her standing alone on the dance floor.

"Jeez, lady, is that what you mean by a park?"

The cabbie's incredulous question put a merciful end to Colleen's recollections. She snapped her eyes open, grasping at the chance to concentrate on the present, even though she knew she was only postponing the inevitable. Like it or not, she was going to have to deal with the caldron of feelings her encounter with Gavin had stirred up.

But not yet. "Pardon me?"

"I said, is that the park you were talking about?" He waved at the dark patch of ground that stretched between the lighted brownstones like a dark gap between a row of pearly teeth.

"Yes, it is."

"Huh." He met her gaze in the rearview mirror as he slowed the taxi and pulled to the curb. "Where I live, we'd call that a vacant lot."

She did her best to look serene. "Everyone is entitled to his opinion." Besides, she hadn't a doubt that once the bulbs she'd planted came up this spring and she added a few trees, a couple of birdbaths and a bench or two, it would look much more parklike, something the cabdriver couldn't possibly be expected to know.

"Yeah, that's true. That's why we live in a democracy."

Frowning, she realized someone was sitting on her front stairs. "Actually, the United States is a republic," she said automatically as she reached for the door handle. "What do I owe you?"

The man rattled off the amount on the meter. "Plus two sawbucks for—"

"Seeing me to the stoop. I remember. But it's really not necessary as it appears I have company. Here's the fare—" she leaned forward and thrust the money at him "—and your twenty, plus an extra five for being so nice." Flashing him a bright smile, she scooted out onto the sidewalk. "Have a lovely night."

"But your old man said—"

"Good night," she said, firmly shutting the door. Then, taking a deep, calming breath and composing herself, she turned just as the shadowy figure climbed to its feet, revealed by the streetlight to be a tall, dark-haired teenager. "Brett? Is that you?"

Hunching his shoulders, the youngster thrust his hands into his front pants pockets. "Hey, Ms. Barone."

Muscles she hadn't known she'd tensed slowly relaxed, while questions crowded her tongue. Oh, dear. Why was he here at this hour? Had he been in a fight? Was he hurt?

In trouble with the law? Had he had another argument with his mother? Or had the woman kicked him out again because she was "entertaining" one of her boyfriends?

Yet as she crossed the sidewalk and started up the steps, Colleen knew better than to ask, at least not right away. Of all the students she counseled at Jefferson High, Brett Maguiness was both the most talented and academically gifted—and the most private.

He was also her favorite, although she was careful not to show it. In her heart of hearts, however, she couldn't deny that there was something about the moody youngster with the guarded eyes that had pulled at her from the instant they'd met at the start of the previous school year.

"Goodness, but it's cold out here." With a shiver that wasn't feigned, she stepped past him to unlock the door to the vestibule. "Have you been waiting long?"

He hiked his shoulders in the nonchalant shrug she considered his trademark. "Awhile."

She let it go, since it wasn't really important. "Well, what do you say we get inside where it's warmer?'' She pushed the outer door open and proceeded to the inner one, trusting him to follow.

Moments later they were walking down the short hallway to her ground-floor apartment. The sound of a violin concerto drifted sweetly from the floor above. Brett made a vaguely rude noise. ''Sounds like the geezer's having his usual wild night.''

''The geezer has a name, and you know it,'' she said mildly. ''It's Mr. Crypinski.'' The older man, a retired transit worker, owned the converted brownstone and lived on the second floor.

''Huh. Creepinski is more like it.''

She glanced at the teenager, startled by the rancor in his voice. ''Did something happen between you two?''

''Nothing important.''

''Then you won't mind telling me about it.''

He rolled his eyes. ''Fine. If you gotta know, I buzzed him and asked if he'd let me in so I could wait for you in the vestibule. And you know what he said? He said that I might have you fooled but he knew a shiftless young thug when he saw one.''

"Oh, dear. I can't imagine..." Though gruff, her landlord had never been anything but kind toward her. Yet she also knew Brett well enough to know he never made things up. "I'll talk to him."

"No."

"Brett—"

"No. He's probably hoping you'll do just that so he can call me a wuss or something. So just forget it, all right?"

She considered an instant, then nodded. "Okay." She'd simply have to find a different way to approach the problem, she decided as she worked the locks on the front door and pushed it open. Switching on a light, she shed her coat and hung it and her purse on the brass wall rack. She turned, glad to be home in her very own space.

Not that there was a lot of it, she acknowledged. Like the lot it was built on, the converted brownstone was long and narrow front to back. Her portion of it consisted of the postage-size entry, with the bedroom, bathroom and utility room stretching down one side of the house, and the living room, kitchen and pantry down the other.

What it lacked in size, it made up for in character, however. The old wood floors had aged to a burnished, golden hue and the high plaster ceilings boasted ornate crown molding.

But Colleen's favorite feature was the bank of floor-to-ceiling windows at the far side of the living room. Her brother Joe might consider "all that glass a break-in just waiting to happen," but Colleen loved being able to look out on her small garden. Like the park next door, it wouldn't be long before the first crocuses began to appear, followed by the constantly changing tableau of blooming flowers, bushes and trees that would go on until the first fall freeze.

"Would you put the kettle on while I go change?" she asked Brett. She could hardly wait to shed her high heels and panty hose.

"Sure."

"Help yourself to a glass of milk or a soda. And there's some lasagna in the fridge if you're hungry."

"Who made it?"

Headed toward her bedroom, she stopped, turned and made a wry face at him. "My sister."

"Great."

Amused, she watched as he hurried toward the kitchen. Due to the brownstone's high ceilings and wide doorways, she could see him perfectly well as he turned on the light and yanked open the appliance door. "Someday my cooking's going to improve and you're going to be sorry for your attitude," she warned.

He straightened and turned, a casserole dish in one hand, a carton of milk in the other, and flashed her a grin. "I'm not holding my breath."

Even as she warmed at the sight of that rare, sunny smile, her stomach clenched. The brightly illuminated kitchen revealed what she hadn't seen before. The corner of the boy's right eye and the cheek below were bruised and puffy.

She parted her lips to ask what had happened, then clamped them shut. She and Brett had been down this road before during the past six months and she knew what to expect. At her very first question, his smile would vanish and the usual guarded look would come over his face. Next he'd claim that he'd run into a door, or something else equally as lame. Then he'd make an excuse to leave.

And if she reported, as she had the last two times, her suspicions that he'd tangled with one of his mother's boyfriends, he'd vanish. He'd go to ground on the streets, not showing up at school for weeks. And when he finally did return, he'd stick stubbornly to whatever story he'd told initially.

"Hmm." Somehow she managed a smile. "Well, don't say I didn't warn you." And with that she twisted around and slipped into her room. Shutting the door, she leaned back against it and allowed herself a sigh of frustration.

Darn it! How could she justify collecting a paycheck, much less live with herself, if she couldn't find a way to provide help when it was needed? Brett was such a good kid at heart, but if something in his life didn't change soon and for the better, there was a more than good chance she'd lose him. He already had two strikes against him—an absent father and an alcoholic mother. Add to that his tendency to keep things bottled up inside, and it was a recipe for disaster.

If only she could find—and convince him to accept—a good foster home. Or even provide him with a role model, someone to show him that real men didn't have to resort to violence to get their way, that he could rise above his beginnings if he stayed in school, applied himself and didn't give up.

Like a genie escaping a bottle, an image of Gavin popped into her mind. With absolute clarity, she recalled the warmth that had crept into his voice when he'd talked about the older man who'd helped him get started in the hotel business.

Transfixed, she wondered why she hadn't thought of it before. Of course! What Brett and the rest of her kids needed were mentors. People who came from similar backgrounds, who'd faced some of the same things they confronted every day and had succeeded, anyway. What's more, Gavin would be the absolutely perfect match for Brett.

She tried to push the idea away, but it wouldn't budge.

Yet lodged with it was the recollection of the coolness that had been in Gavin's voice when he'd spoken to her, the reserve with which he'd treated her, the hurried way he'd said goodbye the instant it was politely feasible. A dull ache blossomed in the region of her heart as she faced a truth she'd been trying to avoid for hours.

Whatever feelings he'd once had for her were dead. The best thing she could do for both of them was keep her distance so they could both get on with their lives.

And yet, if he could help Brett…

She instinctively glanced heavenward. "I don't know if this is part of Your plan for me, but I'm not making any promises," she warned Him, her feelings as tangled as a ball of yarn tossed into a roomful of kittens. "Except that I'll think about it."

For now that would have to be enough.

A nun.

Gavin stared unseeingly at the columns of January revenue figures laid out on his desk.

A *nun.* The word—and all it implied—had been rattling around in his head for the past four days, surfacing at odd moments to ruin his concentration.

And he was damned if he knew why. After

all, as he'd proved at Nick's wedding reception, Colleen meant nothing to him.

It was just… He didn't like the idea of anybody locking themselves away, wasting vital years of their life, in a convent. It was the twenty-first century, for God's sake. Women had choices. And though he'd never thought about it before now, it seemed pretty obvious that prior to making a commitment to the Church, a young woman like Colleen should be required to have some real life experience.

Oh yeah? Like what? Sleeping with you?

Terrific. On top of everything else, now he was being ambushed by his own mind—or what was left of it. Irritated, he slapped the report shut, shoved back his chair and climbed to his feet, then paced over to the large windows that overlooked the street forty stories below. A nerve ticked to life in his jaw.

Who would've thought that after all this time something as tame as dancing with Colleen would be enough to kick his hormones into overdrive? Much less that just thinking about her days later—the fragile hollow at the base of her throat, the slight weight of her hand in his, her faint but never forgotten lily-

of-the-valley scent—could make his temperature rise and his skin feel tight?

Not him, that was for damned sure, he
thought grimly. If you'd asked him a week ago
what he thought about Colleen, he would have
replied flatly, "I don't." And now he couldn't
seem to get her out of his mind.

There was a soft rap on his door. "What?"
he barked, impatiently shoving a hand through
his hair.

His secretary poked her head in. "I'm sorry
to bother you, but I buzzed the intercom and
you didn't answer—"

"What is it, Carol?"

"A Ms. Barone is here to see you. She
doesn't have an appointment, and I told her
you were busy, but she asked me to tell you
she only needed a few minutes."

For an instant he felt nonplussed, as if his
thoughts had somehow conjured up Colleen.
Then the moment passed and his normal prag-
matism kicked in. Whatever the reason for her
sudden appearance, seeing her again could
only be a good thing. In the clear light of day,
on his own turf, he'd no doubt be able to con-
sign her to where she belonged—in the past.

He walked back to his desk and sat. "It's okay. Show her in."

Quickly masking her surprise, his secretary inclined her head. "You're the boss." She backed away, then returned moments later, ushered his visitor to a chair and discreetly departed.

Having learned the power of silence, Gavin took a good look at the woman who'd been in his thoughts far too much lately. Her finery of Saturday night was gone. Today she was casually dressed in low-heeled boots, slim-fitting black slacks and a fuzzy, pale peach turtleneck sweater. An inexpensive-looking black wool coat was folded over her arm, a small black satchel slung over her shoulder.

She looked great.

"Hi." Her smile was tentative. "I know I should have called, but—"

"What do you want, Colleen?" The words came out harsher than he intended, but he didn't care.

For a split second she appeared taken aback. Then she quickly gathered her composure. "I'd like to talk to you."

"About what?"

Perched on the edge of her chair, she laced her fingers together. "Actually, I have a favor to ask."

"I see." He didn't see at all. What could she possibly want from him? He couldn't think of a thing. Unless…

He thought again about their turn on the dance floor the other night. Hell, maybe he wasn't the only one who'd felt hot and bothered by their encounter. Maybe she'd experienced a similar rise in temperature and was interested in finally finishing what they'd started all those years ago—

"It's not for me, really, but for my kids. The ones from my school."

The prickle of anticipation he was feeling vanished, replaced by self-disgust. When, exactly, was he going to learn? Colleen hadn't wanted him when they were younger, and obviously nothing had changed.

He reached over, opened the appropriate desk drawer and pulled out his checkbook. Flipping it open, he picked up his pen and angled a hard look at her. "How much do you want?"

Her eyes widened. "Pardon me?"

He held her gaze. "I said, how much? You can spare me the pep talk about whatever project you want the money for or how great the kids are. Just give me the bottom line."

"Oh, dear. Obviously I'm not explaining myself very well. I don't want your money, Gavin. I want *you*." A faint flush rose in her baby-smooth cheeks as she appeared to realize what she'd just said. "That is, I want your time," she hastily clarified. "I'm putting together a mentoring program, and I need you."

She needed him? For all of ten seconds he felt the siren call of being wanted. Then his sanity kicked in. "No."

She went on as if he hadn't spoken. "I have a student, Brett Maguiness. He's smart, special, but he needs a man in his life, someone he can look up to, who's carved out his own success—"

"No." He'd be a bigger fool than he already was if he let a little flattery sway him. "I'll be glad to donate money if it'll help, but I can't spare the time." Not that he would if he could. It was entirely out of the question. The last thing he needed was involvement in an endeavor guaranteed to bring Colleen and him together on a regular basis. Not when by merely walking into a room she could make his libido attempt to hijack his brain.

"This is a boy on the brink," she continued. "He desperately needs someone like your Mr. Sutherland." Reaching across the desk, she touched gentle fingertips to the back of his tensed hand. "Please, Gavin."

Sex drive screaming, he looked into her dark blue eyes and for a moment felt as if he were drowning. Sternly he reminded himself she was not to be trusted, that the one other time he'd given in to temptation and allowed her close to him, she'd ripped out his heart.

It was a hell of a shock, then, when he opened his mouth to tell her to leave and, instead, heard himself say, "When would you want me to start?"

Three

He'd blown it.

Gavin angled a swift gaze sideways at Brett. The boy sat stiff and silent on the Porsche's sleek black leather seat, his face ever-so-slightly averted, his gaze fixed on the view outside with seeming fascination.

Given that they were traveling on a section of road surrounded by warehouses and that rain was pouring from the inky February sky in sheets, Gavin doubted the kid was admiring the scenery.

"Ugly night out," he commented, taking yet another stab at conversation.

"Uh-huh."

"The wind's coming out of the north. Maybe we'll get snow tonight."

Brett continued to look out the window. "Maybe."

And maybe I'll drop dead, which might give you something to talk about, if only briefly. With a frustrated shake of his head, Gavin considered the wet, shining pavement and tried to pinpoint the exact moment things had started to go sour.

How about the second you clapped eyes on Colleen again?

He shoved the renegade thought away. As much as he'd like to blame this on her, he couldn't. For starters, *he'd* approached her at Nick's reception. What's more, it had been *his* decision to let her into his office. And she sure as hell hadn't been holding a gun to his head when he'd opened his big mouth and agreed to this mentoring thing.

But at least he was consistent in his use of poor judgment. Take earlier tonight. When Colleen had shared some ideas with the adult volunteers who'd gathered at the high school on how best to break the ice with the kids they were mentoring, he'd blown off her words, convinced he didn't need her advice.

He'd been right, too. At first.

Though unmistakably wary at their initial introduction, Brett had relaxed a little when he'd seen that, unlike some of the other mentors who'd chosen to wear suits and ties, Gavin had dressed in jeans, a plain black sweater and a black leather jacket. And like any other red-blooded teenager, the boy had been enamored with Gavin's silver sports car the instant he'd laid eyes on it.

Not that he'd fallen all over himself oohing and ahhing or anything. Instead, with all the nonchalance of someone who rode in a $100,000 car every day, he'd yanked open the door, slung himself onto the glove-soft seat, taken in the custom-made burled-walnut dashboard with its polished steel dials and murmured, "Nice."

At the time, Gavin had found the kid's determined cool amusing. Now it didn't seem the least bit funny. On the contrary, it stood out as the high point of the evening. And it was his own damn fault. Colleen had advised him and the others to keep this first meeting simple, go someplace in the neighborhood for coffee and conversation, and let the youngster set the tone.

And what had he done? He'd taken Brett downtown to the Independence, given him a tour of the hotel, including the view from the penthouse he called home, then ushered him into the main dining room for a five-star dinner.

He had to give himself credit, though. Not for nothing was he known in the business world as a mind reader, as well as a tough negotiator. Once they were ensconced at his favorite table, it had taken him only fifteen or twenty minutes of conversation—with Brett's contribution consisting of half-a-dozen mumbled *yeahs* and *nos* accompanied by a handful of dismissive shrugs—to get the message.

When it came to mentoring, he sucked.

Now that it was too late, he could see that instead of showing the teen that where a man came from didn't matter as much as where he ended up, he'd yanked the kid out of his comfort zone, dragged him into foreign territory, then practically put him on display. And though it hadn't been his intent, he suspected he'd managed to look like a self-absorbed jerk in the process.

So? It didn't work. So what? Look at the upside. Now you can tell Colleen you gave it a shot and missed the target by a mile. You can say goodbye, adios, see you later.

There was only one problem with that. And it happened to be sitting beside him.

He tightened his grip on the steering wheel and took a left, headed for the westernmost Fort Point Channel bridge and Jefferson Heights.

The truth was he wanted a shot at making a difference in this kid's life. And not because of Colleen, but despite her—something he'd realized once she'd left the other day and he'd had time to think about his sudden decision to volunteer.

For as long as he could remember, work had dominated his life. Recently, however, though no less busy, he'd been feeling restless, out of sorts, vaguely dissatisfied with his life. He didn't have any family obligations—his mother had partied herself into an early grave years ago, he'd never known who his father was, and last summer Elliot had finally lost his long battle with cancer. Plus, he'd experienced enough real hardship in his life to know he currently had nothing to bitch about. Given that, the answer to his dissatisfaction had seemed obvious: do something for somebody else. To that end, recently he'd been considering getting involved in a number of good causes, from the Make-A-Wish Foundation to Habitat for Humanity.

Instead, he'd chosen to take on a tough-as-nails teenager.

He slowed the car slightly at the approach to the bridge, then slowed even more as a strong gust of wind buffeted the bridge and the brake lights on the car in front of him flashed. Narrowing his eyes, he told himself to concentrate on his driving, but he couldn't entirely block out the voice in his head.

The one saying, *Yeah? And the instant things don't go your way, you decide to blow out? Get real, O'Sullivan.*

Well, hell. With sudden decisiveness, he accelerated as the car left the bridge and

switched lanes. He passed through the next series of traffic lights, then took a right.

Brett shifted to look at him. "You turned
too soon. I told you to drop me on Market.
You *do* know where Market is, don't you?"

"It's been a while, but yeah, I do," Gavin
replied evenly. He sensed the kid's impatience, but he deliberately didn't say anything
more.

A good thirty seconds passed. Finally the
boy gave vent to his exasperation with a loud
sigh. "So? Where are we going?"

"There's something I want to show you."

Suspicion instantly colored the young voice.
"What?"

"Relax, kid. I've got my faults, but whatever you're thinking isn't one of them. And
before you say anything…" He raised a hand
to forestall the attitude he could see building
on the youth's face. "—I don't expect you to
trust me—" *not yet, anyway* "—but you
ought to have a little more faith in Ms. Barone."

"I do," the boy said defensively.

"Then relax, okay?" Frowning, he stared
hard at the dimly lit street, trying to get his

bearings. He thought for a moment he'd passed his destination, then saw a second later that he hadn't.

The property at 121 Calhoon Street hadn't changed much. The brick facade was still dingy and crumbling, just the way he remembered. All the front windows were boarded up, with only a glimmer of light leaking here and there to suggest that anyone actually lived inside. Black plastic trash bags spilling garbage were heaped around the entrance and piled on the crumbling sidewalk, where a few scraggly weeds poked up in defiance of the winter weather. As a final touch, a soiled mattress shedding its stuffing rested at a crazy angle against the stoop, impaled on the finial of the one iron balustrade still standing.

Gavin brought the Porsche to a stop, staring at the building he'd deliberately avoided for more than sixteen years. He braced, waiting for the familiar sense of shame and disgust; instead, all he felt was a sort of sadness for the boy he'd been.

The discovery was oddly liberating. "See that?" he said to Brett, nodding at the neglected building.

"Yeah."

"When I wasn't in emergency foster care, that's where I lived the last few months of high school. It's pretty typical of the sort of places my mom and I called home over the years."

Lips pursed, the boy considered a moment, then turned to Gavin and regarded him through narrowed eyes. "So? You don't live there anymore."

Gavin met his gaze straight on. "And nobody's more thankful than I am for that. But the point is, I do have some idea of where you're coming from. I realize we haven't gotten off to the best start, but I'd like another chance."

Brett turned his gaze back to the crumbling tenement. He was silent so long and his expression was so blank that Gavin was on the verge of losing hope by the time the boy finally gave an elaborate shrug. "Sure. Why not?"

Relief flooded Gavin, but he knew better than to show it. "Good." Doing his best to match the kid's offhand manner, he put the car into gear and headed back the way they'd come. He turned onto Central and within a few minutes had reached Market Street. Pulling into the first open spot he saw along the curb, he let the engine idle and glanced over at Brett. "You like basketball?"

"It's okay."

"Would you be interested in going to Saturday's Celtics game?" Tied for the lead in the Atlantic Division, the Celtics were playing the Knicks, their longtime rival. The game had been sold out for weeks.

True to form, the boy did his best to look blasé, but there was a spark of interest in his eyes he couldn't disguise. "Yeah, I guess."

"Okay. I'll check the game time and give you a call, all right?"

"Sure." Brett shoved open the car door and climbed out onto the sidewalk. He took a step, then hesitated. Squaring his shoulders, he turned and ducked his head so he and Gavin were eye level. "I don't…that is, well, thanks. For dinner and—" he made a vague, all-encompassing gesture "—stuff."

"No problem."

A sudden gust of wind blew the teen's dark hair into his eyes and he impatiently shoved it away. "And, uh, if you've gotta plan ahead or something, I guess it'd be okay if you picked me up on Saturday. If you want."

The admission amounted to a display of trust, and Gavin knew it. Encouraged, but aware that to show it would be a major breach of 'hood etiquette, he merely nodded. "Sure."

"Okay, then. I'll see you." With a brief nod, Brett straightened and walked away.

Gavin watched him go, filled with satisfaction. Hell, who was he kidding? If he'd been twenty years younger, he'd have been tempted to punch the air with his fist.

Instead, he reached for his cell phone, only to stop midmotion as reality struck. Just who did he think he was going to call? He couldn't think of a single one of his high-powered friends who'd understand what he was feeling. Particularly when he had no intention of discussing what passed as his childhood with them.

He shook his head at his own foolishness, telling himself to grow up and forget this uncharacteristic urge he had to share what had just transpired. After all, it wasn't as if he had any options. Did he?

It was an unfortunate question, he realized the instant a certain female image sprang to mind. Scowling, he put the Porsche in gear, waited for a break in traffic, then pulled into it.

No way was he going *there*.

Was he?

The harsh burr of the doorbell gave Colleen a start.

Stretched out on the faded imitation-Persian rug before the fireplace in her living room, she brought her head up at the urgent sound.

Outside, the wind was putting on a show, perfectly still one second, tossing raindrops against the windowpane and plucking fretfully at the sashes the next.

Inside, everything was peaceful, herself included. If the phone calls she'd received in the past few hours from various adults and kids were any indication, the mentoring program was going to be a success.

She'd love to take credit, but she knew who was truly responsible, and was thankful to Him for His guidance and for helping her make wise matches. Not to mention—she gave a slight shudder as a spate of sleet tattooed the courtyard—seeing fit to hold back the storm until after the meeting.

The buzzer sounded again, and with a resigned sigh she rose to her feet. Her intercom had died a few weeks ago, and she kept forgetting to tell Mr. Crypinski. Hugging her arms to herself, she stepped out of her cozy apartment and into the chilly hall, catching a distorted glimpse of dark hair and the back of a leather jacket through the mottled glass of the entry sidelight. With a pinch of concern, she hurried down the hall and yanked open the door. "Brett?"

Her visitor swiveled around. "No."

"Gavin!" How could she not have known? He was taller than Brett. Taller, broader of shoulder, narrower of hip. And in a category of his own when it came to being intensely, maturely, blatantly male. "What are you doing here? Is everything all right?"

"Yeah. I just thought I'd...report in."

"Oh." Raindrops clung to his dark hair. She watched, distracted, as a bead of water surrendered to gravity, dropped from his hair onto his cheek, then lazily rolled to the edge of his jaw. "You're soaked." To her chagrin, her voice sounded a little hoarse.

"Yeah. It's coming down pretty good."

"You'd better come in." Scooting back, she swiveled around, embarrassed by her reaction to him and praying he hadn't noticed. Yet despite her chagrin, she couldn't stop the tingle of awareness that tickled her spine as he followed her back down the hall and into her apartment. Heat painting her cheeks, she all but dashed to the bathroom.

She snatched a bath towel off the rack, fighting the urge to bury her head in it. *Really, Colleen! Grow up and quit acting like you're seventeen.*

It was excellent advice. Determined to follow it, she let out her breath, straightened her spine and turned.

And promptly bounced off Gavin's chest as she found him blocking the doorway.

"Oh! I didn't know you were there!" Despite her good intentions, she was helpless against the pleasure that zinged through her as he reached out to steady her.

Bravely, she ignored it, forcing herself to smile in the face of his dark, intent gaze. "I was thinking earlier how fortunate it was that the storm held off for the meeting. That everyone had time to get home before it really got ugly. But now here you are. All wet.'' Heaven help her, but she was babbling. The last time she could remember doing that was when Mother Superior had walked in on her doing her impression of the bishop, complete with an exaggerated Irish accent and his trademark steepled hands. Unnerved, she began to blot the moisture from the front of Gavin's jacket with the towel. ''You must be freezing—''

His hand came up, manacled her wrist. ''I'll do it,'' he said quietly.

She looked down at his long fingers. His skin was a shade darker than her own, his hands big but also elegant, his nails clean and clipped. For some reason, the sight of them made her even more acutely aware of the bathroom's diminutive size. And of how close they were standing.

And that she was anything but cold herself.

She released the towel as if it was on fire. ''Of course. I'll…'' Her voice failed for a moment. ''I'll just go make us some tea.'' Sliding her hand free of his grasp, she sidled past him with every intention of bolting for the relative safety of the kitchen.

"No."

The abruptness of his tone jerked her around. "I'm sorry?"

His dark eyes were impossible to read. "Don't go to any trouble for me. I don't plan to be here that long."

"Oh."

"I just want to talk to you for a second about Brett."

"Of course." She made a heroic effort to match his businesslike manner. "Why don't we go into the living room?" *Where you can warm up. And I can cool off. And where I'll be able to put some space between us until I can control my juvenile reaction to everything you say and do.*

"Great."

She crossed the hallway and entered the front room, where she headed for the small, upholstered, isolated armchair placed at right angles to the couch. Sitting, she curled her legs beneath her and tried to focus on the fire. Yet the room was so small she couldn't not see Gavin as he shrugged out of his jacket and tossed it over the umbrella stand inside the doorway. Or notice the way his well-defined biceps bulged and flexed beneath his thin black sweater as he rubbed his hair dry, finger-combed the silky strands into place, then tossed the towel on top of the jacket.

He took a look around. "This is…nice."

Something about the way he spoke suggested that he was surprised, which for some inexplicable reason helped restore a little of her usual equilibrium. "Thank you. How did it go with Brett?"

"Fine."

"Really?" *Way to go, Colleen. Could you sound any more surprised?*

But rather than take offense, Gavin gave a sigh, his mouth twisting in a self-deprecating smile. "Actually, that's a lie. Most of the night was pretty awful. I took him to the hotel, bought him dinner and did a first-rate job of making him feel out of place."

"Oh, dear."

"Yeah. But then later, on the drive back, I decided to give something else a try." He paced over to the windows, forcing her to twist around to keep him in sight. "I wanted him to realize that he and I do have some things in common... I showed him the place Lynette and I lived my last years of prep.''

For a moment she couldn't think what to say. While she'd known ever since being introduced to Gavin that he was from Jefferson Heights—he had, after all, been a scholarship student when Nick first brought him home and introduced him to the family—he'd always flatly refused to discuss specifics, much less show her or anyone else in her family where he actually lived.

So what? Surely you're not so petty you'd envy him and Brett the common bonds of youthful poverty and poor parenting?

Of course not.

''Did it help?'' she asked with genuine concern.

''Yeah. I think it did.'' He turned, walked over and sat down on the couch. ''At least he's willing to give things another chance. We're going to take in a Celtics game this weekend.''

''Gavin, that's wonderful!'' Impulsively she reached out and gave his forearm a squeeze.

The warm curve of muscle beneath her fingertips immediately went rigid, while his smile grew equally stiff. "I don't know about that, but it's an improvement over the mess I made of things earlier." He glanced at his wristwatch, then abruptly stood, sliding free of her touch in the process. "Hell, look at the time. It's after ten. I've intruded enough on your evening. I should get going."

What on earth was the matter with her? Every time he got the least bit close she either bolted or, worse, acted as if he were a sheet of paper and she a first-grader learning to finger-paint.

She scrambled to her feet. "I'm the one who ought to apologize," she said hastily, following in his wake like the tail on a kite as he strode over to get his jacket. "I should've told you more about Brett, made sure you understood how complicated he is. Not that he isn't terrific, with so much potential, but—"

"You don't have to sell him to me, Colleen." His voice unexpectedly curt, he stopped and turned. "If Brett wants me to, I'll be there for him. And when I make a commitment, I keep it."

She jerked to a halt, stopped as much by his slight emphasis on *I* as her desire not to crash into him. Not sure whether he was alluding to her decision to leave the Church or their breakup or both or neither one, she felt his words nevertheless cut straight to her heart. "Yes, of course. I didn't mean…I wasn't implying…that is, I wasn't trying to insult your integrity. I'm sorry."

Their gazes locked and the sudden silence in the room was deafening. As if from very faraway Colleen heard the fire snap, followed by the faint scrape of a tree branch against the window.

"Damn it, don't look like that," Gavin said fiercely.

She wasn't certain what it was he saw in her expression, but she was very certain she wanted to keep to herself the emotional turmoil he caused her. She lifted her chin. "I'm not. And don't curse."

"Don't you tell me what to do."

Having grown up with four brothers, she was fully versed in the folly of saying anything to the male of the species that resembled a challenge. Yet she couldn't stop the imprudent streak that seemed to seize control of her tongue. "Or what?"

His dark eyes hooded over. "Or this."

Clasping her upper arms, he lowered his head and in the next instant his mouth settled possessively over hers.

Four

——

The pleasure Colleen felt was immediate and stunning.

Pinpricks of delight raced down her spine at the hard warmth of Gavin's hands, the firm silkiness of his lips, the heat radiating off the solid angles of his muscular body.

For half a second she wondered what she was doing. Then she realized she didn't care. It had been so very, very long since she'd felt Gavin's touch. Oh, how she'd missed it. How she'd missed him.

She drank in his scent like a woman finding water after weeks in the desert. He smelled clean, like rain, shampoo and lemon drops, with a dash of something uniquely male that went straight to the core of her, making her feel weak in the knees.

But then, he'd always had that effect on her, from the very first time Nick had brought him home. Standing unobserved on the upper curve of the front stairway, she'd watched as her teenage brother's new friend had gotten his first glimpse of the sparkling floors and gleaming woodwork of her parents' entry.

As always, there'd been a tall vase of freshly cut flowers on the console table that faced the door. Though Nick had been too busy talking to notice it, she hadn't missed the way the newcomer had reached out and hesitantly touched the creamy petal of a deep-throated lily. There'd been a sort of wistful reverence to the gesture that had called out to her, touching a place in her heart.

As if he, too, had felt that tug of connection, Gavin had suddenly looked up. In the long moment they'd considered each other, Colleen had been overcome with an uncanny sense of familiarity, as if she'd always known him and understood his heart, his dreams, his strengths and vulnerabilities. Although she hadn't understood what was happening to her at the time, years later at college, when she and Gavin had finally acknowledged there was more between them than mere friendship and a mutual affection for Nick, she'd realized she'd fallen in love with him at that very first meeting.

Now it was years later—and nothing had changed.

Crowding closer, she raised her arms and tangled her fingers in his thick hair. Her pulse jumped as her thighs brushed his and her breasts met the hard wall of his chest.

She heard a soft little sound midway between a moan and a whimper, and vaguely recognized her own voice. Under different circumstances, with a different man, she would've been mortified. But this was Gavin. The only man she'd ever wanted. Without hesitation, she parted her lips for the probe of his tongue, savoring the bloom of heat that had her clenching her thighs as his tongue softly breached her mouth. With an instinct as old as time, she arched her back and crowded even closer, shivering with nervous wonder as the unmistakable thickness of his erection thrust against her.

Only to discover, too late, that apparently she'd made a mistake.

With a muffled curse, Gavin abruptly terminated their embrace and jerked away. "Damn it, Colleen! What do you think you're doing?"

She bit her throbbing lower lip, thinking the answer couldn't be any more obvious if she'd held up a flashing neon sign that read "Wildly enjoying kissing you and thinking I wouldn't mind doing more."

And yet it was clear from the look on Gavin's face that would definitely *not* be an acceptable thing to say. Struggling valiantly to rein in her jangling senses, she tried to decide what would be a more diplomatic but still-honest answer. "I…your kiss…it caught me by surprise. I didn't think that you…that is, I didn't expect that I…and then, it just felt so—"

He threw up a hand like a cop halting traffic, putting what Colleen could only view as a humane stop to the fit and start of her words. Her relief vanished, however, when he said, "This is all my fault. I was out of line to take advantage of your innocence that way. Way out of line."

"Oh, but—"

"I shouldn't have come here. I knew that, but I came, anyway. Now the best thing I can do is leave." Shoving a hand through his already tousled hair, he twisted around and snatched up his jacket.

"But, Gavin—"

"I'm sorry, Colleen."

Without giving her a chance to say more, he strode to her front door, and had it open and was passing through it by the time her addled brain accepted that he really meant to go. "Gavin, wait!" She scrambled after him. Dashing out of the apartment, she raced down the hall and finally caught up with him in the entryway. "Please." Although logically she knew she was incapable of physically restraining him, she reached out and grabbed hold of his shoulder, anyway.

A shudder went through him at her touch and he spun around. *"Don't."*

She snatched back her hand, startled by his vehemence. "I'm sorry."

"Aw, sh—" He clenched his teeth as he bit off the curse. "Do *not* apologize, Colleen. You've got nothing to be sorry about. Like I said before, I'm the one at fault here."

She opened her mouth to protest, then shut it as it occurred to her that if she ever wanted to see him again, and she did, this might not be the best time to tell him he had no reason to apologize, either. That she'd wanted to kiss him ever since the wedding reception, and that far from being a hapless victim he'd overpowered with his virile magnetism, she'd more than welcomed his embrace.

She dampened her lips; the Almighty was no doubt going to get her for what she was about to do. "If you're truly sincere about believing you were out of line, there's a way you can make it up to me."

Gavin suddenly looked just the slightest bit wary. "Yeah? And what's that?"

"My family's having a little get-together to launch the newest Baronessa gelato flavor. Come with me."

Gavin stared at her as if she'd lost her mind. "You're kidding, right?"

"No."

"Under the circumstances, I don't think that's a very good idea."

"On the contrary. It will be nice and public and will give us a chance to talk in depth about Brett and the challenges he's facing. It's not as if it would be a...a date, or anything." Poor Father Brennan. He was going to get an awful shock when he heard her confession on Sunday.

Gavin considered her for a moment so long it felt like an eternity, then heaved a sigh. "When is it?"

"Friday." Her hopes skyrocketed, only to plummet as he yanked open the door.

"I'll think about it, okay?"

"But how will I know—"

"I'll call you." And with that the door banged shut and he was gone.

Frustrated in more ways than one, Colleen let loose a sigh of her own. Terrific. Now, in addition to everything else, every time the phone rang for the next few days she was going to have to deal with a case of yo-yo stomach.

Apparently the Lord wasn't wasting any time getting her started on her penance.

Some little get-together.

Taking a sip of champagne, Gavin lowered his wineglass and considered the scores of people crowding the reception area of Baronessa's main corporate headquarters.

In addition to most of the Barone family and dozens of their longtime friends and key employees, a number of local restaurateurs and dignitaries were in attendance, including several national food writers. And because today just happened to be Valentine's Day, a little fact Colleen hadn't seen fit to mention when she'd asked him to come and he'd completely overlooked when he'd agreed to attend, a sizable number of the Boston press was covering the event, no doubt considering it good local color.

God knew, the family had spared no expense. Dozens and dozens of huge bouquets of red roses in genuine cut-crystal vases decorated the room, giving it an air of festive elegance. Add the quintet of ornate fountains spouting champagne and the constantly circulating tuxedo-clad catering staff, and he had to give the Barones credit. They knew how to throw a party.

Under different circumstances Gavin might even have enjoyed himself. Say, for example, if he'd been here because the family was courting his business.

But that wasn't the case. Hell, no. No matter what kind of twist he tried to put on it, he was here tonight because of Colleen.

He considered her as she stood a few feet away, listening intently to her younger sister Rita, who was talking and gesturing animatedly.

At first glance, Colleen, the oldest of the Barone daughters, looked perfectly respectable. Her makeup was a study in elegant understatement, just a kiss of color at her eyes, cheeks and lips. And the gleaming, slightly tousled cap of her hair was exceedingly casual compared to some of the other women's more ornate upsweeps or geled, cutting-edge hairdos. Likewise, her wine-colored dress with its high neck and long sleeves was outwardly demure and almost plain.

Until you noticed that it was made of some sort of stretchy lace material that clung to her every slender curve. And that it exposed tantalizing glimpses of smooth, peachy skin every time she moved. Which was about the same time you began to wonder how much of the plum color glistening on the full curve of her lips was lipstick and how much was just her. And then, try as you might, you couldn't help but remember how silky her unlaquered hair felt against your fingertips, and how...

Whispering a curse, Gavin tossed back the last of his bubbly. There was a stir at the far end of the room, and grateful for the diversion, he dragged his gaze away from the pale, vulnerable curve of Colleen's neck and along with everyone else, turned to watch as her father, Carlo, took center stage on a low dais. Facing the crowd, the older man waited for silence before he spoke.

"Welcome, friends," he said, smiling genially. "On behalf of my family and everyone who works at Baronessa, I thank you for coming tonight."

Gavin felt a tingle run down his spine and knew, without turning his head, that Colleen had come to stand at his side.

"We at Baronessa pride ourselves on making only the finest gelato from the highest-quality ingredients from around the world," Carlo continued. "To that end we are always extremely selective before we introduce a new flavor, testing and tasting and tinkering with the recipe until we are one hundred percent certain it will live up to the Baronessa reputation for excellence.

"And as I'm sure you all know—" Carlo leaned forward, as if imparting a great secret to his closest friends "—that means that only a very few, very unique, very special new flavors get the privilege of becoming part of our line.

"And that is why we are so very proud to introduce to you tonight the newest jewel in the Baronessa crown." With a crook of his fingers he beckoned to the left, and a procession of waiters holding high over their heads silver trays loaded with scoops of deep raspberry-colored dessert nestled in sparkling glasses began to enter the room. "We've named it passionfruit.'' He gave a dramatic flourish, a sudden twinkle lighting his eyes. ''And when better than St. Valentine's Day to unveil it, eh?''

There was a burst of appreciative laughter. It was quickly followed by a spontaneous swell of applause as the Barone patriarch gave a genial nod and exhorted everyone to enjoy the new icy treat as the waiters began to move through the crowd distributing it.

Gavin turned to Colleen. ''That was a pretty good show. I can see your father hasn't lost either his flair or his enthusiasm for the business.''

''Yes and no.'' She glanced at the older man, and Gavin didn't miss the way her face softened as she watched him accept a bowl of his company's newest creation. ''Papa loves everything about it and always will, from actually making the gelato to marketing it to scooping cones at the gelateria on Hanover Street. But when it comes to the nuts and bolts of the day-to-day operation, Nick, Joe and Gina have taken over more and more of it the past few years.''

Gavin gave a slight shrug. ''I guess it's

bound to happen as his generation ages and ours grows up." He paused. "I heard about Joseph losing his wife. That must've been tough."

She nodded, her expression sobering as she considered her always serious second-eldest brother. "It was, but he's doing all right. Although now that Nick and Gail are settled, I suppose he'll be Mother's next matrimonial target." Her lips quirked mischievously. "That is, if she doesn't find out about Rita first."

He raised an eyebrow in question. "Rita?"

"Uh-huh. It seems someone sent my little sister an anonymous gift today, of all things. She appears to have acquired a secret admirer and is going crazy trying to figure out who it is. But not nearly as crazy as she'll be if Mother finds out about it and decides to 'help' her discover her mystery man's identity."

"It doesn't sound like your mom's changed much." Gavin did his best to make his voice light, but it wasn't easy. Moira Barone had been coolly polite but nothing more when he and Nick had become friends, and as a teenager, each time he'd visited the Barone brownstone he'd always suspected that the second he left she'd made a beeline to the silver to count it.

And though later on, her opinion of him had never become an issue since he and Colleen had broken up before they'd gotten around to informing her family they were a couple, he was pretty damn certain Mrs. Barone would not have considered him a suitable suitor for her daughter.

As if reading his mind, a shadow passed briefly over Colleen's face, only to vanish as she determinedly summoned a smile. "No, I'm afraid you're right. One can always count on Mama to be Mama—just like death or taxes. Although—" her smile grew more genuine "—if you ever quote me as saying that, I'll deny it to my very last breath."

To his surprise, Gavin found he couldn't help but smile back, which sent a jolt of uneasiness through him. He was also surprised by the accompanying thought that Colleen was no longer the young woman he'd known more than a decade ago. She'd changed.

Well, yeah, Einstein, what did you expect?

Up until not too long ago, she was a nun. That's bound to change anyone.

"Oh, dear."

The totally unexpected note of alarm in Colleen's voice jarred him out of his reverie. Pushing his unsettled thoughts to the back burner, he shifted his focus and took a good look at her, concerned as he saw that her eyes were wide with growing alarm as she glanced around at the surrounding crowd. "What's the matter?"

"I don't know. But there seems to be something wrong. Look at Mr. Marino." She indicated a short, paunchy gentleman who looked to be about her father's age.

Sure enough, the older man appeared to be in distress. His face was red, his eyes watering, his breath coming in raspy gasps as he stared accusingly at the ice-cream bowl still clutched in one hand. Tossing his spoon away with a clatter, he reached over, snatched a champagne glass off the nearest table and took a hearty gulp, only to promptly begin to sputter even harder.

Nor was he alone, Gavin realized as he took a quick survey of the crowd. Dozens of people toward the front of the room—those who'd been first to be served Baronessa's new dessert—were showing various signs of distress, albeit less severe than Mr. Marino's, from scrubbing at their mouths, to indelicately spitting spoonfuls of gelato back into their bowls, to coughing as they struggled to get air, to fanning their faces and dashing tears from their eyes.

"Call 911," Gavin said to Colleen. "There's something in the ice cream that shouldn't be there."

"Oh, but that can't be—"

"Make the call," he ordered crisply, "and we'll argue about it later." He waited a second for her to head off to find a phone, then crossed to Mr. Marino and slipped the bowl out of the older man's unresisting hand. Dipping a finger into the gelato, he touched it lightly to his lips.

In less time than it took to light a match, the affected part of his mouth felt as if it had encountered a blowtorch.

"What the hell is going on?"

The alarmed sound of his old friend Nick's voice turned him around, and he found the other man standing no more than a few feet away, his legs splayed in a fighter's aggressive stance and a combination of concern, frustration and anger darkening his good-looking face.

"I think something caustic's been added to your gelato," Gavin said, keeping his voice down since he didn't want to alarm the people around them. "Maybe some sort of pepper, judging by the way my lip feels right now, numb and tingling at the same time. For almost everyone, it doesn't seem to be causing anything more than discomfort." He glanced over at Mr. Marino, who seemed to be having some trouble breathing. "But that gentleman seems to be getting worse."

"Did anyone call 911?" Nick couldn't hide the alarm in his voice.

"Yes, Colleen did. The paramedics should be on their way." Gavin clapped his hand on his friend's shoulder. "In the meantime you might want to make some sort of announcement telling everyone to lay off the champagne. If it is a pepper or some sort of derivative, booze will just make the burning worse.

A piece of bread or a cracker would be better.''

"What does this look like, the Fourth Street Deli?'' Nick demanded. Despite his tension, he reached out and shook Gavin's hand. ''Thanks. I promise I'll buy you a drink when this is all over and you can tell me how you got so smart.''

"You've got yourself a deal.'' Glad to have been able to help, if only a little, Gavin watched Nick stride away, purpose and determination in his every step as he began rattling out orders to a variety of people, including several of his brothers and sisters.

Stripping off his jacket and tossing it over a chair in anticipation of following Nick's lead, Gavin realized how much he'd missed his friend these past few years, missed his energy and intelligence and his basic goodness.

But not nearly as much as he'd missed Nick's little sister, he belatedly realized as he turned to find Colleen standing only an arm's length away, watching him with unmistakable admiration in her eyes.

Twelve years ago, he would've done just

about anything to see her look at him that way.

He made a sudden vow that for tonight, at least, he wasn't going to let her get away.

Five

There was nothing quite so pathetic as a thirty-two-year-old virgin plotting seduction, Colleen reflected as she stood in her kitchen hours later, waiting impatiently for the teapot to whistle. Every neuron in her body tingled and twitched at the thought of Gavin O'Sullivan waiting for her in her living room. Just as they had throughout the evening, especially when she watched him commandingly take charge of the scene at Baronessa headquarters. During that whole time she couldn't stop thinking of what she'd like to do when they were alone later.

She wished she could believe that after the debacle of the gelato-tasting earlier tonight, the evening could only improve. Yet she had a strong suspicion that when it came to matters of the flesh or, she supposed, most anything else, it didn't quite work that way.

If only she had more experience. Heavens, if only she had *any* experience. She was a relatively intelligent woman; why had it never occurred to her after she'd left the order to find someone on whom she could practice her feminine wiles?

Well, let's see… Could it be because no one except Gavin has ever interested you that way?

She suppressed the urge to roll her eyes, but just barely. After all, it was her tendency to follow her heart, instead of using her head that had resulted in her present predicament.

Not that bemoaning her past—or, more precisely, her lack of one—was going to improve matters. Yet even so, she couldn't seem to stop wishing there was some way to make certain that if she made the first move tonight, it wouldn't end up like her and Gavin's last encounter, with him bolting for the door.

Unfortunately if there was one thing she'd learned over the past dozen years, it was that absolutely nothing, with the obvious exception of God's love, came with guarantees.

Good grief, Colleen, with just a smidgen more effort you're going to talk yourself out of a moderate case of nerves and into a full-blown panic attack. And won't Gavin find that alluring?

She had a vision of herself running into the living room babbling that confession was good for the soul and demanding to know if Gavin found her the least bit attractive, because she really, really, really wanted to kiss him silly and more. So much more.

She gave a violent start as she heard a floorboard creak. Freezing in place, she held her breath, then realized it was only Gavin moving around in her living room. With a slight shake of her head, she exhaled and raised her hands to the fiery heat throbbing in her cheeks.

The mere idea of putting herself in such an emotionally charged situation might have been laughable if she'd been in the mood to see the slightest humor. But she wasn't exactly the dancing-on-the-edge type, and with each passing moment she became less and less certain what Gavin's reaction would be if she actually had the courage to follow through on her desires.

It was not a comforting thought. Even so, a persistent thread of sensual excitement kept drawing her mind back to the enticing image of his mouth. And to the way his every movement hinted at the hard muscle beneath his smooth, olive-toned skin and how the most innocent touch of his long-fingered hands made her nerves sing with pleasure—

The shrill of a ringing phone snapped her out of her growing fantasy that, with any luck, she was going to finally make love to Gavin tonight.

Oh, sure, she thought as she reached for her cordless phone. And right after that she was going to sprout wings and fly. "Hello?"

"Hey, Col, it's Nick."

Relief flooded through her at the sound of her brother's voice. "Thank goodness. I've been hoping you'd call. Is everyone okay? How's Mr. Marino?" The last she'd seen of the neighborhood friend of her sister Gina he was being taken away in an ambulance. "And is Papa all right?"

"Papa's fine—if you don't count his being mad as hell about what happened. Everyone's okay, but the doctor wants to keep an eye on Mr. Marino. Apparently he was allergic to whatever was put into the gelato and he had some trouble breathing. They call it anaphylaxis."

"I still can't believe it really happened," Colleen said. "Thank heaven he is going to be all right. That could have been tragic."

"Don't think I haven't thought of that," Nick said grimly. "We were just lucky Gavin happened to be there and could give us a head start on what to do."

"Yes." Even though she knew it was silly, she felt a sort of possessive pride every time she thought about how calm, controlled and effective Gavin had been in the face of the crisis. "We were."

"Yeah, well, be sure and tell him thanks."

She wasn't quite sure how to respond to Nick's certainty that Gavin was there with her.

Thankfully she was saved by the shrill whistle of the tea kettle. "Nick, I've got to go."

"Okay. But do me a favor and tell Gavin I'll call him tomorrow."

"Sure." Disconnecting, she set the phone on the counter and turned off the burner, then reached for the French coffee press, which she'd already filled with freshly ground coffee beans. While the coffee steeped, she got down two cups, some napkins and a tin of cookies and assembled a tray. Then, telling herself firmly that she wasn't going to let her brother's unintended interference put a wrench in her plans, she picked up the tray, took a deep breath and headed for the living room.

Seconds later she concluded that breathing was highly overrated. And that while just a little while ago she might have truly believed she was much too conservative and inexperienced, not to mention repressed, to actually follow through on her kitchen fantasies, that was no longer true.

All it took was one look at Gavin. Because while she'd been working herself into a lather in the other room, he'd shed his coat, loosened his tie and undone the top few buttons of his shirt.

Now, sprawled comfortably on the center of the couch, his legs stretched out and his hands clasped loosely behind his head, he was the picture of potent masculinity. And, she acknowledged, her dream lover come true.

"Gavin?" Her voice sounded every bit as tremulous as she felt.

"Yeah?"

"Nick called. He said to say thanks and wanted me to let you know that it looks as if everyone's going to be fine."

"Good."

She swallowed, her mouth suddenly feeling desert-dry. "I—I have a question."

"Okay. Shoot."

"Do you really want to have a cup of coffee?"

He glanced from her face to the tray in her hands and back again. "Hey, listen, if there's some problem, if you're worried you made it too weak or too strong, it's no big deal—"

"That's not it."

"Oh." He considered her, clearly puzzled. "Okay."

She felt his gaze like a brand as she walked the few feet to the sideboard, set down the tray, then turned and, heart jammed in her throat, approached the couch.

He studied her face, then cocked his head slightly to one side. "So, you want to tell me what's going on?"

"Want to?" She grimaced. "Not really. But I will." And before she could lose her nerve, she closed the distance between them. "The truth is, I don't want anything to drink. And I don't want to sit here and make polite conversation.

"What I want—" She stopped to clear her throat. "The only thing I want is you." In one decisive motion she swung a leg over his thighs, straddling them, slid her arms around his neck and her bottom onto his lap, and claimed his mouth with her own.

She braced for his reaction, her heart in her throat.

She didn't have long to wait. For the space of a heartbeat every muscle in his body tightened, and then to her profound relief he made a raw, primitive sound low in his throat, wrapped his arms around her and met her kiss with his own.

Time lost all meaning for Colleen. She wasn't sure how long they kissed, whether it was seconds or minutes or hours. Nor did she care. The only thing in the whole wide world that mattered was Gavin; his taste, his touch, the wet heat of his mouth.

When finally they came up for air, she felt as if every nerve ending in her body was on fire. She blinked, knowing there was something she needed to tell him and wondering what on earth had happened to her verbal skills. Her mind was a blank. "That was nice," she ventured.

Gavin clearly wasn't in the mood for conversation. "Oh, yeah," he murmured. In the next instant he nuzzled her neck with his lips, honing in on the hollow behind her ear.

The warm lick of his tongue followed by the cooler tickle of his breath sent a shock of pure pleasure shooting through her. Feeling blissfully weak, she let her head loll back, allowing him greater access even as she again tried to remember what she'd wanted to say.

A wisp of recollection drifted across her

mind. "There's—" she gasped as his teeth closed with gentle firmness on her earlobe "—something I need to tell you."

"Yeah?"

He nibbled at the lower curve of her ear. To her stupefaction, that relatively tame action made her nipples instantly begin to throb, while a feeling of warmth and wetness blossomed at the apex of her thighs. It was so unexpected that her mind blanked out again, and it was a minute or two before she could speak.

Not that what she wanted to say seemed as urgent now as it had just a few minutes ago. Still… "I'm wearing panty hose."

"What?"

"You know, panty hose? The kind that comes in the little plastic packages at the grocery store. I'm so sorry, but…I thought you should know."

He was silent just long enough for her to start to wonder if she'd been right to tell him when he abruptly leaned back to stare at her. "Why on earth would you think you had to tell me that?" he demanded.

He sounded so incredulous that for the first time she felt a little foolish. "Well, you've dated all those glamorous models and gorgeous actresses and I'm sure they all have silk panties and gorgeous underwear and garters and lace, but I—I don't.''

Without warning, he gave a muffled bark of laughter. ''Oh, yeah, that's a real cold shower, all right.'' He stroked a rough-tipped thumb down the curve of her cheek. ''Baby, you could be dressed in sackcloth and ashes—or better yet, nothing at all—and I'd still think you were the sexiest woman on earth. You seem to have forgotten that I've wanted you since I was seventeen years old.''

''Oh, Gavin. Really?''

''Sure.''

''But you never said…''

He gave a slight, dismissive shrug. ''How could you not have known? I was crazy about you. And unlike you women, that's a pretty hard fact for us guys to hide.''

As if to prove his point, he rolled her beneath him and settled himself in the cradle of her thighs. Even through the barrier of their clothes, there was no missing the rock-solid length of his erection pressing against her. ''I want you. Colleen, I want you so much.''

''Me, too,'' she replied, finding it hard to talk due to the combination of relief and anticipation surging through her. Locking her hands around his neck, she urged him closer.

Yet to her surprise he momentarily resisted. Instead, he lifted himself up on one elbow, slid his hand down her thigh until he found the hem of her dress, then slipped his fingers beneath it. Ignoring her indrawn breath, he slowly ran his warm palm up the inside of her thigh.

''As for these—'' there was no mistaking the flame of satisfaction that lit his eyes as he reached the crotch of her silky hose and his hands brushed tantalizing against her ''—no problem. No problem at all.'' With clever fingers he lightly began to stroke her, intuitively seeming to know just the motion and the pressure to please her.

One did not shake off thirty-two years of good-girl behavior, however, without making one token, knee-jerk act of resistance. Which was why she found herself automatically lifting her hand with some sort of hazy, totally lacking-in-conviction idea that he really shouldn't be doing *that*.

Then he gently pressed down and rotated his thumb dead center against the one place on her entire body screaming loudest to be touched.

It was as if the rest of her ceased to exist. Her hand fell bonelessly back to the couch as every nerve in her body made a mass migration to the tingling, tightening, escalating swell of sensation beneath Gavin's fingertips.

She couldn't move, couldn't think, couldn't utter even the tiniest sound as her entire being strained toward an elusive need that stubbornly seemed to lurk just a fraction beyond her reach.

And then Gavin slid a little lower on the couch, shifted his head and clamped his mouth around one of her nipples straining through the lace dress and sucked at the same instant he rotated his thumb against her again—and pushed her over the edge.

Pleasure unlike anything she'd ever felt rocketed through her. It claimed every muscle and every nerve ending, every inch of bone and patch of skin. And it seemed to go on forever.

And ever.

And ever.

By the time the tempest finally passed thousands of seconds later, she felt amazed, transformed, exhausted, exalted and reborn.

And happier than she'd been in a long, long time.

It was a Sally Field moment if there'd ever been one, she decided as she found herself thinking, *He likes me. He really likes me.*

It seemed like something she really ought to share. Not the Sally Field part, of course, although she couldn't stop the smile tugging at her lips as a little voice in her head insisted that he had to care about her to have done something so intimate. But surely he had every right to know that she thought the entire thing had been amazing. That *he'd* been amazing.

"Gavin?" Opening her eyes, she looked down, her stomach hollowing with a combination of tenderness and awe at the sight of his head cradled against her breast.

"What?"

"That was…incredible."

"I'm glad you think so." He lifted his head and twisted his neck to meet her gaze, and her heart did a wild little somersault.

Because in stark contrast to the languid satisfaction she hadn't a doubt was plastered all over her face, the line of his mouth was taut and the slash of his cheekbones pronounced, while his dark eyes glittered with raw desire.

A little drumbeat of anticipation kicked up inside her, miraculously banishing her previous lethargy. "And why is that?" she inquired in a throaty voice that didn't sound at all like hers.

"Because." In one lithe move his feet hit the floor at that same time that he scooped her up and into his arms. "That was just the beginning."

"It was?"

"Oh, yeah. There's not a whole lot you can count on in life—" he straightened, lifting her as if she weighed nothing and began to walk, carrying her out of the living room and down the short hall in the direction of her bedroom "—but you can stake your life on that."

So far, so good, Gavin thought as he bumped open Colleen's bedroom door with his hip.

Somehow he was managing to control himself, to walk and talk and act like a civilized grown-up despite the near-savage need pumping through his veins and making his heart pound like a jackhammer.

He shifted sideways as he crossed the threshold to ensure he didn't inadvertently scrape Colleen against the frame, filled with the old protective instinct she'd always inspired in him. The one that until half an hour ago he'd been one hundred percent certain was not merely dead but buried six feet deep. The one that now appeared to have magically resurrected itself.

And wasn't that just perfect? Because at the same time, he was caught in a vise of desire stronger than any he'd ever experienced. So compelled was he to touch, taste and bury himself inside this one particular woman that the mere thought of being thwarted made him feel frantic and desperate and more than a little dangerous.

And he didn't like it. He didn't like it one bit. Because although he could no longer recall the specifics that had prompted it—only that it had predictably involved his mother abandoning him yet again to pursue her own selfish pleasures—he'd long ago vowed never to care too much about anything or anyone.

Yet here he was, frantic with need. Hell, he was so turned on by the mere act of holding Colleen in his arms that his body, like that of some randy, inexperienced teenager, was on the verge of embarrassing him. And all because of a woman who'd already stomped his heart into the ground once, more than proving she couldn't be trusted.

And yet as he looked down into her soft blue eyes, he knew that he would never allow anything to hurt her.

The realization sent a deep wave of uneasiness surging through him.

"Gavin?"

Just the sound of his name on her lips was as tantalizing as any caress. His body jerked in eager response, and the effort it took to control it put an abrupt end to his disturbing thoughts.

"Are you all right?" she asked.

"Sure. Why wouldn't I be?"

"I don't know." She pursed her lips in contemplation and it took all of his willpower not to just toss her down on the bed, rip away the bare minimum of clothes that would give him access to what he wanted most and plunge himself deep inside her. ''You just seem a little…tense.''

No kidding. His entire body from his hair to his toes hurt from the effort of keeping himself in check, and there was a fine trickle of perspiration trailing down his back, further proof of the escalating cost of his restraint. ''Yeah. I suppose I do. I've waited a long time for this. For you.''

Her eyes momentarily widened and then she reached out to cup the side of his face in one fine-boned hand. ''Me, too,'' she said softly.

He appreciated the sentiment. Still, the more cynical side of him, the part she'd had no small part in helping to create, seriously doubted she truly understood what she'd put him through all those years ago.

The whole time they'd been together he'd had to constantly rein himself in, denying the howling needs of his testosterone-flooded body. Yet he'd assured himself over and over that it was worth it, persuaded that what they had would last forever and that he could wait—he *would* wait—to make her his wife before claiming her innocence.

It had been his willing gift to her, one of the few he could give her and a testament to his belief that she was the antithesis of the women around whom he'd grown up. He'd believed with all his heart that she was pure, gentle, *good*.

Right up until the minute she'd told him that it was over. That they both needed to concentrate on school. That, when it came right down to it, they weren't right for each other.

But that was then and this was now, he reminded himself. He was no longer a welfare kid from the projects, going to school on a soccer scholarship, working multiple jobs to make ends meet.

Just as Colleen was no longer a sheltered young innocent, as she'd so amply demonstrated in the living room just minutes ago.

And although sometime in the past few days the last lingering little sting of being dumped by her had vanished, he wasn't so foolish as to believe that by being together now they could turn back the clock or recapture what they'd lost.

But there was no reason they shouldn't enjoy tonight. He knew he intended to. And as his body wasn't the least bit shy about reminding him, it was past time they got started.

Reaching the end of the bed, he set Colleen on her feet and unclasped her hands from around his neck. Then in one fluid motion he reached down, grasped the bottom edge of her stretchy little dress, pulled it up and over her head and tossed it aside.

She made a little sound that was part gasp, part protest and part laugh. "Gavin—"

"No." He pressed a finger to her lips. "Don't say a thing. Just…let me do this."

Her blue eyes searched his, and whatever she saw there caused her expression to abruptly sober. She swallowed, then, her gaze still locked on his face, nodded.

He reached around, unsnapped her bra and slid it away, then hooked his thumbs in the waistband of her panty hose, slid them down and snagged the side of her panties and peeled both garments to her ankles. He gave her just enough time to grip his shoulders for balance and then sent her shoes sailing away. The remainder of her undergarments followed seconds later.

He straightened, took a step back and looked.

Instantly he was grateful that he regularly worked out. Otherwise he probably would've dropped dead from a heart attack.

She was perfect. Petite, but willowy. Sleek, silky-skinned, delicately boned. She was more beautiful than he'd ever imagined, and over the course of seventeen years, he'd imagined, a lot.

Her breasts were small, but exquisitely shaped, tipped with pale pink nipples that were currently beaded like priceless pearls. Beneath the smooth plane of her stomach, the perfect dimple of her navel, a neat triangle of ebony curls seemed to point the way to his ultimate destination.

The second he could breathe again, he yanked his shirt over his head, heedless of the sound of popping buttons, stripped away his pants, briefs and socks and eliminated the distance between them.

Then he caught her to him with an arm to her waist and one to the top of her thighs and lifted her up. Their lips met and clung. Having felt her silky wetness through her clothing out in the living room, he didn't hesitate. Knowing she was more than ready, he bent his knees and with one powerful thrust sheathed himself inside her.

"Oh! Gavin, oh!"

Her exclamation of shocked pleasure was the most potent of aphrodisiacs. Not that he needed any added stimulation. Lowering her onto the bed, settling deeper into the notch of her thighs, he had to fight a primitive urge to say to hell with control and just do whatever it took to accomplish his own pleasure.

Except that he wanted…more. He wanted Colleen twisting and bucking beneath him, he wanted her shuddering and shaking, he wanted her shouting his name as she came.

Bracing on his forearms, he came up on his knees, searching for just the perfect angle. Knowing he'd found it when she gave a surprised little shudder, he tore his mouth from her lips and traced a line with his tongue from her throat to the shallow valley between her breasts.

"I…that's… I didn't realize…" Her breathless attempts to talk ceased abruptly as he licked one tightly budded nipple, gently blew on it, then locked onto it with his mouth and sucked. Hard.

With a strangled cry she lifted her hips and took him as deeply as she could, then did an instinctive bump and grind that was as old as time.

It did him in.

With a deep, guttural sound of his own, he lifted himself up and began to move, out and then back in, harder and faster, faster and harder. The small of his back hollowed, the bands of muscle that sheathed his solar plexus clenched, his biceps burned.

A rictus of pure, possessive satisfaction tugged the corners of his mouth as he heard her breathy moans and felt her strong interior muscles clench and release around him.

This is the best sex I've ever had in my life. Nothing's ever felt this good, this right.

It was as if he and Colleen were the perfect fit, absolutely made for each other.

It was his last rational thought before his climax hit him with the force of a runaway train, carrying him into a void of pure, mind-numbing pleasure.

Six

"So there you are."

Seated at the end of the richly patterned brocade sofa that graced her father's cozy study, Colleen looked up from the magazine she'd been reading as her younger sister Gina swept into the room.

In a ritual instituted by their mother, Moira, when Colleen, Nick, Ryan and Joe, the four older kids, had been teenagers, barring death or imprisonment the entire family was expected to sit down to dinner together at their

parents' Beacon Hill _____ cond Sunday
of each month _____ her's wrath.

Not s_ _____ s excellent.
And us_ _____ joyed the
chance _____ nd sisters
and get _____ ves.

But n _____
thinking _____
helping b_ _____ ment.
And how sh_ _____ for the clock
to strike seven-thirty, the earliest acceptable
time for post-dinner departure. Or that as
usual, God seemed to be having some fun at
her expense, since the time, which usually
flew by at these little get-togethers, currently
seemed to be hobbling along with all the speed
of a three-legged tortoise climbing Mount Ev-
erest.

''I wondered where you were hiding.'' With
her usual efficiency, Gina made a quick survey
of the room, then headed to the fireplace,
where she stooped down in order to open the
screen. Taking a stick of applewood from the
bin on the hearth, she tossed it onto the dwin-
dling flames before straightening and turning
to address Colleen. ''What happened? All the

arguing and shouting finally get to be too much for you?''

Colleen shook her head and a little regretfully slid the magazine—a copy of *American Bride* that she assumed had originally belonged to Nick's new wife, Gail—onto the end table. "Of course not. Besides, you know what Mother always says, 'Barones do not shout. They discuss.''' She tipped up her chin in a lofty way that was a dead-on imitation of their maternal parent "'Albeit with passionate persistence.'''

Clearly caught off guard, Gina let out a surprised sputter of laughter, and some of the tension seemed to drain out of her. Plopping down on the sofa next to Colleen, she kicked off her shoes and stretched out her long, slender legs. "Thanks. I needed that. I'm pretty sure it's the first time I've laughed in the past forty-eight hours." Unable to contain a slight shudder, she leaned her head back against the cushion, squeezed her eyes shut and let out a heartfelt sigh. "Lord, what a nightmare."

There was no need for her to explain that she was referring to the Valentine's Day disaster; Friday night's debacle had been the dominant topic most of the night. And since Gina was Baronessa's VP in charge of marketing and public relations, it had fallen on her slim shoulders to deal with the press the past forty-eight hours and do what she could to minimize the damage done to the company's reputation. She'd been in the thick of every discussion.

Colleen leaned over and gave her sister a quick hug. Pulling back, she met Gina's troubled gaze. "It'll be all right," she said softly. "Just give it some time. You're doing a great job."

"I don't know about that," Gina said with a sigh. "Every time I think about all those people getting sick because some twisted creep put habanera peppers into the gelato, I want to hit someone. And who ever even *heard* of a burning-hot pepper that's colorless and odorless and flavorless, anyway?" Her slim, elegant hands curled into fists. "It was probably one of those sneaky, underhanded, weasel-faced Contis."

Colleen checked her instinctive protest. Although there was no proof that the feud with their family's long-term archenemies was behind what had happened Friday night, feelings for and against the theory were running high.

While Nick, as chief operating officer, insisted it was his obligation to remain neutral until he had all the facts, their father, Carlo, cousins Daniel and Derrick, and Gina herself obviously were convinced what had happened had to be the work of the Contis.

Their brother Joe and cousin Claudia, on the other hand, were more inclined to believe that one of Baronessa's competitors must have been behind the malicious act.

Most unexpected of all, however, had been Maria. Almost ten years younger than Colleen and the baby of the family at twenty-three, the very capable manager of the Hanover Street gelateria had out of the blue unexpectedly defended the Contis, causing a mild uproar and a lot of raised eyebrows.

Colleen wasn't sure what she believed. Like Nick, it wasn't in her nature to rush to judgment. And she had faith that a certain Higher Power would see to it that things eventually got sorted out and justice prevailed.

Plus, at the moment she happened to be

more than a little preoccupied with her own life.

As if reading her mind, Gina suddenly turned to her. "You certainly didn't have much to say at dinner one way or the other."

Colleen met her sister's lovely violet eyes and shrugged. "I guess I don't see the need. I'm confident that you and Papa and Nick and Joe will get to the bottom of it."

Gina shook her head in a show of disbelief. "You know, sometimes I can't believe we're related. You're always so sensible and serene."

Don't I wish, Colleen thought wryly. Serene was the very last word she'd use to describe herself ever since the incredible night she'd spent with Gavin. Instead, she felt like one of those tiny figures inside a well-shaken snow globe—totally adrift and completely clueless as to which way was up and which was down.

"Although," Gina mused out loud, tilting her head a fraction as she considered her sister, "tonight you do seem a little distracted. And once or twice you've had the strangest little smile on your face." He gaze abruptly sharpened. "It doesn't have something to do with your seeing Gavin O'Sullivan again, does it?"

The small brass clock on the mantel chimed. Colleen glanced at her watch, saw that it was finally half-past seven and scrambled to her feet.

"You're imagining things," she said, trying not to wince as she added *lying* to her growing list of recent sins. She slipped on her shoes, leaned over and gave a startled Gina a quick hug. "But I love you, anyway," she said. "And don't worry so much. Everything will turn out all right."

"But, Colleen, wait! Where are you going?"

She flashed her sister a sunny smile. "Home."

The last place Colleen expected to find Gavin and Brett was out behind the brownstone in the garage with Mr. Crypinski.

In the three years she'd lived there, she'd never been allowed into the small, detached building with its boarded windows. Her landlord had always kept it securely locked.

Colleen had to admit that Mr. Crypinski's

protective, secretive behavior had caused her no end of entertaining speculation. What could he have in there? she'd often wondered. An alien spacecraft? The world's largest collection of old magazines? A gigantic ball of string? Or perhaps there was a cache of super high-tech spy equipment because behind his gruff, taciturn facade the older man was actually a suave secret agent, South Boston's very own James Bond. Although even she realized that last was a definite long shot.

But now, as she stood in the garage's open doorway looking in at the scene, which was as bright as day thanks to a bank of lights overhead, Colleen finally knew.

And it was even better and more unexpected than anything she'd ever imagined.

Smack dab in the center of the concrete slab floor was a car. And not just any car. Having been blessed with four brothers, Colleen knew a classic 1961 Thunderbird when she saw one.

And this one was a beaut. Looking as if it had just rolled off the line and onto the showroom floor, the candy-apple-red convertible boasted a mirror-polished chrome grill, gleaming hubcaps, pristine white sidewall tires and a red-and-white leather interior.

By itself, it would have been impressive enough. But even more astonishing was the sight of Brett, sitting in the driver's seat, his hands on the wheel. And beside him in the passenger seat was Mr. Crypinski—the same Mr. Crypinski who probably hadn't spoken more than a hundred words to her the entire time she'd known him—gesturing with actual animation while going on at length about his pride and joy's various attributes.

Rounding out the surreal tableau was Gavin. Perched on the edge of the back seat, the sleeves of his navy V-neck sweater pushed back to expose his forearms, which were resting atop the seat in front of him, he appeared engrossed, seeming to hang on the older man's every syllable.

It was…amazing. Unbelievable. More than a little wonderful.

And people don't believe in miracles, Colleen thought in bemusement. Apologizing for her fellow man, she sent a heartfelt word of thanks heavenward.

A second later, as if sensing her presence,

Gavin abruptly looked over and spotted her. "Hey," he said. Although his voice was casual, something in the way his gaze played over her made her heart skip a beat and took the chill out of the night air.

"Hey, Ms. Barone," Brett echoed, doing his best to match Gavin's controlled cool, only to blow it with his next sentence. "Isn't this *tight?*"

"Yes. It certainly is."

"Mr. C's telling us all about it. Did you know that it can go from zero to sixty in under ten seconds? And that Elvis Presley owned one just like it?"

She shook her head. "No. I didn't."

"Well, he did. I can't believe you never told me about it."

There was a faint note of accusation in the boy's voice, and Colleen realized it didn't have anything to do with Elvis, but about what he believed to be her failure to confide in him regarding the car's existence.

Before she could decide on the best way to respond, however, her landlord surprised her all over again, this time by coming to her defense.

"Now hold on," he said to Brett. "The truth is, she couldn't say anything to you because she didn't know anything." He sent Colleen an apologetic look, then turned back to face the boy. "I never thought to show her the car 'cause I just plain didn't think she'd be interested. This baby here—" he gave the T-Bird's glossy dash a fond pat "—well, it's kind of a guy thing. Or at least that's what Edna, my late wife, always said."

To Colleen's fascination, the other two "guys" immediately nodded and both knowingly murmured, "Ah," as if the older man's explanation was a perfectly acceptable defense for behaving like a male chauvinist.

She knew she ought to be offended, yet in this instance it just didn't seem that important. Not when it was so clear that the three of them were caught up in some serious male bonding.

That had to count for something, given that until she'd walked in here a minute ago she'd never in her life known three more stubbornly solitary individuals. Something very good indeed. And the last thing she wanted to do was put a damper on their good time. At least not tonight.

Not that she intended to roll over completely. Crossing her arms, she fixed her best expectant look on Brett, the one she'd worked hard to perfect during her tenure as a nun, and waited.

The boy managed to avoid her gaze for all of ten seconds, then finally looked over at her. "Sorry," he mumbled.

"Apology accepted. Did you get your homework done?"

He nodded.

"Good." Rubbing her hands down her arms, she manufactured a little shiver. "Now, I'm going inside. It's way too cold out here."

She turned and took a step, then stopped and looked over her shoulder. "Oh, I almost forgot. My mother sent one of her German-chocolate cakes home with me. You're all invited to come have a piece when you're done here."

With that she made her exit, wagering they wouldn't last outside another fifteen minutes.

As it turned out, she underestimated the lure of dessert.

They were at her door in under six.

* * *

Moira Barone might not be his favorite person, but Gavin had to give her credit.

The woman knew her way around a kitchen.

"Wonderful cake," he said to Colleen as he set his empty plate down on the coffee table in her living room. With a satisfied sigh he stretched out his legs and slouched down on his spine on the sofa.

"Are you sure you got enough?"

On the surface the question sounded sincere, but he was beginning to relearn the nuances of Colleen's personality, and one sideways look at the banked amusement in her eyes as she sat in the chair to his right, her bare feet curled beneath her, told its own story.

"Yeah. Three pieces was a bit of a challenge, but then, I like living on the edge." He'd also managed to outstay Emmett Crypinski and Brett, which had been his goal all along. For the usual male reason—the desire to get a particular woman into bed—he was in no hurry to leave. "So how was your dinner?"

She made a face. "Noisy."

"Any word yet on who's responsible for what happened Friday night?"

She shook her head. "No. Just a whole lot of opinions."

"Huh. Well, your family has certainly never lacked those."

To his gratification, the corners of her mouth tipped up. "Truer words were never spoken. But I'd suggest you try not to look quite so smug."

"And why is that?"

"Because as I was leaving tonight, Mother informed me she wants us to get together this week."

"Us who?" he said, suddenly wary.

"Who do you think? You and me and her and Papa. She said that unless she hears otherwise, she'll expect us for dinner this coming Thursday."

"Swell."

She sent him one of those mischievous smiles that always played hell with his insides. "Don't worry. I told her I couldn't possibly make a commitment without talking to you first. And as far as I'm concerned, we don't have to do anything just because Mother commands it. We can have dinner anytime. I'm thinking that February 2054 sounds about right.''

He couldn't help it, he laughed, his equilibrium restored, along with a curiosity about just what Colleen's mother had in mind. ''No, let's go. I can handle your mother.''

''Really?''

He nodded.

''Okay. If you're positive.''

''I am.''

''Now I have a question.''

''Shoot.''

''How did you ever wind up being so chummy with Mr. Crypinski?''

''Emmett?'' He shrugged. ''I don't know. He came by to fix your intercom, heard Brett and me discussing my Porsche, and out of the blue he got all bent out of shape, claiming there was no way some fancy foreign import could hold a candle to a real American car. That made Brett get on him, asking what made him such an expert, and the next thing I knew, we were on our way to his garage. And then once we actually clapped eyes on the T-Bird, things sort of snowballed from there.

''Brett asked him some question, and he

started going on about his baby's finer points, and…well, you heard them. It was like once they got started, neither one of them could shut up.''

''Amazing,'' she murmured. ''Just a couple of weeks ago Mr. Crypinski wouldn't even let Brett into the house.''

''Yeah, well, in this neighborhood it pays to be cautious.''

''But tonight the two of them really seemed to be connecting,'' she said, disregarding his rather pointed remark.

Gavin considered the thoughtful look on her face and decided he'd let the other matter drop—for the moment. ''I got the feeling that Emmett's lonely. And he said a few things that made it pretty clear he's been keeping tabs on Brett for a while.''

''Really…'' Her voice trailed off, and it was obvious from her arrested expression that something ingenious was going on in her mind.

He settled more deeply into the couch and found himself thinking, as one minute turned into two, that despite its well-used appearance, this particular piece of furniture was extremely comfortable. Which was more than he could say for the handsome taupe leather sofa that occupied his own living room at the Independence.

Which reminded him… "Colleen?"

"Hmm?"

"Tell me something."

"What?"

"Why *are* you living here? In a place like this?"

She looked over, focusing on him. "I'm not sure I know what you mean. It's my home."

He gazed steadily at her, letting his silence do the talking.

"Well, it is." She suddenly sounded just the slightest bit defensive. "Plus, it's close to school and shopping, which is convenient since I don't drive. And I like that I don't have to share space with lots of other people the way I would in a bigger apartment building."

He conceded the merits of her argument. "All right." Then he drove home *his* point. "But it's still Jefferson Heights."

"So? That happens to be where I'm employed. And in case it's somehow escaped your notice, they don't exactly pay school social workers a ton of money.''

Try as he might, he couldn't keep out the edge that suddenly crept into his voice. ''And what? You're saving your trust fund for your old age?'' He knew damn well that each of the Barone kids had received a million dollars when they reached twenty-one. During the time they'd been together he'd been acutely aware of Colleen's upcoming windfall. And his utter lack of one.

Yet to his surprise, rather than taking offense, Colleen suddenly laughed. ''Oh, Gavin, I'm sorry. I thought you knew. I gave it away.''

''You gave what away?''

''My trust money. Before I entered the convent, I signed it over to the Church to start a scholarship fund for inner-city kids.''

He felt his jaw sag and clamped it shut. Still, he couldn't stop the shock shuddering through him. ''You gave away a million dollars?''

She nodded.

''Just like that?'' He tried to take it in.

She shrugged one slim shoulder. ''I didn't

need it,'' she said softly, a touch of sadness suddenly stark in her eyes. ''I told you back when we were in college, remember? For me, my life, it's never been about money.''

He sat back and stared at her.

Because ever since Friday night he'd been telling himself that what was between them was purely physical. That his sense of contentment the past two days was due to long overdue sexual satiation and because he and Brett really did seem to be connecting, as evidenced by their great time at last night's Celtics game.

He'd refused to ask any questions about— much less assign any significance to—his postcoital suspicion that Colleen had never been with any man but him.

And he certainly hadn't acknowledged that in just two weeks he'd come to feel more at home in her modest apartment than he ever had in his own swank penthouse—or anywhere else he'd ever lived.

But now...despite the wrong she'd done him in the past, he could no longer deny there was something special about her, something that drew him to her in a way that he'd never been drawn to another woman.

But that wasn't all. There was also the fact that even with him guarding himself against her, in a ridiculously short period of time she'd still managed to breach the substantial wall of defense he'd built around his heart.

The wall she'd brought down once before, only to abandon him, leaving him empty, defenseless and hurting. The one he'd subsequently spent years fortifying and wasn't at all certain he cared to surrender now.

The hell of it was, he realized as he stared at her unguarded face, he wasn't certain he had a choice in the matter anymore.

"Damn, Colleen," he said hoarsely. "What are you trying to do to me?"

Seven

Colleen stared at Gavin's inexplicably grim expression. "I'm sorry, but I'm not sure… I don't understand what you're asking."

Abruptly he sighed. "Of course you don't. Oh, hell, I didn't mean…" He trailed off as if needing a moment to collect himself. When he spoke again, his voice was steady. "Do you trust me, Colleen?"

She felt a rush of relief, since the answer to that was easy. If there was one thing her years spent striving to do God's work had taught her, it was that when it came to putting one's faith in other people, the potential for reward was well worth the potential risk.

Besides, this was Gavin, whom she'd loved for such a very long time, and believed in even before that. "Yes."

He squeezed his eyes shut. "Thank God," he said softly.

She did her best to give him a few seconds before inquiring, "But why are you asking? What's the matter? Did I do something wrong?"

"No," he said instantly, opening his eyes. "It's me. If anyone screwed up, it was me." To her consternation, he rose to his feet and held out his hand. "Come here. Please."

Questions surfaced in her like weeds popping up in a garden after a good rain. Yet instinct told her it was somehow important that she stay silent and simply follow his lead. Taking his proffered hand, she stood and compliantly let him usher her out of the living room, down the hall and into her cozy but dark bedroom.

He reached over and switched on the table lamp.

Encircled by the resulting pool of light, they considered each other. It was so quiet the only sound was their not-entirely-steady breathing.

"Gavin—"

"Shh. Don't talk." He pressed a finger to her lips, then without warning toed off his shoes and shrugged out of his sweater and T-shirt. Her heart began to thump. "Friday night," he said quietly, tossing his clothes to the floor. "I thought... I was pretty preoccupied. It didn't occur to me that you'd never made love before. But you hadn't, had you?"

There was enough self-disgust in his voice that for a moment she was tempted to lie. Except that their gazes were locked and she knew she'd never pull it off. She shook her head. "No," she reluctantly admitted.

"That's what I thought."

"But it didn't matter," she protested. Surely he knew that she'd loved every moment of everything they'd done that night. "It *doesn't* matter. It was wonderful—"

"Yeah, it does matter," he contradicted, cutting her off. He undid the fly of his jeans, slid down the zipper and shucked off the rest of his clothes. "Because if I'd known, I'd have done things differently. For instance…"

He stepped so close that despite her clothes she could feel the heat radiating off him. Then he bent his head and began to lazily forge a link of kisses from her temple to her jaw. "I would've gone a whole lot slower." His tongue rimmed her ear, making her shiver. "I would've taken my time and made sure of your pleasure."

"Oh, but you did—"

"No. Maybe later. But not that first time." Deftly he unbuttoned her blouse and peeled it away, then managed to relieve her of the rest of her garments while also continuing the delicious torture he was inflicting with his mouth.

"I should've taken the time to tell you how much I love your breasts. The way they fit into my hands—" he cupped her "—the pale pink color of these—" his thumbs rubbed circles over her tightly beaded nipples "—the way they pucker at my touch."

"Oh, my gosh…" she said weakly.

"And then there's the way your waist curves in." His palms slid down her sides, his thumbs tracing her midline and the dip of her navel, gliding lower until only the tips of his little fingers rested against the lowest curve of her hips. "You're so damn delicate, Colleen. It turns me on."

"Gavin—"

He ignored her breathless little protest and feasted at the curve of her throat with his lips. Feeling as malleable as modeling clay, she let her head fall back to give him better access.

"So does the smoothness of your skin." His voice was a deep rasp abrading her nerve endings. "And how fast you get wet when I touch you here." With one finger he parted the dark curls between her thighs and stroked her.

She shuddered, her body feeling exquisitely overloaded. "Don't," she murmured weakly even though she was certain she'd die if he actually stopped now. "You shouldn't... I can't... It feels too... Oh, my, too..."

"Good?" he supplied. "I know, baby," he whispered, resting his damp forehead against her flushed skin. "Believe me, I know."

Even so, that didn't stop him from suddenly moving away.

"Gavin!" she wailed, her lashes fluttering up at the rude discovery that the only thing more excruciating than his teasing touch was the lack of it.

"Easy," he soothed, catching her by the wrist and drawing her with him as he backed toward the bed. "Hang on just a second. I promise you won't regret it."

His calves bumped against the side of the mattress and he sat. Then, before she completely understood what he intended, he was lifting her up. Laying back, he brought her down on him, impaling her on the silky thrust of his erection.

The sheer pleasure of it stole her breath.

But that didn't begin to compare with the joy that swept her as she looked down at his face. Because for a few seconds his expression was completely unguarded, allowing her to see the fierce tenderness, the intense emotion stamped on his features.

It gave her hope for the future. And the courage to follow her instincts.

Reaching down, she twined her fingers in

his, glorying in the strength of his powerful body. She met him halfway as he thrust upward into her, feeling herself getting lost in his gaze, feeling a compelling need to commit to memory every inch of his handsome, precious face.

Perfectly matched, they increased their pace. As they rocked together, their bodies coming together each time a little faster, a little harder, Colleen felt a rising pleasure that belonged to them alone.

Clamping down on her lower lip, she struggled to hold back, wanting to wait for him, wanting them to come together.

And then the moment came. With a strangled gasp he freed his hands and grasped her hips, pressing her down at the same time that his back hollowed and his body bucked. He surged upward, his whole body straining as he pumped himself into her, filling her with his seed.

Pleasure overtook her. Crying out, she gave herself up to the waves of sensation crashing through her. And finally gave voice to her heart.

"I love you," she whispered, tears of happiness filling her eyes as he locked his arms around her and cradled her close and she heard the reassuring thump of his heart against her ear. "I love you, Gavin. I always have. And I always will."

"I must say, I had no idea Elliot Sutherland once had a hotel in addition to the Independence," Colleen's father said before taking another sip of his after-dinner coffee. Setting the thin porcelain cup down on its platinum-ribbed saucer, he absentmindedly traced the outline of one of the finely embroidered flowers that adorned the Irish-linen tablecloth.

"And in Phoenix, of all places. But it certainly turned into a piece of luck for us that he did—and that he sent you to work there, Gavin. A pepper is the last thing I'd have suspected would be used to ruin gelato. Your experience and quick thinking helped save the day. If I failed to say it before, thank you."

"There's really no need, sir," Gavin replied, looking totally at ease as he lounged back in his chair at the long, burled-walnut table. "As the saying goes, I just happened to be in the right place at the right time—and the person to think of it first."

"You're being too modest, but I can see I'm making you uncomfortable, so we'll drop the subject for the moment. Why don't you tell me, instead, about this rumor I hear that you may be acquiring the old Commodore Hotel up on the North Shore?"

It was Gavin's turn to look impressed. "How did you learn about that? No one's supposed to know except my banker and my CFO."

"You get to be my age and you're bound to have a few inside sources," the older man said with a twinkle in his eye. "Although, if you don't mind a word of advice, you might suggest to your banker that he could use a more discreet assistant."

Gavin nodded. "You can bet I will. First thing tomorrow morning."

Listening with half an ear as the two men she cared for most in the world continued to talk business, Colleen wondered if it was possible to be too happy.

The past few days had been some of the most carefree and enjoyable of her life. The mentoring program, though still in its early stages, was going exceedingly well. And then, just yesterday, she'd had a very interesting talk with Mr. Crypinski regarding Brett.

There was also her ever-increasing closeness to Gavin, which figured heavily into her contentment. He'd spent every night at her place since Sunday, and though they were both on their best behavior and she knew that at some point they were going to have to address the hurt she sensed he still harbored regarding their past, in every other way their relationship was better now than it had been then.

And though she thought that was mainly because they were finally adults, she also had to admit there were times when her heart felt so childishly light it wouldn't have surprised her if it had taken flight like an untethered helium balloon.

Giving her arm a gentle squeeze, her sister Gina claimed her attention. Leaning close, she whispered, "Congratulations. I was afraid that by dropping in unannounced—and as Mom made quite clear, uninvited—Joe and I were intruding on your big moment. But honestly, Colleen, I wouldn't miss this for the world.''

"What are you talking about?''

"You and your beautiful Irishman.'' She inclined her head at Gavin. "It looks like Daddy likes him. And so does Mom, for that matter.''

Colleen involuntarily sneaked a quick glance at her mother and with a surge of relief saw that Gina seemed to be right. Moira was listening thoughtfully to the men's conversation, nodding from time to time when she agreed with something and appearing surprisingly content.

"As for the two of you,'' Gina went on, a rare teasing note entering her voice, "you're a little scary. Every time you look at each other you glow like a pair of floodlights.''

Colleen bit down hard on her lower lip at the burst of laughter that wanted desperately to escape. Not until she was sure it was corralled did she turn her head to glance warningly at her sister. "You little brat. Knock it off.''

"Why, Colleen Barone.'' The younger

woman did her best to look innocently bewildered. "Whatever are you talking about?"

"You know very well," Colleen admonished. "No more poetic images. Please. Not tonight."

"Oh, all right."

She returned her gaze to the men, but not before she caught her sister's laughter-laced whisper, "Spoilsport."

Her lips quivered so much that it was a moment before she could focus on the conversation. When she finally did, it was at almost the same instant that she sensed Gina coming to attention beside her.

"What did you just say, Dad?" Baronessa's VP of marketing and PR demanded to know.

Her father glanced over at her, his expression mild but unyielding at the same time. "Nothing you need to worry about, sweetheart. I was just remarking to Gavin that we could use a little help with public relations at the moment. And he was saying that he has a friend, a young man named Flint Kingman—" Carlo glanced at Gavin to confirm he had the name right, and Gavin inclined his head ''—who specializes in just this kind of corporate damage control.''

Joe, who was sitting across the table next to Gavin, nodded, ignoring Gina's suddenly stormy expression. ''I've heard of him,'' he said, addressing his remarks to the other two men. ''Doesn't he have a reputation of being a kind of a wonder boy when it comes to controlling the media?''

With an apologetic look at Gina, Gavin nodded. ''Yes, he does. In general he's very good at whatever he puts his mind to.''

''Perhaps you wouldn't mind, then, if I had my secretary call yours tomorrow for his phone number?'' Carlo inquired.

''By all means,'' Gavin said courteously.

With a gesture that was all the more ominous for its very deliberateness, Gina pushed away her plate and dropped her napkin beside it. With an impatient shove to her chair, she stood. ''Could I see you in the library, please, Father?''

With the faintest of sighs, Carlo nodded. ''Of course, Gina. If you'll excuse us?'' he said to the others.

Everyone nodded except Joe, who stood, instead. "Since this is about Baronessa business, I think I'll come, too, if it's all the same to you, Papa."

"Certainly." Looking just the slightest bit harried, Carlo quickly shook hands with Gavin and thanked him for coming to dinner, came around the table to give Colleen a buss on the cheek and whisper in her ear that he loved her, then marched in the direction of the library with his other two children in tow.

"Well," Moira, always the perfect hostess, said brightly into the sudden silence. "That was rather awkward, wasn't it? I do apologize for Gina's behavior, Gavin. Sometimes she can be very strong-willed. I must confess I simply don't understand from whom in the family she gets it."

"Yes, of course," Gavin murmured politely. He glanced at Colleen, then in quick succession at the door and his watch, his expression carefully neutral.

"Did I mention I have an early staff meeting, Mother?" Colleen said quickly. "We really should be go—"

"Oh, nonsense." Moira waved one elegant hand. "I haven't even served dessert yet."

"I'm sorry, but we really can't stay."

Moira hesitated the merest instant, then nodded graciously. "Very well. If you can't, you can't. But at least let your Mr. O'Sullivan finish his coffee. Surely you have time for that, darling?"

Colleen softened. As crazy as her mother sometimes made her, she knew the older woman's heart was in the right place; like most parents, Moira simply wanted what was best for her children—regardless if it was what *they* wanted. "Of course."

"Oh, good." Smiling, Moira turned up the charm, and the next ten minutes passed quickly.

Finally, however, Colleen motioned to Gavin and rose. "Thank you so much for having us, Mother," she said sincerely. "Dinner was wonderful, as always."

The three of them started toward the entry, stopping briefly at the hall closet so Gavin and Colleen could retrieve their coats.

"She's right, Mrs. Barone," Gavin said graciously. "If you ever decide you want a job, come see me. You'd be a draw in any of my kitchens.''

"Why, thank you, dear.'' Moira smiled, her beautiful eyes alight. "But I think I'd probably better stay around here. Although he'd never admit it, Carlo wouldn't last a day without me to look after him.''

"His gain is my loss,'' Gavin said gallantly as they reached the front door.

Moira seemed to consider him for a moment, then reached out and gave him a pat on the shoulder. "I just want to say...I was wrong about you, Gavin.''

Although his pleasant expression didn't change, Colleen didn't miss the thread of tension suddenly drawing him tight. "Were you?'' he inquired politely. "In what way?''

"Despite your unfortunate background and all my dire predictions, you've grown up into a fine man, just as Colleen always claimed you would. I do hope you know it was never you personally that I objected to. It's just...Carlo always had such dreams about Colleen entering the religious life, and you both were so young. I hope you can see your way clear to understand that we simply wanted something different for our daughter.

"And really, I'm sure if you'll take a little time to reflect, you'll see that in some ways we did you a favor. After all, surely you wouldn't have felt nearly the drive to succeed that you obviously have if you'd married Colleen. And at least now you can honestly claim that the success you've had is your own."

Gavin's expression was so rigid by now that Colleen thought it was a miracle he could talk. "You're one hundred percent right about that, Mrs. Barone. Good night."

Assisting Colleen down the outside stairs with a hand to her shoulder, he walked tensely beside her to the Porsche, unlocked the passenger door and waited as she climbed in. Then he carefully shut the door, walked around the hood and slid into the driver's seat.

"Don't forget your seat belt," he gritted out as he locked his shoulder harness into place, turned on the ignition and pulled out.

He didn't say another word for a good ten blocks. Then he abruptly changed lanes and pulled off the main boulevard they'd been traveling and onto a residential street. Lips pursed, he scouted the area ahead, then pulled smoothly into the first open space at the curb.

Pulling on the parking brake with a jerk, he switched off the engine before finally turning to face her.

"Why, Colleen?" he demanded. "Why the hell have you let me think for all this time that you didn't love me enough to stick things out? Why the hell not just tell me it was your parents who objected all along?"

Eight

On some level, Colleen realized, she'd been waiting for Gavin to ask her this very question ever since he'd first approached her at Nick and Gail's reception.

Not that there'd been a logical reason for such an expectation. After all, she'd never told anyone about the afternoon all those years ago when she'd answered the imperious rap on her dormitory-room door and opened it to find her mother standing outside.

Just as she'd never repeated a word of their

subsequent conversation, the one that had pre-
cipitated her decision to end things with
Gavin.

Or shared how, once she'd finally stopped
crying hours later, she'd sat awake in the dark
the entire night, trying to plan exactly what she
was going to say to him, while doing her best
to anticipate his every argument and decide
how she'd counter it.

"So?" he said impatiently now. "Are you
just going to sit there? Or are you finally going
to have the decency to explain? You owe me
that, Colleen, at least."

He was right, of course. She squeezed her
eyes shut, asking the Almighty once more for
the wisdom to choose the right words. And
praying that whatever else happened, she
wouldn't hurt Gavin more than she already
had. Because if she did, she didn't think she
could bear it.

She took a deep, steadying breath. "First, I
want you to know that it's not fair to blame
my parents for what happened. Despite the impression Mother may have given you tonight,
ending things was my decision—and mine
alone."

"So what are you saying? That I should just forget everything she said tonight? That the truth is your mother couldn't wait to have me for a son-in-law?" He made a rude sound. "I don't think so."

"You're right. She didn't think we should be together, much less marry. But not for the reasons you think."

"Oh yeah? I can't wait to hear this."

She felt a prickle of irritation and did her best to ignore it. "When she came to see me, back while we were in college, she told me she'd heard we were dating…and that people were saying it was serious.

"And yes, Gavin, she was concerned. About me, but also about you. She said she'd known you since you were seventeen, and that no matter what I thought, I hadn't lived long enough to appreciate how hard your life had been—or understand how deep your pride ran. She feared that being with me would ultimately destroy you."

Gavin made another rude noise, but Colleen ignored it. "After all, she pointed out, I would have a million dollars. If we used it to live on, you'd be labeled a gold digger. But if I gave it away, you'd blame yourself for not being able to provide me with the kind of luxuries I'd grown up with. There was no way you could win.''

''Right. So what you're saying is, you dumped me for my own good? Because you cared about me so much?''

''Yes! No! Darn it, Gavin, don't twist my words!''

''Me?'' he shot back incredulously. ''Listen, sweetheart, I'm not the one who pledged my undying love, then went off to become a nun. Or did you only do that to please your father?''

This time she felt a definite surge of temper. ''Papa may have hoped I'd find my place in the religious life, but the last thing he ever wanted was for me to feel pressured or coerced. And I wasn't. By the time I fell in love with you, I'd been hearing God's call for a long while. I knew He had plans for me, I just wasn't sure what. And as it turned out, ultimately I made a mistake.'' One she'd paid for with hundreds and hundreds of hours of soul-searching and heartache and prayer.

''Yeah? Well, that makes two of us. Because while all this is fascinating, it still doesn't explain what's been going on the past few weeks. Or does it? Tell me, Colleen, what am I to you…really? Just another Barone-family charity project?''

She knew he was angry. But try as she might to tell herself that he didn't really mean what he was saying, his words cut to her heart. ''Of course not,'' she flashed back. ''But as long as we're on the subject, maybe I ought to ask you the same. Because while I know that I hurt you all those years ago, for which I'm truly, genuinely sorry, it's also true you didn't put up much of a fight to keep what we had. One bump in the road and you were gone so fast you practically left scorch marks on my carpet.''

He didn't give an inch. ''At least I don't tell people I love them when I don't mean it.''

''I wouldn't know,'' she retorted, trying to keep the hurt out of her voice. ''Since recently you haven't felt compelled to say those words to me. Which pretty much tells its own story, doesn't it?''

He didn't answer. Instead, looking straight ahead, he lapsed into a stony silence. Then he started the car and pulled onto the street. There was no mistaking the unyielding set of his jaw, which was perfectly visible every time they passed a streetlight.

Yet Colleen didn't care. All she knew after they'd traveled a few more blocks was that she found the silence unbearable. "Where are we going?" she demanded for lack of a better question.

Gavin gave a harsh, humorless laugh. "*We* aren't going anywhere. I'm taking you to your place. Then I'm going to the Independence. Where I belong."

She took one last stab at finding some kind of common ground. "If we could just talk rationally about this—"

"I don't think so, Colleen," he interrupted harshly. "Whatever's happened between us, now, in the past, whenever, it's over. You can bet the rent money on that."

Once again he turned his attention back to the road, not saying another word until they finally reached her place. Pulling to the curb, he reached over, shoved open her door and sat back. "Be sure and tell your mother thanks for dinner,'' he said with an edge of sarcasm that was razor-sharp.

He impatiently drummed his fingers against the steering wheel, looking less approachable than Mount Kilimanjaro in a blizzard.

While Colleen wasn't a quitter by nature, she realized she didn't have anything left to say. Her heart breaking, she did the only thing she could. Clinging desperately to what little was left of her composure, she climbed out of the car and forced herself to walk away.

She managed to make it all the way to the vestibule before the tears came.

Poised in the doorway of her office, which had in a previous incarnation served time as a broom closet, Colleen considered the piles of paperwork stacked in precarious towers on every possible horizontal surface.

If these files were lions and this was the Colosseum, I'd be the afternoon snack, she thought bleakly, not particularly surprised when even her minor attempt to amuse herself fell flat.

But then, in the week since she and Gavin had last spoken, that was pretty much the way everything had gone, she reflected, picking her way around the piles to reach her desk, which was actually an old closet door one of the janitors had thoughtfully placed atop a pair of two-drawer file cabinets.

In point of fact, it was actually a rather apt description of her life recently. As well as a fairly accurate picture of the state of her heart.

Both were flat. Utterly and completely without buoyancy. Bleak, humorless, leaden.

Goodbye, bright helium balloon. Hello, tasteless, wizened, hit-by-a-steamroller pancake.

But at least she was going to participate in one happy ending, she reminded herself as she sat down on the hard wooden seat of her creaky swivel chair. Reaching over, she plucked a file from the top of the nearest pile and set it carefully down in front of her.

Brett's name, in her own familiar handwriting, filled the index tab, and for the first time in days she felt an urge to smile.

Although it had taken some doing, she'd managed to hack through a jungle of red tape and get the Department of Child Services to sign off on a plan that would declare Brett an emancipated teenager and still provide him with a good, stable home while allowing him to spend regular time with his mother.

If he agreed—and the fact that it was his decision to make was the very best part, in Colleen's opinion—he'd have supervision, but not too much; he'd get to live with someone who genuinely cared about his future; and he wouldn't have to change schools or leave Jefferson Heights, both of which he'd repeatedly made clear to her mattered to him.

God Bless Emmett Crypinski, she thought a little mistily. Her gruff but secretly marshmallow-hearted landlord hadn't hesitated when she'd approached him with the idea.

Sure, why not? he'd said with one of his familiar shrugs. The kid wasn't really so bad, and he himself wasn't getting any younger. He wouldn't mind having someone around who could help out occasionally. And since she'd be just down the stairs, it wouldn't be as if he'd have sole responsibility for the boy, now would he?

All Colleen had left to do was sell Brett on the idea. Which shouldn't be that hard, not once she let it drop that Emmett had said it might not be a bad idea to teach the youngster to drive, as the Boston traffic was starting to be too much for a man his age.

With an amused shake of her head, Colleen took one last fond look at the worn file cover. Although she hadn't had to compile the usual caseworker studies or dozens of other documents in triplicate, since this was to be more a gentlemen's agreement between Emmett, Brett, herself and the State of Massachusetts, there were a few things she did want to clarify with Brett one more time, such as his birth date, his father's last known whereabouts, any phone numbers where his mother might be reached in case of an emergency.

Plus, it probably wouldn't hurt to toss out the notes she'd scribbled to herself the past few months as she'd pondered how best to see that the boy got the kind of future he deserved. Those sorts of things were always open to misinterpretation, so it would no doubt be best for everyone if they got filed in the garbage can.

Except that somebody had already beat her to it, she saw as she opened the manila folder.

Her heart, which had actually felt lighter for the past few minutes, sank like a stone. Be-

cause there was only one person she could
think of who would've found the file contents
of interest.

And that, unfortunately, was its main subject.

Gavin stepped briskly out of the elevator.
With his head of security, James Maddux,
bobbing along in his wake like a tin can tied
to a bumper, he set off at a brisk pace down
the carpeted corridor, trying hard not to lose
his temper.

"At this point the last thing that concerns
me is cost," he informed Maddux in no un-
certain terms. "Just go ahead, have Lee Ellen
in personnel set up the interviews and hire as
many people as you think it's going to take.
Our first priority—always—has to be guest
safety.

"You know where I stand on this, Jamie.
We've discussed it before. If our guests don't
feel secure when they climb into bed at an
O'Sullivan hotel, then none of the rest of it
matters. Not our gourmet food, our beautiful
accommodations or our first-class service. And
I'm getting tired of having to repeat myself.

Almost as tired…'' Sweeping into the reception area that fronted the executive offices, he grabbed the sheaf of papers that Carol, his secretary, was holding out for him with one hand, while at the same time motioning her not to interrupt when he saw her part her lips to speak. ''Not now,'' he murmured without breaking stride. ''I'm making a point.''

''But—''

He ignored her protest and picked up with Jamie. ''As I said, I'm almost as tired of having to go over the same points again and again as I am of the whole damn place going to pieces every time I take a few mornings or afternoons off. So do your damn job, would you? Because that's why I'm paying you.''

Satisfied that he'd made his point, he pushed open his office door and sailed inside.

Only to be brought up short as he saw a familiar figure standing at the windows, looking out. ''Brett? What in blazes are you doing here?''

''I'm sorry, sir.'' Carol, appearing more than a little flustered, skidded to a stop beside him. ''But I did try to warn you. First he showed up without an appointment, then he barged right in like he owned the place and insisted you wouldn't mind if he waited inside. Are the two of you related, by any chance?''

Gavin sent her a cutting look that had her beating a swift retreat, but not before she sent him a saccharine smile warning that, unlike the rest of the staff, she was done putting up with the foul mood he'd been unable to shake the past week.

''I'll hold your calls,'' she informed him in a dulcet tone of voice.

''You do that.'' He waited until he heard the door shut before he approached the youngster who continued to stare moodily out the window. ''What's up? Is something wrong? I didn't forget we had a lunch date, did I?''

Brett slowly shook his head. Shoving his hands into his pockets, he turned. ''Naw. I just came by to let you know I'm not going to be around for a while.''

''Ah.'' Clamping down on his escalating alarm, Gavin nodded, then walked over and sat down on the nearest of the two leather couches that formed one of several casual conversation areas in the big room. ''So.'' He stretched out his legs. "Where are you going?"

Brett shrugged. "I'm not sure, exactly. But somewhere for sure."

"Well, that sounds like a hell of a plan. You want to tell me what's going on?"

The kid remained silent, but just for another few seconds. Then he cracked, information spilling out of him like the yolk from a dropped egg. "It's Ms. Barone." Leaving his post at the window, he paced toward Gavin, anguish and anger mixed on his young face. "Man, I thought she was different! I thought I could trust her. But now—now I know she's just like all the others," he exclaimed.

Yeah? Well, I could've told you that, an ugly little voice in Gavin's head whispered.

Except when it came to Brett, she *did* care. Gavin knew it, with an utter, clear-down-to-the-bone certainty he didn't think to question. "What exactly did she do?" he asked carefully.

"I thought she was my friend," Brett responded bitterly. "I explained to her that I couldn't just take off, move across town or somewhere to live with a bunch of strangers and leave my mom here alone. As bad as things get sometimes, she still needs me to check up on her, to make sure she eats and has a place to live and stuff like that. And Ms. Barone, she seemed to get it.''

''So what did she do?'' Gavin repeated.

''She sold me out! I went into her office today, to talk to her about…stuff.'' For the first time the boy avoided Gavin's gaze, and with a slight shock Gavin realized that most likely the ''stuff'' the kid had wanted to discuss with Colleen was him. ''But she wasn't there.

''So I was waiting around, just hangin', when I knocked over this pile of papers, and there, right on top, was my file. And inside—'' Brett stopped, his young mouth trembling slightly before he regained control ''—inside there was this stuff about how smart I was, but I was too young to know what I wanted, much less needed, and then there was a list of phone numbers with the one for the State Foster Care coordinator circled and a note that said to be sure and give him a call, let him know that things were proceeding…'' He shook his head.

Gavin frowned. As tempted as he was just

to agree with the boy, to let his own feelings about Colleen take precedence over logic, there was something wrong here.

"Think about what you're saying," he said slowly. "Why would Ms. Barone go to all the trouble of putting together the mentoring program if she was secretly planning to send you off to who knows where? It doesn't make sense. Besides—" the next words came harder, for all that he knew in his gut they were true "—I don't think she'd do that. It's not Colleen's nature to betray people she cares about."

Hell, had he really said that? Did he mean it?

Telling himself firmly that this wasn't the time for such questions, he forced himself to concentrate on the issue at hand. "Plus, why would she think it would be best if you left the Heights? Not that it wouldn't be—" he sent the boy a look that effortlessly quelled Brett's instinctive protest "—but that's not the point.

"The point as far as you're concerned is that Colleen's made it her home. She really believes that as long as you try hard enough, good can come out of anywhere. Although where she came up with that particular piece of fantasy is anyone's guess.''

''Yeah, right.'' Brett gave him the sort of get-real look only a teenager could pull off. ''That's easy enough. It's you. Even old Mr. C figured that out. He said something real sappy, like how he thought you were her inspiration for seeing to it that us kids got a fair shake. Or something like that.''

Gavin stared hard at the boy. No way, he told himself immediately, was he going to start putting stock in some kid's opinion. Much less that of an old codger like Crypinski.

After all, neither of them knew the whole, unvarnished truth. Not about his and Colleen's past. Much less about what had gone on between them these past few weeks.

And yet he couldn't entirely quell the sudden hope stirring to life inside him. Or stop himself from wondering… What if by some chance they were right?

He sank more deeply into the chair.

''Aw, hell,'' he murmured as he slowly began to look at the past few weeks from an entirely different perspective.

What in God's name had he done?

Even more importantly, if he could somehow drum up the guts, was there any way he could fix it?

Or had he already thrown away the best thing he'd ever had in his life for the second time?

Nine

"**I**'m so sorry, Mr. Crypinski." Swallowing hard because she absolutely was not going to cry, Colleen gazed fixedly through one of her living-room windows at the barren display of her garden outside. "This is all my fault. I didn't want to get up his hopes until I was sure I could make this thing with you happen, so I didn't take him into my confidence—not that I'm trying to make excuses. And now he's out there in the dark, all alone, and no doubt convinced I betrayed him."

Her landlord made a noise that sounded suspiciously like what it was—an unimpressed snort. "You've never been a ninny, Colleen, and now is not the time to start. Not only has Brett grown up on some of the toughest streets this city has to offer, but given his proclivity for dropping by here at all hours of the day and night, I can definitely assure you he's not afraid of the dark.

"As for the other, if he's got so little character he'd assume the worst without giving you the benefit of the doubt, not to mention a chance to explain yourself, then the young fool deserves whatever happens to him. And as long we're talking plain, the same goes for that rich, hotshot boyfriend of yours who's suddenly MIA."

She stared at the old man in amazement, so stunned by his uncharacteristic outburst she couldn't think what to say.

Not that he seemed to need prompting. "That's how I see it, anyway. And don't think I haven't seen enough *Oprah* to know even an old guy like me is entitled to his opinion."

"Yes, of course you are. I certainly didn't mean to imply…that is…" Good heavens, she was practically stuttering, trapped between competing urges to laugh and cry.

Not that her companion appeared to notice. "You know what your problem is, missy? You're like my Edna, God rest her soul, too nice for your own darned good. You're always trying to take care of somebody, when maybe you ought to be letting that somebody take some care of you part of the time." Then his ears turned a fiery red as if he just realized how much he'd revealed. "Now if you'll excuse me, I need to check on my dinner."

"Yes. Of course." Trailing in his wake for no good reason except that she wasn't quite ready to be alone, Colleen followed him toward the door—only to practically leap a foot as the buzzer unexpectedly sounded.

Since he was closer by more than a yard, the building's owner reached out and pressed the intercom button. "Who is it?"

There was a lengthy pause, and then Brett's familiar voice said uncertainly, "Mr. C?"

"Well, it's not Santa Claus."

"Oh, thank you, God," Colleen murmured, her hand pressed to her heart.

"Sorry, Mr. C. I must've hit the wrong button. Will you let me in? I need to talk to Ms. Barone.''

''You're right about that,'' the older man retorted, hitting the release no more than half a second before he yanked open the apartment door and stepped into the hall. ''And that's not the only person you're going to be doing some explaining to,'' he muttered.

Since Colleen's only thought at that moment was to make sure with her own eyes that Brett was all right, she followed him out into the corridor.

Only to take a step back as she caught sight of Gavin standing behind Brett like a silent shadow.

''Oh.'' She experienced a momentary sense of dislocation, as her emotions seemed to open ranks and split into two different camps.

Part of her was overwhelmed with relief that Brett was all right.

The other part was wholly focused on Gavin, drinking in the sight of him, examining his expression, his stance, the placement of each strand of his hair, doing everything it could to commit his image to memory.

To her dismay, Mr. Crypinski started down

the hall toward the entry, bearing down on Brett and leaving her feeling both alone and exposed. "It appears to me that you and I need to have a little talk."

With complete disregard for the teenager's yelp of objection, the former transit worker clamped his hand on the boy's shoulder, spun him around and began propelling him up the stairs toward his own second-story apartment.

Neither Gavin nor Colleen moved. Nor did they utter a sound.

Gavin, however, was having a field day berating himself. *She looks pale. And tired,* he thought, feeling as if an invisible hand were squeezing his heart. *And I'm an idiot.*

He took a step forward. "Hey."

She swallowed, her eyes looking big in her face as she stared at him. "Hey yourself."

"Are you okay? I mean, I suppose I should've called you when Brett showed up at the hotel, but it just sort of slipped my mind. I guess I thought it would be best all around if I simply drove him over." *Not to mention that it gave me an excuse to see you.*

"I'm fine. I just…I didn't expect…I guess I'm surprised to see you."

"Yeah, well, I don't blame you." He watched, frowning, as she hugged her arms to herself and rubbed her bare forearms with her palms. "You cold?"

The instant he said it he had a sudden desire to give himself a slap in the forehead. "Yes, of course you are," he answered himself, shrugging out of his coat as he advanced on her. "Here. Put this around you and let's get you the hell out of this drafty hall."

Despite the fierceness of his words, his hands were gentle as he wrapped her in his coat, then turned her around and herded her back into her apartment. "You really ought to hang a sweater on that wall rack by the door," he admonished, only to curse himself soundly when a quick sideways glance at her face as they awkwardly negotiated her narrow hall revealed that she was biting her lower lip to keep it from trembling.

"Colleen, *caraid*. Please. Stop looking so sad. I know I've been one hell of a giant fool, but I swear if you'll just give me one more chance, I'll spend the rest of my life making it up to you. Please, Colleen. As God is my witness, I love you. I always have and I always will, and all I'm asking for is some time to prove it.''

''You...you called me your darling,'' she said with a sort of wonder, turning toward him as they reached the relative warmth of her small living room.

''What?''

''*Caraid.* That's what it means.''

''Yeah, of course.'' He gave a little shrug, not about to admit that its precise meaning was news to him, that all he'd known for sure when he'd said it was that it was an endearment of some sort and the only fit-for-mixed-company Gaelic word in his vocabulary. Besides, whether he'd intended it to or not, it was exactly what she was to him. ''Just like I know how they spell the word for *stupid* in this particular neighborhood.''

A slight frown formed between her brows. ''Is it spelled differently here than in the rest of Boston?''

''Oh, yeah. Or maybe not. Beacon Hill or Southie, it's still spelled O-S-U-L-L-I-V-A-N.''

For the longest time, she gazed up at him, not saying anything, and then one corner of her mouth curved, just for a second. "Oh, Gavin, no. That isn't true—"

"Don't argue with me, Colleen. Only the world's biggest fool would let the only woman in the world meant for him almost get away not just once, but twice.

"I love you, Colleen. And I know we've got lots to discuss, lots to work out, but I don't want to spend another moment of my life without you. Make me the happiest man on the Eastern seaboard. Tell me you'll marry me."

Her face lit up, and then his coat slid in a heap to the floor as she raised her hands to cradle his face and he swept her into his arms. "Yes," she said fiercely, using quick kisses for punctuation. "Yes, yes, yes!"

But it wasn't until her mouth finally settled against his that Gavin knew everything was going to be all right.

There would be a lot to work out and discuss over the next days, weeks, months and years.

But as long as they had each other, he knew everything else would be all right.

*   *   *   *   *

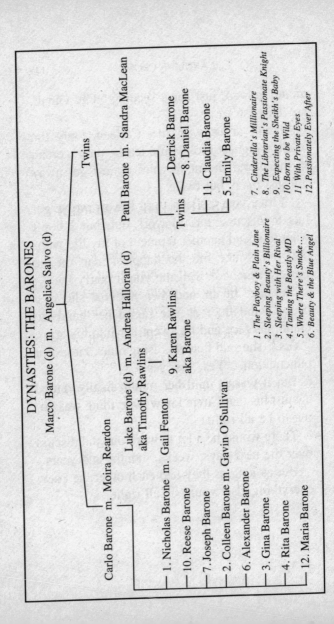

DYNASTIES: THE BARONES

Marco Barone (d) m. Angelica Salvo (d)

Carlo Barone m. Moira Reardon

Luke Barone (d) m. Andrea Halloran (d)
aka Timothy Rawlins

9. Karen Rawlins
aka Barone

Twins

Paul Barone m. Sandra MacLean

— Derrick Barone
— 8. Daniel Barone

Twins

— 11. Claudia Barone
— 5. Emily Barone

— 1. Nicholas Barone m. Gail Fenton
— 10. Reese Barone
— 7. Joseph Barone
— 2. Colleen Barone m. Gavin O'Sullivan
— 6. Alexander Barone
— 3. Gina Barone
— 4. Rita Barone
— 12. Maria Barone

1. *The Playboy & Plain Jane*
2. *Sleeping Beauty's Billionaire*
3. *Sleeping with Her Rival*
4. *Taming the Beastly MD*
5. *Where There's Smoke…*
6. *Beauty & the Blue Angel*

7. *Cinderella's Millionaire*
8. *The Librarian's Passionate Knight*
9. *Expecting the Sheikh's Baby*
10. *Born to be Wild*
11 *With Private Eyes*
12 *Passionately Ever After*

DYNASTIES: THE BARONES
continues…

*Turn the page for a bonus look
at what's in store for you in
the next Barones book—
only from Silhouette Desire!*

Sleeping with Her Rival

by Sheri WhiteFeather

will be on the shelves in March 2004.

Sleeping with Her Rival

by

Sheri WhiteFeather

Gina Barone wasn't in the mood to party, but she sipped a glass of chardonnay—praying it wouldn't irritate her stomach—and worked her way through the charity mixer, feigning an I'm-in-control smile.

She knew it was important to be seen, to hold her head high, especially now. Gina was the vice president of marketing and public relations for Baronessa Gelati, a family-owned Italian ice-cream empire—a company being shredded by the media.

Something Gina felt responsible for.

Moving through the crowd, she nodded to familiar faces. Although she'd come here to make her presence known, she thought it best to avoid lengthy conversations. A polite greeting was about all she could handle. And with that in mind, she would sample the food, sip a tiny bit of wine and then wait until an appropriate amount of time had elapsed before she said her goodbyes and made a gracious exit.

"Gina?"

She stopped to acknowledge Morgan Chancellor, a business associate who flitted around the social scene like a butterfly, fluttering from one partyer to the next.

Morgan batted her lashes, then leaned in close. "Do you know who asked about you?"

Gina suspected plenty of people were talking about her, about the fiasco she'd arranged last month, the Valentine's Day publicity event that had ended in disaster.

Baronessa had been launching a new flavor called passionfruit, offering a free tasting at their corporate headquarters. But pandemonium erupted when people tasted the gelato.

An unknown culprit had spiked the ice cream with a mouth-burning substance, which they'd soon discovered was habanero peppers—the hottest chillies in the world.

And worse yet, a friend of Gina's who'd stopped by the event at her invitation had suffered from an attack of anaphylaxis, a serious and rapid allergic reaction to the peppers.

She'd nearly killed someone. Inadvertently, maybe, but the shame and the guilt were still hers to bear.

Gina gazed at Morgan, forcing herself to smile. "So, who asked about me?"

"Flint Kingman."

Her smile cracked and fell. "He's here?"

"Yes. He asked me to point you out."

"Did he?" Gina glanced around the room. The crème de la crème of Boston society mingled freely, but somewhere, lurking amid black cocktail dresses and designer suits, was her newly acquired rival.

Anxious, she fingered the diamond-and-pearl choker around her neck, wishing she hadn't worn it. Flint's reputation strangled her like a noose.

The wonder boy. The renowned spin doctor. The prince of the PR world.

Her family expected her to work with him, to take his advice. Why couldn't they allow her the dignity of repairing the media damage on her own? Why did they have to force Flint Kingman on her?

He'd left a slew of messages at the office, insisting she return his calls. So finally she'd summoned the strength to do just that. But their professional conversation had turned heated, and she'd told him to go to hell.

And now he was here.

"Would you mind pointing him out to me?" she asked Morgan.

"Certainly." The redhead turned to glance over her shoulder, then frowned. "He was over there with that group of men, but he's gone now."

Gina shrugged, hoping to appear calm and refined—a far cry from the turmoil churning inside.

"I'm sure he'll catch up with me later," she said, wondering if he'd attended this party just to intimidate her.

If he didn't crawl out of the woodwork and

introduce himself, then he would probably continue to spy on her from afar, making her ulcer act up. It was a nervous condition she hid from her family.

"If you'll excuse me, Morgan, I'm going to check out the buffet."

"Go right ahead. If I see Flint, I'll let you know."

"Thanks." Gina headed to the buffet table to nibble daintily on party foods, to pretend she felt secure enough to eat in public. No way would she let Flint run her off, even if she wanted to dart out the door.

Balancing her food and a full glass of wine, she snuggled up to a floor-to-ceiling window, set her drink on a nearby planter ledge and turned to gaze at the city. Rain fell from the sky, and lights twinkled like pinwheels, casting sparks into the brisk March air.

She stood, with her plate in hand, admiring the rain-dampened view. And then she heard a man speak her name.

The low, vodka-on-the-rocks voice crept up her spine and sent her heartbeat racing. She recognized Flint Kingman's tone instantly.

Preparing to face him, she turned.

He gazed directly into her eyes, and she did her damnedest to maintain her composure.

She'd expected tall and handsome, but he was more than that. So much more.

In an Armani suit and Gucci loafers, he stood perfectly groomed, as cocky and debonair as his reputation. Yet beneath the Boston polish was an edge as hard as his name, as sharp and dangerous as the tip of a flint.

He exuded sexuality. Pure, raw, primal heat.

She steadied her plate with both hands to keep her food from spilling onto the floor. Men didn't make her nervous. But this one did.

He didn't speak; he just watched her from a pair of amber-flecked eyes.

"Aren't you going to introduce yourself?" she said, her posture stiff, her fingers suddenly numb.

A cynical smile tugged at the corner of his lips, and a strand of chocolate-brown hair fell rebelliously across his forehead.

"Nice try. But you know exactly who I am."

Like a self-assured predator, he moved a little closer, just enough to put his pheromones between them. She took a deep breath, and her stomach ignited into a red-hot flame.

Damn her nerves, she thought. And damn him.

"I'll stop by your office on Tuesday," he said. "At two."

"I'll check my calendar and get back to you," she countered.

"Tuesday at two. This isn't up for negotiation."

Gina bristled, hating Flint Kingman and everything he represented. "Are you always this pushy?"

"I'm aggressive, not pushy."

"You could have fooled me."

She lifted her chin a notch, and Flint studied the stubborn gesture. Gina Barone was a feminine force to be reckoned with—a long, elegant body, a mass of wavy brown hair swept into a chignon and eyes the color of violets.

A cold shoulder and a hot temper. He'd heard she was an ice princess. A woman much too defensive. A woman who competed with men. And now she would be competing with him.

*   *   *   *   *

▼ SILHOUETTE®
DESIRE™ 2-IN-1

AVAILABLE FROM 16TH JANUARY 2004

LIONHEARTED Diana Palmer

Texan Lovers
Virgin Janie Brewster had always been in love with Leo Hart. But he'd never noticed her as a woman—until she decided to tempt him beyond *all* reason.

INSTINCTIVE MALE Cait London

Heartbreakers
Past experience had taught Mikhail Stepanov to keep his boss's dangerously alluring daughter at arm's length. But once the desperate single mother turned to him, how could he resist?

KISS ME, COWBOY! Maureen Child

Career-woman Nora Bailey was planning to lose her virginity—with relationship-shy, sexy single dad Mike Fallon! This was a challenge Nora would take on both day and…*night*.

THE TYCOON'S LADY Katherine Garbera

The Baby Bank
When Angelica Leone stumbled off the stage at a charity auction and into the arms of tycoon Paul Sterling, she knew he would stop at nothing to get what he wanted—and he wanted her!

CINDERELLA & THE PLAYBOY Laura Wright

When C K Tanner got Abby McGrady to pretend to be his wife to snare a business deal, he never expected the attraction between them—let alone wanting to turn this into something permanent.

QUADE: THE IRRESISTIBLE ONE Bronwyn Jameson

Chantal Goodwin had never stopped wanting ex-love Cameron Quade. So she thought they could have one night of passion and then walk away. But that was before she found out about their baby…

AVAILABLE FROM 16TH JANUARY 2004

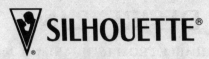 **SILHOUETTE**®

Sensation™

Passionate, dramatic, thrilling romances

ONE OF THESE NIGHTS Justine Davis
MOMENT OF TRUTH Maggie Price
BENEATH THE SILK Wendy Rosnau
PRIVATE MANOEUVRES Catherine Mann
THE QUIET STORM RaeAnne Thayne
HONKY-TONK CINDERELLA Karen Templeton

Special Edition™

Vivid, satisfying romances full of family, life and love

MICHAEL'S DISCOVERY Sherryl Woods
HER HEALING TOUCH Lindsay McKenna
TAKING OVER THE TYCOON Cathy Gillen Thacker
BABY 101 Marisa Carroll
THE WEDDING BARGAIN Lisette Belisle
THE MISSING HEIR Jane Toombs

Superromance™

*Enjoy the drama, explore the emotions,
experience the relationship*

SUBSTITUTE FATHER Bonnie K Winn
THE NOTORIOUS MRS WRIGHT Fay Robinson
THE FIRE WITHIN Kathryn Shay
SHOOTING THE MOON Brenda Novak

Intrigue™

Danger, deception and suspense

DADDY TO THE RESCUE Susan Kearney
PHANTOM LOVER Rebecca York
FAKE ID WIFE Patricia Rosemoor
UNDER LOCK AND KEY Sylvie Kurtz

SILHOUETTE®
SPECIAL EDITION™

proudly presents

a brand-new series from
GINA WILKINS

THE McCLOUDS
OF MISSISSIPPI

*Three siblings find their way back
to family—and love.*

THE FAMILY PLAN
January 2004

CONFLICT OF INTEREST
March 2004

FAITH, HOPE AND FAMILY
May 2004

0104/SH/LC81

SILHOUETTE®
DESIRE™

are proud to introduce

DYNASTIES: THE BARONES

Meet the wealthy Barones—caught in a web of danger, deceit and…desire!

Twelve exciting stories in six 2-in-1 volumes:

proudly presents

a brand-new five-book series from
bestselling author

SHERRYL WOODS

The Devaneys

*Five brothers torn apart in childhood,
reunited by love!*

RYAN'S PLACE
December 2003

SEAN'S RECKONING
January 2004

MICHAEL'S DISCOVERY
February 2004

PATRICK'S DESTINY
March 2004

DANIEL'S DESIRE
April 2004

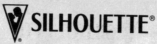

▼ SILHOUETTE®

is proud to present
a brand-new series

The

Country Club

**Dangerous, intense and seductive.
Get ready to be introduced into a world
where wealth is power and deception is rife.**

March 2004	The Country Club: The Debutantes *by Ann Major, Christine Rimmer & Beverly Barton*

Now prepare for more action with the twelve-book series...

March 2004	Stroke of Fortune *by Christine Rimmer*
April 2004	Texas Rose *by Marie Ferrarella* The Rebel's Return *by Beverly Barton*
May 2004	Heartbreaker *by Laurie Paige* Promised to a Sheikh *by Carla Cassidy*
June 2004	The Quiet Seduction *by Dixie Browning* An Arranged Marriage *by Peggy Moreland*
July 2004	The Mercenary *by Allison Leigh* The Last Bachelor *by Judy Christenberry*
August 2004	Lone Wolf *by Sheri WhiteFeather* The Marriage Profile *by Metsy Hingle*
September 2004	Texas...Now and Forever *by Merline Lovelace*

**Look out for more stories from THE COUNTRY CLUB
in Silhouette Desire. Starting with *Shameless*
by Ann Major in December 2004.**

2 FREE

books and a surprise gift!

We would like to take this opportunity to thank you for reading this Silhouette® book by offering you the chance to take TWO specially selected titles from the Desire™ series absolutely FREE! We're also making this offer to introduce you to the benefits of the Reader Service™—

- ★ FREE home delivery
- ★ FREE gifts and competitions
- ★ FREE monthly Newsletter
- ★ Exclusive Reader Service offers
- ★ Books available before they're in the shops

Accepting these FREE books and gift places you under no obligation to buy, you may cancel at any time, even after receiving your free shipment. Simply complete your details below and return the entire page to the address below. *You don't even need a stamp!*

YES! Please send me 2 free Desire books and a surprise gift. I understand that unless you hear from me, I will receive 3 superb new titles every month for just £4.99 each, postage and packing free. I am under no obligation to purchase any books and may cancel my subscription at any time. The free book and gift will be mine to keep in any case.

D4ZED

Ms/Mrs/Miss/Mr ....Initials...................................
BLOCK CAPITALS PLEASE

Surname ....

Address ....

....

....Postcode...................................

Send this whole page to:
UK: FREEPOST CN81, Croydon, CR9 3WZ
EIRE: PO Box 4546, Kilcock, County Kildare (stamp required)